stories, seven novels, and ten collections during a career spanning forty years. He is a past recipient of the World Fantasy Award and the British Fantasy Award, and his 2014 novel *Blood Kin* won the Bram Stoker Award. His latest novel, *Ubo* (Solaris, 2017), is a dark science fiction tale about violence and its origins, featuring such historical viewpoint characters as Jack the Ripper, Stalin, and Heinrich Himmler. *Yours to Tell: Dialogues on the Art & Practice of Writing*, written with his late wife Melanie, also appeared from Apex Books in 2017. A sampling of his best short stories can be found in *Figures Unseen: Selected Stories*, also published by Valancourt.

Also available by Steve Rasnic Tem

Figures Unseen: Selected Stories

THANATRAUMA

stories by

STEVE RASNIC TEM

VALANCOURT BOOKS

Thanatrauma by Steve Rasnic Tem
First edition 2021

Copyright © 2021 by Steve Rasnic Tem

Published by Valancourt Books, Richmond, Virginia
http://www.valancourtbooks.com

ISBN 978-1-954321-04-5 (hardcover)
ISBN 978-1-954321-05-2 (trade paperback)
Also available as an electronic book and an audiobook.

Set in Bembo Book MT Pro
Cover by Vince Haig

CONTENTS

Thanatrauma

The limitless sky outside Andrew's bedroom window was the hue of soured milk and mushrooms. It wasn't an unusual sky for a cold, late autumn day, with the fallen leaves dark and shredded, streaking the lawns, turned into a decaying filth encrusting the edges of things.

Last night someone had turned over the trashcans put out for this morning's collection. Up and down the street the large green cans lay on their sides, garbage spilling over the sidewalks and out into the lanes. He wondered who could have been so angry, or in these times was it a sign of the carefree? Everyone would think a gang of young people did it, but sightings of sick raccoons had been reported in the neighborhood the past few weeks. Wasn't it more likely to be one of them? A flyer stuck in his door had provided a phone number to call in case of a sighting, and a warning not to approach, as raccoons were known carriers of rabies.

To make matters worse, vehicles had driven through this cold variegated sludge and dragged the trash everywhere. Some of his neighbors were already out there vigorously trying to make things right. He'd neglected to put his own trash out; it slipped his mind regularly. Still, he needed to lend a hand.

But he hadn't talked to any of these people since his wife's passing. And now, several years later, how could he even begin? There was far too much that should have been said.

On such days he longed for snow to cover everything, to provide some semblance that the world had been made fresh.

But more often than not the snow did not come, and he'd choose to close the curtains rather than look outside. Which he did now, in case one of his neighbors looked up at the window and saw him spying on all their efforts.

From inside his body came a soft noise like something breaking. He could feel his deadened flesh falling away, bones slipping and sour organs spilling out. Still, he managed to move forward despite his demise.

It bothered him, how sensitive he was to changes in the weather, to colors, to atmosphere and mood. It was hard to say how he really felt about anything.

He'd rearranged his bedroom several times in the years since Marge's death. He'd first gotten rid of the bed and all the bedding. He'd given their daughters the chest of drawers, the twin nightstands, her armoire, her clothes and jewelry. They'd been happy to receive them, although they didn't understand why he'd wanted to let her things go so quickly. He didn't know how to explain, but he felt his life depended on it.

Later he'd removed key pieces from the living and dining rooms—the ones she'd liked the most—and given them to various thrift shops. He and his wife had had similar tastes so it was necessary to replace some of the furniture with styles not at all to his liking. He wanted no reminders. As a result some mornings it felt as if he had awakened in a random hotel. Who had chosen such bland artwork? He must have ordered it online, although he couldn't remember actually doing so. Desert scenes, mostly, a fried egg sun over plains of crumbling whites. The American Southwest, or perhaps Australia, or some alien world.

Andrew went over to his dresser and sorted his prescriptions and supplements. He re-read the yellowing paper specifying the proper amounts. He had no idea why he couldn't remember them, but he could not. He dutifully consumed his pills with three full glasses of water. He had no idea what might happen if he neglected to take them. He doubted that it would be anything dramatic, but he wouldn't take the chance. His primary focus of late was to avoid suffering. His ancient physician had told him, "You're actually pretty healthy, considering. Hell, you're in better shape than me!"

His eyes began their involuntary flutter. He clutched the edges of the dresser as anxiety grabbed onto him and shook. Several bottles fell over, a half-empty glass. He would have a mess to clean up. "Nerves," the physician called it. One of these bottles was supposed to take care of his nerves, but often did not. Of course, Andrew had never revealed to his doctor all his symptoms.

His hands appeared claw-like, the skin stretched. When had his wrists gotten so skinny? He'd been trying to lose weight, but feared that some of his weight loss might be involuntary. How could you tell the difference? He supposed if he suddenly died he would have his answer.

His vision blurred slightly. Great hunks of flesh began to disappear from his arms and legs. They looked like partially eaten chicken wings and drumsticks. It was enough to put one off meat, but he figured he needed the protein. He gazed down at his naked body. Numerous bits were missing, others dripping. He felt the beginnings of nausea, made his hands let go of the dresser, and ran to the bathroom.

Once he'd emptied his system sufficiently the visions disappeared. He stared at himself in the mirror. Mirrors had become largely useless. They rarely showed him anyone he could recognize.

He went back into the bedroom and sat on the edge of the bed. He'd have to do something about the smell. He hated how his body smelled even at the best of times. He was tempted to crawl back under the covers but would not allow himself that escape. Again, he sensed that his life depended on it.

He should eat something, although he couldn't think of anything he was hungry for. Something pre-packaged perhaps. Something processed to the point that it was no longer recognizable. Anything that didn't look as if it had once been alive.

Marge had been unable to eat the last month of her life. Not crackers, not even gelatin. She'd put something in her mouth and chew but her throat would not permit her to swallow it down. She had simply lost all desire for it. Similarly, she lost all desire for his touches, his stories, his speech, their daughters' speech. Marge could no longer bear to listen, and eventually, to talk. She began to live in a world where such activities no longer had meaning.

He struggled to understand and accept. They'd always talked things through. He assumed he would stay with her until the very end, that she would talk to him, and he would answer.

In the hospital they fed her this cream-colored liquid in plastic bags through a tube leading into a vein above her heart. They'd sent her home with a supply of these refrigerated bags and shown him how to prepare and administer them once daily, how to attach the tubing and how to disinfect. They told him the bags contained a mixture of nutrients and chemicals. It filled their bedroom with a grainy smell. He recalled a similar smell when he'd been a young man working near a dog food factory.

Every day he would talk to Marge and tell her what he was doing as he prepared her daily meal: the steps required to reduce the chances of infection, the attachment of the tubes, the readying of the pump. Marge still had nothing to say, but periodically she would say "yes"—whether out of politeness or as some part of her own internal process he did not know. He was terrified, of course, of making a mistake, of doing something that would make it worse for her, but each day he still did what he'd been instructed to do. And her belly did swell over time, although he wasn't sure that it was from nourishment.

Eventually Andrew dressed, got in his car, and obtained a burger and some fries via a drive-thru. Once home he pulled the meal apart and examined it: the bun had a plastic sheen and the perfectly circular patty resembled no meat he'd ever seen before. He gobbled everything greedily. The accompanying soda burned down his throat gratifyingly.

Although retirement required no scheduling on his part, no necessary destination or progress toward any sort of goal, no need to ever leave the house really, Andrew had still instituted a regular routine as a way of giving some minimal structure and meaning to his life. Meals and sleep occurred at the same times every day, as did reading the newspaper or a book, as did brooding, as did panic.

As it did every day following lunch the wallpaper in the living and dining rooms began to peel from the top, long curling bits dropping down to reveal great patches of black mold underneath. Wall board began to buckle and dark insects crawled out of the resulting gaps. There were drips everywhere as paste and paint began to liquefy. There were other things as well: vermin and tiny creatures he had no name for living in the walls, coming out to reveal themselves. But he never looked at these too closely, as a previous glance had shown they bore the faces of dead friends and relatives.

Andrew made some coffee—hard to think of it even remotely as food—and carried it out into the back yard. He sat in an ancient wooden chair beneath a naked maple and drank it while gazing at the mass of wreckage the yard had become.

Marge used to spend an enormous amount of time out here; he had not. He'd hired a man to rake the bulk of the leaves and haul them away. Dead flower heads bent the gray stems of the ravaged beds leaving jagged ends pointing at the sky. A stiff breeze lifted wire-like branches and made them rattle, broken bits joining the debris piles beneath the bushes. He regretted not paying the man enough to simply take everything away.

Nature made its own trash, and it used to be Marge's chosen role to deal with it. Andrew had become accustomed to letting it lay. Since her death the back yard had accumulated a collection of broken pots, ice-cracked plaster statuary, rusted garden implements, rotted cushions, and objects whose names and functions had escaped his memory. Marge would have been ashamed, and he was ashamed to realize her opinions were no longer relevant to him. She should have managed to stay alive if she'd wanted some say.

But was it really so bad? Andrew felt both drawn and repelled. Some day he might just take a nap out here, and whatever crawled his way was welcome to anything it could grab.

But he supposed it would be bad if his daughters found him that way. Perhaps he would pass away peacefully in his sleep. That's what everyone hoped for, wasn't it? No suffering, and a little bit of dignity?

When the visiting nurse first met Marge lying so quietly, making such a small shape in the bed, she'd said, "Your mother ..." and both alarmed and angered, Andrew had interrupted, "My *wife*." Another time he might have been flattered, although now he could not imagine when.

After several weeks at home Marge entered a period of even more intense silence, and no longer replied "yes" to his recitation of her food preparation, nor did she ask him to adjust her pillows or apply ointment to her lips. She slept, or he assumed she slept. Sometimes he would ask her questions and she would reward him with a vague nod. Frequently he studied her for signs of breathing, and he changed her adult diapers as necessary, although she gave him only minimal cooperation. The nurse on her daily visits reassured him this was to be expected with the increase in her pain medications.

Eventually there came a day when the sounds of her breathing returned, but they were labored, occasionally violent, and frightening. The nurse came to the house after he called, and let him know that again, this was normal, she wasn't in any distress. This was to be expected as the body shuts down. The end would be relatively soon, so perhaps he wanted to call their daughters for a final visit?

Their daughters came, and cried, and left again, and Andrew was left with Marge and her body and her breathing.

Andrew had gone downstairs to eat something. A can of tuna fish, which thankfully did not look like fish, but more like very soft, flavorful wood chips, like mulch for the neglected flower beds.

When he returned to their bedroom he discovered that everything was silent, back to where it had been before this last stage, and he felt almost relieved. He stared at her for a while, and unable to find those vague indications of breath, he approached, and lay down beside her, and touched her, and tried to gently shake her awake. He knew she wouldn't come awake, but he still felt that was what he was supposed to do.

He needed to call his daughters, and then he would lie with her for a while until they came, but there was this stench, and he didn't want his daughters to have to deal with that on their final visit. Marge would have hated that, and he thought he needed to do something, or else what kind of husband had he been, what kind of father?

He readied a clean diaper and some wipes, and he gently turned her, but hadn't anticipated the imbalance she possessed now, or her inability to participate, and she flopped over onto her face and a kind of sludge flowed out of her mouth, the rank contents of her stomach he supposed, but he really had no idea. He was completely ignorant, and here he had made this terrible mistake, and it had broken him, what he had done, how he had let her down, and he cried out in pained confusion, and tried to roll her back as gently as he could, but nothing about her felt right or normal, and her chin went down, and now he had more to clean. So he grabbed every rag and towel he could find to soak it all up, blotting and wiping it away, crying and cursing himself, and what he could not wipe away he tried to find ways to hide by folding and bunching the bedclothes and towels around her, all of which he knew he must throw out once they'd taken her away.

Andrew must have dozed off outside in the yard, because suddenly he was blinking his eyes against the changing sunlight. The sky appeared to be melting, great gobs of it dropping away like soaked tissue wherever the sun broke through the clouds. But he was just tired. He never seemed to get enough sleep. He'd even forgotten how much he was supposed to get. What had his physician said? "As much as you can." That old man was useless, but perhaps the appropriate physician for Andrew in this phase of his life.

It had been years since he'd had his eyes checked. No doubt his prescription needed updating, or did you reach a point where very little improvement was possible? Perhaps he simply needed more sugar. He looked at his wrist but he must have left his watch by the bed. Was that his hand with all the skin hanging from every finger, as if he had forced his way through a mass of cobwebs? He looked away and gazed at the lawn, where great masses of dirt were churning. At any moment he expected an arm to pop out of the soil.

He looked at his hand again. It was an ugly, emaciated thing, this old man's appendage, but at least its covering of skin was more or less intact again. But he was alarmed at the apparent thinness of its skin—he could see almost every vein and joint. Sometimes as the body declines it breaks our sense of time. Had he read this, or simply experienced it?

Marge had always loved his body, or at least that was what she had said. Now he could not imagine how that was possible—he couldn't stand the look of it, the smell of it. Did everyone else smell their own stink the way he did? He considered that perhaps they didn't, otherwise they'd be unable to show themselves in public.

He heard a murmuring beyond the bushes from where his neighbors had their lawns, and lives. He tried to put down his coffee cup and climb out of the chair but the cup was no longer in his hand. He searched the ground around him but found only mushrooms, hundreds of them showing their dirty faces to the sky. Of course it was their season, but he hadn't noticed them when he first sat down.

He stood and made his way across the lawn, walking carefully because he didn't want to step on any of the mushrooms. Although he couldn't imagine there being any danger in it the prospect repelled him. He almost stumbled over an old log by one of the dead flowerbeds. He remembered how he had placed it there under Marge's instructions. Now it had dark, spongy pieces falling away and a spread of moss over one end. Moss crept up the bases of several other trees in the yard—some of it a bright, almost phosphorescent green, and some of it dark and dry-looking, like spreading patches of dead skin. The sight made him want to rub his arms, but when he tried it hurt, as if the skin were loose and detaching itself from the muscle underneath.

He thought of Marge, and how in her last days she had seemed this old, rotted log, and he hated himself for it. She had been his beautiful wife. Should he call the man back to remove this log, or would that only make him feel worse? Suddenly he was at a loss as to where he should step. A tumble of bleached flesh and internals had spilled from one of the flowerbeds, gummed together with translucent membrane. It smelled both sweet and sour. It alarmed him that he suddenly felt hungry, thinking of seafood, which at one time he had loved. He had an impulse to drop to his knees, bend and fill his mouth with its rankness. It was like leaping off a cliff, not caring at all.

He looked again. It was ordinary dead vegetation; how could he have thought otherwise? Nothing here that reminded him of human flesh, although there in one corner, sunlight stirring some cobweb, some network of filament, seemed vaguely familiar. He immediately looked away.

A sharp pain on the back of his right hand. He raised it, making a fist. Some sort of wasp was stinging the same place again and again, aggressive in its attack. Odd—he hadn't seen any wasps in a few months—weren't they out of season? It turned its tiny head and appeared to glare at him, its multi-faceted eyes far bigger than they should have been. He shouted and shook the thing away. Now in terrible pain he stumbled toward the back door.

One of the outdoor lamps had separated from the wall and now lay in pieces to one side of the back door. Broken glass scattered like a spray of ice. When had that happened and why hadn't he noticed it before? At one shattered end a pile of crushed insects—moths and mayflies and the like—lay with their bodies roasted by the bulb. More invisible flying things buzzed at him. He cried out and struggled with the knob, finally jerked the door open, slamming it shut behind him.

Both daughters stayed at the house until the hearse arrived. The nurse had given him some names of funeral homes, and once he'd made his selection she made the initial call. While his girls cried over their mother's body he waited in his study. He thought he simply wanted to honor their privacy, but in a moment of clarity realized he couldn't bear to witness that moment. He had no idea if this made him a bad person or not.

When the men arrived he went downstairs and let them in. He was surprised to see their black suits and ties, and the long black vehicle parked in his driveway. Andrew wasn't sure exactly what he'd expected, but he hadn't expected this TV-like scene. They were quite circumspect, and one practically whispered that they needed his signature before they could come inside. He signed, but did not read the paper on the man's clipboard. He showed them upstairs, and they said hello to his daughters. The one who had done all the talking said the family might not want to be in the room as they removed the body. His daughters insisted on staying, while he retreated into the room next door. He stood there, waiting, unable to sit down. He heard a sliding sound coming from the bed, and one of his daughters made a sudden, soft sob. He did not know what she had seen, and would never ask.

It had been explained to him that the transporters would take the body to a central place, a "hub," where it would wait with other bodies until picked up by the designated funeral home. He could not imagine such a place, and he knew that Marge would have hated the very idea.

In his bathroom Andrew poured disinfectant over the sting, and then waited there cradling the injured hand with the other until it stopped burning. Then he took a long shower. He'd started taking multiple showers every day after Marge died. He wondered if that was bad for the skin. He really should look it up. It wasn't that he felt dirty, or in any way unclean. He simply liked the release it gave him. There seemed to be a kind of exchange, the heat, the liquid passing into his flesh even as some aspect of his flesh—some tension, some secret—passed into the water, striking the tiles beneath his feet and disappearing down the drain. He wondered if it were possible to stay under the water for so long the body eventually disappeared. He would have to look that up as well.

When the snow finally did come it was almost a surprise. It filled the sky rapidly with bits of white—as if the world were rapidly disintegrating to reveal the blank backdrop beneath. Andrew wandered from window to window, opening all the curtains, eager for some new view. Snow quickly packed the lawns, piled up against the fences, gathered along the edges of limbs, highlighting then weighing them down. By the time it stopped late in the day there was at least a foot of heavy, wet snow, maybe more. The world lay hushed and lifeless beneath its sheets.

Inside the house the rooms filled with brilliant snow-glare. There was nothing flattering in its revelations of dust and grime accumulated since his wife's death, the spaces left empty from furniture removed, the aging stacks of laundry and unopened mail. Had he really been living this way?

He glanced out an upstairs window into the back yard. Snow had erased almost everything, an emptiness bounded by fence. But there, a man was climbing over his fence, his face turned up defiantly in Andrew's direction.

He pulled on his slippers and raced down the stairs. He grabbed the poker from the fireplace and went through the porch and the door and into the back yard. He kept the poker raised, stepping awkwardly through the snow, watching for the man's footprints. The snow was churned by the fence, but Andrew could find no distinct trail.

His feet were completely swallowed up by the white, but he didn't really feel that cold. There was a chill, certainly, stiffening his skin and making him blush, but nothing that he couldn't handle. He'd handled so much already, and he was doing just fine, wasn't he?

The old chair under the maple had finally collapsed, pieces of it protruding above the snow.

He wasn't sure where to go. He heard a terrible sound of breathing behind him and swung, throwing himself off balance, sprawling into the snow. Something dark and furious leapt over him, attaching itself to the fence. Andrew jerked his head up. An old man was perched on the top of the fence, staring at him. It didn't seem possible—surely that fence was too flimsy to support the weight of a man. And yet there he was, staring at him wide-eyed and shaking. Andrew felt suddenly weak and dizzy, and struggled for breath. His chest felt as if it might erupt.

Then the old man turned his head, changing into a raccoon, its long tongue hanging out. Was it ill? Andrew didn't even know what he was supposed to look for.

The raccoon bounded from the fence and landed beside

him. Andrew covered his face, but the raccoon didn't touch him. He heard it race across the snow, scramble over something, and then nothing. But Andrew still kept his face covered, listening, refusing to move until he'd heard something more.

"Sweetheart," he said after some time had passed. "Please."

There were the sounds of distant traffic, the soft whisper of wind across the snow, a dripping suggestive of an imminent thaw, and then, possibly, *yes*.

Field of Shoes

He stumbled into the field a little past midnight after taking a wrong turn off the lane. He'd been at the local bar, and stayed later than intended. All his old friends had stories to tell about when they were young and walked easily about the planet. They'd asked him how he was doing now that his family was gone. He'd said *fine, fine*, as if saying it twice made it more true.

He didn't notice the shoes at first, until he tripped over the first one or two. He gazed out over the field with his failing eyesight, saw all the variegated forms, the rough shapes like clods of plowed ground. Then the moon slipped out of the clouds and he could see them: row after row of them, hundreds in no particular order, spreads and piles of shoes as far as he could see.

He staggered out into the middle of them. He couldn't help himself even though it didn't seem the safest thing to do. His arthritis was bad and his crippled legs didn't move so well, but how could he witness such a thing and not be drawn into its center?

There'd been a little girl in his life once, and back then she's been obsessed with shoes. She'd slip into her mother's or her daddy's and trudge around the house that way, and if she saw either of her parents barefoot she'd chase them down with their shoes in hand, shouting "where's your *shoes*?"

These shoes also had no feet attached, no legs, no body of any kind. They were entirely separated, lost, unowned. There was quite the variety of them on display: pumps, and flats, brogues, Oxfords, loafers, high-heel sandals and rain boots, every possible variety of sneaker and athletic shoe, ancient cowboy boots in leathers domestic to exotic.

But none of them came in pairs. As much as he looked he couldn't find a single mate.

That little girl had been his granddaughter, and she was the first one lost to him: disappeared into the streets when she reached a certain age, and her mind ventured down a certain mysterious path. That had been decades ago, and he had no knowledge of her final destination.

Her parents eventually decided to go swimming in the ocean, choosing to leave their shoes behind on the rocky shore. He'd kept those shoes a long time and through a series of moves until finally losing track. He wondered if he might find them here, if he cared to search that long.

As the clouds changed there was a great reshuffling in the balance of dark and light, some shadows disintegrating into a burning brightness even as other shadows spread and consumed. This brought a shimmer of illusion into the field, a phantasma of movement as footwear stirred to attention, becoming upright as they began to search for their owners.

The old man stumbled to get out of their way, wanting no part of this dance or ritual or whatever it might be. Experience had taught him long ago that nothing good ever came out of imagining.

His wife had kept hundreds of pairs in closets and cupboards. She'd joke and declare it her only sin. It went without saying that if he only had her back he'd buy her hundreds more.

But before he could explore that tired subject he stumbled out of the field as quickly as he'd stumbled in. He turned around and turned around again, but the only field visible was a field of houses, packed wall to wall and porch to porch, a hundred shuttered doors and a thousand windows staring back at him.

He might have said something then if he'd had anything left to say. Instead he listened for the wind, and the stream of distant traffic, and that multitude of shoes endlessly walking away.

The Dead Outside My Door

Some days the dead drifted: the ones empty of viscera, whose skeletons had worn wafer-thin, whose remaining skin was like parchment. They were as vague and insubstantial as memories imperfectly recalled. Sometimes the slightest breeze picked them up and tumbled them along the ground or flew them like kites. Jay suspected no one flew kites anymore and he didn't have the words to express how sad this made him.

He saw only this limited sample of the world, but he assumed only the dead gathered in groups. He couldn't imagine more church picnics or basketball games, sports of any kind. People—assuming there were others alive in the way he was alive—now understood what they always tried not to know, that they lived their imperfect lives alone.

The wind blew the dead into mangled clumps or dangled them from trees, still animated, gesturing their unconscious dismay. For the past few months, a semblance of a human being hung from the top branches of the hemlock across the road. He'd watched its slow dissolve into fluttering, translucent wisps of skin, so like a deteriorating plastic bag.

This new normal was not as it was once portrayed in the movies, the TV shows, the comic books. Not at all. He and his brother had had lengthy arguments over who was best prepared in the event of a zombie apocalypse. They didn't know what the hell they were talking about.

Jay considered it essential all this be documented. Perhaps there were others writing this down or making recordings, but he couldn't be sure. He had no illusions about his own importance, or his talent. At least he could put words on paper. He said them out loud first until they sounded right, then he wrote them down. At times they never sounded right, no matter how many ways he said them, and he would get discouraged, and behind. He might go a couple of weeks without writing, and then he had to rely on memory. Certain observations were lost, but those probably weren't the important ones. He kept talking even if he wasn't writing the words down to pretend he was having actual conversations.

He would talk to himself for hours and it all sounded quite wonderful, and he'd become drunk on the words and forget to write them. Or his hands would cramp near the end of a long session and he could no longer read his own handwriting. All in all, he was a poor selection for the role of scribe, but there had been a serious lack of volunteers.

"The dead are unaware. They've been blessed that way. At least that is my hope. If they have an awareness, even a small one, that's too terrible to think about. It's springtime, at least I think it is. I haven't been outside in months and if Mom and Dad owned a calendar, I haven't been able to find it. But the windows are full of green, and the air carries spring's odor of sweetness, the scent of flowers and moist breezes, and underneath all that, rot, the stench you get when the ground breaks open after a long, deep winter. And now, unfortunately, the corrupt smell of human decay, everywhere.

"In Southwest Virginia spring usually means oaks and maples budding into life, fresh produce in the restaurants, outdoor music concerts, walls of mountain laurel along the paths, weekend trips to the catfish pond, explosions of rhododendron, the pleasing smell of honeysuckle, violets and fleabane, wild red geraniums, azalea bushes, flowering dogwoods with white and pink blossoms. It has always been beautiful country. In many ways it still is. I have to say I've never seen so many different shades of green as I can see here in my windows.

"When I say the windows are full of green, I mean that literally. Every year when growing season comes the weeds and the vines and the bushes are so aggressive, they cover the house in no time. I get tired of hacking them away. I can't keep up. All the windows are covered by a couple of years' worth of vine, the dead stuff closest to the glass, the new green stuff on top, sending feelers inside. I keep the attic window relatively clear, so I can get air into the house. Of course, it's an old house and air leaks in anyway, so I figure that means this ailment isn't airborne, right? Otherwise I would have turned already unless I'm immune. I don't really know, and I have no one to ask. Some day I will have to get out there and cut all the growth away, otherwise it'll pull the house apart. At least I think so. I don't look forward to spending extensive time outside."

Besides the burgeoning growth, the dead were more in evidence this time of year. Jay didn't know why—maybe they didn't like the cold. He had never believed Mother Nature had any sort of intelligence, or any sort of consciousness, but some chain of events must have been triggered, an unknown tipping point surpassed.

His brother had hated the cold. When Ryan was a kid, he couldn't wear enough sweaters and socks. This past winter Jay had been sorely tempted to go outside and throw a blanket over Ryan. He never did. Through the sidelights by the front door he could see his brother's body greening up, splotched with moss and lichen and ground covers supplying modesty patches where his shorts had rotted away. Ryan's head still moved aimlessly. He appeared to be looking at the front door, looking for Jay. Jay avoided gazing at his brother, afraid their eyes might meet.

"The day I saw Ryan sprawled near the front steps I wanted

to rush out and drag him inside. But I didn't. I didn't want to take the risk. Besides, he wasn't the same Ryan anymore, I didn't think. I wish I could be sure.

"I don't know how long he'd been there. I almost never looked out those windows. His feet and one arm were missing. I wondered if some predator carried them away. I don't see how he could have made it this far without feet. But he hasn't gotten any closer. I don't think he can.

"I figure he was trying to get home the way I was. I just got here first. Mom and Dad weren't here. Maybe they went out to find us. I'll never know. But they never came back, and now I can only hope I never see them again.

"Ryan would have been a lot better at this. He was good with his hands, and knew about wells and electricity and plumbing, running a farm, raising food, using a compass. He'd have been a great Robinson Crusoe. I read *Robinson Crusoe*, and Defoe's other novels, but never learned anything practical from them. Dad would have wanted Ryan to run this place. He would have been disappointed with how I've let everything fall apart."

Jay's getting to the farm first had been a matter of luck. He'd already been on his way, his car packed with all he owned. He'd just dropped out of college in his senior year, six months before graduation, a graduation which wasn't going to happen anyway. He was still figuring out what he was going to tell his parents, but it was a long drive. He had time to figure out an explanation for why he was disappointing them once again.

He knew he shouldn't be there anymore. He didn't know what he could do with an English degree anyway. Oh yeah, chronicle the end of humanity.

He'd just left the Richmond city limits, west on Interstate 64, when he saw people driving off the highway, accidents everywhere. He tried to get off at Charlottesville, but all the exits were jammed. Near Waynesboro he saw his first pile of bodies, along with some struggling to free themselves from dead weight and tangled limbs. He stopped the car and tried to help a young woman, but there was something wrong with her. She didn't try to attack him. Again, not like in the movies, but she scared him, because she seemed to be losing bits of herself, leaving them in a trail behind her in the grass.

His cellphone was useless. On I-81 he tried tuning up and down the dial, getting rational snippets, but no answers. It was his last exposure to mass media, and he didn't expect to encounter it again in his lifetime.

It took him an embarrassing length of time after he arrived home to realize all their farm animals were gone. Maybe his parents liberated them before they went looking for their sons, or maybe it was something more sinister. Maybe there was a simple explanation he hadn't thought of. It was a question Jay was never able to answer.

"Ryan should be the one recording this. He was the star. He always had practical strategies for almost every situation. He was the one who had the best ideas about what we could do if the zombies ever came. Of course, he was completely wrong about that, but maybe he'd have better ideas now.

"Is this an epidemiological event, a metaphysical catastrophe, or the result of warfare? Ryan would be the first to say it doesn't matter. The world has turned back to a time when no one knew anything about anything, so they made up explanations as they went along."

Jay never knew the time, or if the kitchen wall clock was ever correct. He knew eventually he would run through his parents' huge store of batteries, and then it would fail.

If he'd been thinking clearly, he could have created a calendar from the beginning, even if it were simply marks on a wall. He could remember neither the day nor the date he first arrived. He knew there were ways using instruments or astronomical knowledge to figure those things out, but he possessed none of those skills.

In his new world there were warm days and cold days, days with more sun than others, days which were longer or shorter than others, days when it rained, days when the sky was beautiful and he was tempted, but didn't dare, to go outside.

There were frequent electrical outages. This caused him great anxiety since electricity powered the pump for the well. Eventually he would lose power. That he had it now seemed a miracle; wasn't some sort of maintenance required? He had no idea how things worked now, but then he never had. He didn't dare hope there were people still running things.

Within months of his arrival home, his life before began to feel like a dream. He couldn't quite believe he had ever attended classes, gone out to movies, or had friends. After the first year he began to entertain the possibility he might have hallucinated that entire other life. A lifetime in isolation was a difficult fate. Imagining a former life which included people seemed a logical remedy.

"I still have enough food for six months or so if I'm careful. Mom and Dad kept years of it: jars, bottles, and cans stuffed into every corner of the cellar. There's some meat left in the big freezer. But at some point, obviously, I'll have to leave. I'll have to go exploring outside.

"The dead don't bother you. Again, nothing like the movies. The few times I had to go out, to unload the car, to retrieve stuff from the barn, I was clumsy. I made noise. I even screamed once when one of them surprised me. They don't notice you're there. The dead don't care. But I don't want to have whatever it is they have.

"I have no idea how it all works, how you get infected. If it's not the air, then maybe it's the touch, or something else. Certain people get it right away and a few people can't get it at all, although I haven't seen anyone else who wasn't dead. At least I don't think so. Maybe it's something we don't even have words for. No pronouns, no nouns, no adjectives, no verbs—maybe nothing I can say has anything to do with what is happening to the world."

The narrow, paved road through the farm was rarely used. It was an access road to smaller farms and properties beyond, and another, bigger road leading into Tennessee. It was unpaved the year Jay was born. They had their buildings and the garden on this side of the road. The other side was all hayfields and pastures for the cattle. They'd never had many visitors. Most people were just passing through.

The dead often arrived two or three at a time, sometimes in a group of a dozen or more, most on the road, and a few came out of the distant fields. Many wore pieces of clothing. Others didn't even have their skin.

Most of the dead staggered on, to the farms and lands beyond, but several stopped here, where an accumulation of them remained. Did they know he was here, though they paid him no attention? They lay down in the yard, or they lingered among the trees, or leaned against the barn. They stood out in the fields like noble scarecrows, until bit by bit they went away, perhaps stolen by the animals Jay never saw.

During the previous late fall and winter, a lesser number of the dead came with the weather. The wind blew them in, or they drifted out of the clouds with the snow, or they arrived like hail and shattered when they hit. Clouds rolled in and clouds rolled away, stars appeared, snow drifted, and the empty dead floated by.

"I know little about the human body. I doubt I could pass a basic anatomy test. I know nothing of pathology, or of the stages of decomposition, but what I see out of the attic window makes no sense. From up here, surrounded by my family's aged possessions, relics of a world that is no longer, I get a pretty good view of our farm: the yard, the barn, the sheds, the empty chicken coop, the weed-filled vegetable garden, the endless pastures. All of it smothered in green and a vinery brown, the land overgrown and the structures collapsing.

"And scattered throughout: the dead, like Halloween decorations, grotesque marionettes, pale ornaments dangling from trees, broken bits moving in a corner or ditch. These ghastly memorials show an unlikely variety in rates of decay—I wish there were a doctor I could speak to for some logical explanation. Why do some look so healthy, as if they were sleepwalking, or just staggering down to the fridge for a glass of milk, and others appear to have been in the ground for years, recently dug up and whatever's left of them somehow animated?

"For many of those walking the roads their locomotion seems an impossibility. They shouldn't be able to sustain themselves mechanically as the connective tissue and the joints begin to fail. A hand drops off, an arm. Some do collapse because their legs will no longer support them, and they literally fall to pieces.

"Even many of the relatively fresh-looking ones degenerate at a rapid rate. By the time they get from one edge of our property to the other an accelerated decay has reduced them to almost nothing.

"I've watched how, for a few, a kind of self-digestion occurs. As they wobble down the road their bellies or their groins suddenly split open, and a foul mess of organs drops out. Some look down at this point, watching themselves stepping through their own insides. Others—perhaps the lucky ones—continue as if nothing has occurred.

"So, like the rest of us, the dead are both individuals and part of the herd. It makes sense—each of us suffers a different death, but we all, every one of us, dies. I think maybe I'm not out of the woods yet. I might still come down with this, and at any time.

"I use *us* as if it's a given. I have no idea. I never thought I was special. Now I hope to God I'm not."

Jay utilized his dad's old binoculars to get a better look at their faces. Early on, these faces were still recognizable as once-living personalities, with varying proportions, and individual noses, chins, eyes, and the like. Their features showed a range in expression, although for the most part these were simulations of living emotions, some variation of surprise, shock, or alarm.

Given their ages (although death, like the camera, can add years to a face), he assumed he'd know a few of them from high school or elementary, or he might have seen them in town. He tried not to make comparisons, or think too much about familiar details. This continued to nag him, and when further deterioration resulted in anonymity, he felt relieved.

In some the eyeballs fell out. In others the eyeballs shrank and receded into the skull. Sometimes there was liquification and bloating. Or there was significant aridity and a paper-like appearance. Sometimes a dark leakage from the abdomen would dribble down the legs. Sometimes the skin looked tight and stretched like a drum. In others there was a great deal of skin slippage and teeth falling out. The world of the dead was every bit as unequal and unjust as the world of the living.

In church, when Jay was small, the preacher said when the rapture happens the souls of the believers would be delivered to heaven, leaving their sinful bodies behind. One afternoon he thought he saw the preacher's body lurching up the road. He turned away and went downstairs. He wasn't sure if it was out of respect, but he didn't want to see any more.

Then there had been the girl he'd always wanted to ask out in high school, but never did. He'd been too shy. Lately the dead who appeared on the road were so deteriorated, even if she'd been among them, he would not have recognized her. He was grateful for that much.

"All my life I've dreamed of the dead. Both in waking

dreams and sleeping dreams I have seen them: passing through rooms, gliding across lawns, sometimes perched on rooftops. Sometimes in these dreams they confront me, angry because of something I've done or simply because I'm still alive. I've always come away from these dreams feeling guilty, either because of something thoughtless I said or something heart-felt I lacked the courage to reveal. But the most peculiar thing is that I've never dreamt of the actual dead. The dead people in my dreams have always been living at the time.

"Like everyone else I've lost elderly relatives. We expect grandparents to die, older parents, old men and women in the neighborhood. It seems natural. I loved my grandfather very much; he built this farm from nothing. But the last decade of his life I pulled away from him. I was still glad to see him when I did, but I didn't seek him out. Part of it was I was busy with my own life, and we didn't have as much in common anymore. But I know much of it was because I realized his life was on its way out. He was going to die relatively soon, and I didn't want to be close enough to watch.

"I'm ashamed of that now. I wanted to ask him how it felt—I admit that was more about my own anxieties than anything meant to comfort him—but I wanted to know how it was to lose most of the people you'd ever known, most of the people you'd ever loved, and knowing you were both the last and the next. No wonder the old looked so tired and moved as if they were carrying a great weight.

"I wish I had asked. I could really use that information right now.

"The first young person I knew who died was a popular high school boy who lived on a farm a few miles away. I was in elementary school, but everyone knew who he was—a star player on the high school football team, in the choir at church, and he always smiled and said hello to me even though I was just this scrawny kid he didn't really know.

"His junior year he was on a tractor helping his dad out

when it rolled over on him, trapping him underneath. All the boys drove tractors around here, helping on the family farm. They tried everything to get him out while he screamed until he passed out, but he died under there.

"For years I just couldn't get him out of my head. Anytime anything big happened—a huge snowstorm, an important game, a new *Star Wars* film, the terrorist attack on the World Trade Center—the first thing I thought was *Frankie missed this,* like he missed falling in love, getting married, having kids, having a career. I wouldn't have said it was *unfair* because that's just the way life works. But I thought it was *strange*, the way it all works, a short life and a forever death. For the dead, death just is, I suppose. For the living it's about everything they missed, and what you miss about them. Until now, of course.

"What is happening now is much stranger. I'm glad Frankie died all those years ago, and not recently. I wouldn't want to see him walking around dead, like my brother Ryan before he ended up by the front steps.

"I haven't written down anything in a while. Sometimes I don't see the point. The power has been blinking out a lot lately. The other day it must have been eight hours or more. Pretty soon it will go out for good. I've been lucky to have it this long. But the pump isn't working right, I think maybe because of all the power outages. You can't live without water. I may not know much about survival, but I know that much.

"I've got a backpack filled with some food, a blanket, a knife and a few tools, a change of clothes, extra shoes, some first aid stuff. I'll bring the journal and several pens as well. I'll see new things, so I'll have new things to write about.

"I'm a fool for not thinking more about what to pack for my exit from home. I had the time. I'm a fool for not maintaining my car. But I didn't want to go out there, and who knows if there's any gas to be found, or a clear space to drive.

Lately the dead fill the road. I'll know soon enough. I'll know a lot of things I don't know now. Human beings, we're always learning."

Jay went out the front door the next morning. He left the door open, for another survivor, or as a new space the dead could—whatever. He would have liked to stay and watch that happen. That would have been too foolish even for him.

He would look for a place with a spring—quite possible in southwest Virginia, and if there was a store nearby, he was all set. Problem solved.

He stopped at Ryan's body and watched him for a few moments. The body wasn't exactly moving, but Jay detected a subtle trembling, a vibration, a Ryan quake. His brother had turned his face downward, as if in deep contemplation of the ground and what lay beyond.

The dead in the yard paid no attention. He meant nothing to them. He dwelled in a different universe. There was a pervasive stench which, although not fresh, was deeply unpleasant. He was now close enough to examine the dead more thoroughly, but chose not to, assuming he would have many such chances later.

When he stepped onto the road Jay was pleased to see he would be able to ease past the walking forms without having to touch them. He wasn't sure which direction to take. It made little difference, but he decided to go right first, toward the small towns, for a greater selection of supplies. It did mean going against traffic, for all the dead were traveling the other way. Another thing he'd never been able to figure out—why all in the same direction? There was nothing for them there.

He was so tired. He hadn't slept well in, what? Months. He felt his hands trembling and brought them up to his face. When had they gotten so thin? And spotted? He had brownish spots everywhere. As his mother turned old she used to call those age spots. And skin so thin it looked like tissue. But still he looked better than these poor souls. So many things had happened to him. He was last of his kind.

He became momentarily confused and wasn't sure where he was going. He turned and turned and finally fell into pace with the rest of them.

He felt a great weight pressing on his shoulders. He may have put too much into his pack. He kept moving his feet, but it was becoming increasingly difficult. He was aware when the lower part of his body let go. There was a hushing sound, and a tremendous release. A great sigh rushed through him. He was still thinking. He was still thinking.

Saudade

As his taxi raced toward the dock Lee could see the water between buildings and at the end of streets, filling the space around and beyond distant spits of unfocused land. The ocean smelled like a liquefied cellar. His last time near the ocean was that summer at Myrtle Beach when he was nine. He'd hated the way the sand got between his toes, in his swimsuit, in every private crevice. He'd gone into the water to get rid of the sand, and had been alarmed by the volume and the pull of it. Its murky gray was the color of everything dissolved, everything disintegrated, eaten, and disappeared. He never went into the ocean again.

It wasn't too late to turn around. But his girls wouldn't get their money back. And worse, they'd be disappointed in him.

"Dad, it'll be like riding the bus." Jane had tried to be reassuring, but how could she know? Neither she nor her sister had ever been on a cruise. All they knew was from the TV commercials and the colorful brochures. Lee and his late wife had raised their daughters to be skeptical, but it never quite took.

His cell phone began playing that discordant ringtone Cynthia had programmed to identify her. He fumbled with the buttons and answered. "Hi honey. I'm almost at the dock."

"Great! I'm sorry we couldn't be there to see you off."

Jane shouted in the background, "Bon voyage!"

"Tell her thanks. How's the internship going?"

"It's going *well*, Dad! We're impressing everybody! You'll be proud."

"I'm already proud. You sure you have enough money? You spent so much on this trip."

"We have *savings*, remember? All that stuff you used to say about the *real world*? We listened."

Lee felt himself tear up. It happened easily these days. "OK then. I'll send postcards." He heard inarticulate yelling, laughter in the background. "Cindy, what's going on?"

Cynthia laughed. "Jane wants you to promise you'll warn us first if you're bringing home a new wife." Lee didn't react, and they said their goodbyes. He wished they hadn't pushed him into this.

Stuck in traffic only blocks from the pier Lee pulled out the brochure. *Senior Singles Cruise*. The words embarrassed him. But it had been over five years, and he was very much single and feeling older every day.

If the taxi were late it wasn't his fault. The welcome packet stressed that the ship always sailed on time—it was your responsibility to get on board, both at the start and at all stops along the way. The very idea of being marooned in some Caribbean port—he might just stay on board the entire trip.

But the taxi made good time over the remaining blocks. Dilapidated warehouses were the rule on one side of the road. On the ocean side small and mid-size boats were anchored or dry-docked for repair, their hulls chewed with corrosion, the upper parts and edges stained a coffee color.

At the terminal he waited for hours with hundreds of others on brightly-colored chairs, an experience not mentioned in the brochure. Eventually he found himself heading for the gangway with a large group. A pretty young photographer offered to take his "Bon Voyage" picture. It was only then he realized the looming white metal wall was his destination. He consented only so he'd have one to give the girls. He smiled as if he were already having the best time of his life.

Once inside the ship a small olive-skinned man with a thick accent offered to take him to his cabin. "My bags?"

"They wait for you," the little man said, "please watch your step," and rapidly led him through various openings and a maze of corridors. After a few minutes he had no sense of location or being on the water at all.

The cabin was like other small rooms he'd stayed in at cheap hotels. An undersized bed and a cramped bathroom, a tiny table and chair beneath twin portholes. He wasn't sure what he'd hoped for—something exotic perhaps. But Lee was used to disappointment.

A printed schedule for "Senior Singles" was on the table. He read it with increasing alarm. Dinner was a "Meet Some-one New" event. An equal number of women and men at each table as somehow guaranteed. He'd made a terrible mis-take in agreeing to this.

After breakfast there were classes on dance and casino games, bridge, tennis, other "deck sports," and "Social Skills for Seniors." After a small-group lunch (whatever that was), "cruisers"—oh, *please*—were encouraged to change into sun or swim attire and relax in one of the countless deck chairs. A good quality sunscreen was highly recommended. His daughters had bought him enough extremely high SPF products to protect him from anything short of immolation. In the evenings, after the awkward-sounding dinners, live entertainment was offered, and the optional "romantic stroll around the deck." Lee dropped this schedule into the waste bin. He had brought plenty of books.

He glanced out one of the portholes. The ocean appeared to be in a slow spin around him as the ship headed out to sea. He sat down, struggling not to weep.

For the first two days Lee asked for people's names and occupations. He listened to their stories and laughed at their jokes, and told a few harmless stories of his own. But "his" stories were stolen from people he knew and had nothing to do with him. He wasn't sure why he lied, except he thought these tales more generally appealing. With each small deceit he felt worse.

Staff were always interrogating him, asking if he was having a good time, offering snacks, providing dozens of fluffy white towels every day. Others ran around with buckets of white paint, coating the barest suggestions of corrosion. Every day there were new brown spots, red streaks of oxidation, holes needing to be plugged before passengers noticed.

"I don't believe I've ever seen you out on the deck," a tablemate named Sylvia said at one night's dinner. "But it's the quiet ones you really have to watch out for." She winked at him and laughed. Lee couldn't remember the last time a woman had winked at him.

"Oh, I've heard that saying," he replied, not knowing what else to say. What in the world was she talking about?

The ever-present waiter interrupted. "Is everything perfect?"

Lee looked up and forced a smile. "It was a very good meal."

"Was there something that did not suit you?"

He had no idea what to say. His tablemates spoke of textures, presentation, and the blend of flavors. Surely they were making it all up as they went along?

When the waiter hustled off, that woman, Sylvia, grabbed his arm. Lee stared at her thin fingers, a large ring on each one. "Don't tell me you've found someone *already*, without giving the rest of us girls a chance!" He looked into her red-rimmed eyes and realized how much wine she'd consumed.

"Sylvie! You're *terrible*!" her companion exclaimed, blushing and glancing his way. Suddenly he was in high school again, not understanding what his classmates were getting at. He was unable to speak the rest of the meal. He embarrassed too easily. Had he ever been able to do this? There had been moments, surely, otherwise he could never have married Ann, and raised those two beautiful daughters.

After dinner Lee took an elevator to an upper deck for some air. The motion of the ship was more pronounced at this level, sometimes with a roll that forced him to shift his weight from one leg to the other, or a pitch that almost made him fall, or float off into the air. He knew suicides were sometimes a problem on these voyages, but perhaps some were hapless victims of unintentional flight. He wondered if the onboard shops sold heavier shoes.

At this height the ocean was a boundless expanse of black, borderless width and bottomless depth. There should have been more reflections—the ship was brightly lit. It made a shushing sound cutting through the liquid dark, and the troublesome whispers underneath.

Tonight's moon was low on the horizon, its gleaming reflection painting a path across the water into its very heart. He felt a desire he had no words for.

If he stared into the water long enough he could distinguish blacker areas within the black, moving independently. As the clouds drifted rapidly away and the waves began to rise he saw another cruise ship in the distance, all lit up like an upside down chandelier. Then an arm of the ocean covered it and it disappeared. He waited for it to reappear, unsure of what he had just seen. Finally he turned away, thinking he had misapprehended.

He heard a broken cackle from the deck below, followed by sobs, reassurances. That woman Sylvia and her friend. Lee took a few steps back in case they looked up. He saw a woman a few feet away in a pale yellow gown leaning on the rail. There was something about the set of her shoulders, a certain absorption. From this angle her face looked wet. It alarmed him enough that he was willing to risk embarrassment. He walked over and stood beside her.

The sky was now remarkably clear—a field of stars extended over hundreds of square miles. "You never see this many stars from land," he said. He should have followed that with something, but he had no idea what. The stars ended in a region near the horizon line where lightning rhythmically fractured the emptiness.

"Lovely, isn't it?" She turned her face slightly and she didn't appear to have been crying. Her eyes were large and outlined in black—make-up or not—he couldn't tell. She smelled of some exotic spice, not perfume, but perhaps something she'd eaten. The rest of her was in shadow. He thought she must be both beautiful and unusual. Still, she seemed untroubled. He had misunderstood everything.

"I'm sorry to have interrupted you."

"You thought, perhaps, I was going to jump."

"Oh no, I was just . . ."

"Attempting to measure my mental state. Do not be embarrassed for a kind urge. People do end their lives on these . . . frenetic vacations. They *insist* that you enjoy yourself. And when you do not respond as programmed, a certain desperation ensues."

"I was thinking that very thing earlier. I didn't want to come, but my daughters gave me this trip."

"And you do not wish to disappoint them. You are part of the seniors group, the 'cruisers' I believe they call themselves."

"Terrible, isn't it?" Then she wasn't part of the group. In this light he couldn't tell how old she was—maybe he was making a fool of himself.

"Loneliness is terrible. Loneliness deadens the spirit. A man who has lost his wife knows much about loneliness, I think."

"How did you . . ."

"A band of discoloration on your ring finger. You might have removed the ring as part of some ruse, but you do not seem the type. So either a divorce, or a passing, and I see no signs of divorce in your face."

Lee looked down at his hand. He couldn't see anything—it was too dark for her to have seen. He had taken his ring off over a year ago. "As I've told my daughters, I'm doing okay. I don't need some . . . intervention."

"We have a word in Brazil. *Saudade*. *Estou com saudades de você*. I miss you. But it means much more. It is a profound, melancholic longing for an absent something or someone one loves. However much you attempt to think of other things, it lingers. But you may never have even possessed the thing, or the someone, before. The one you yearn for may be a complete fabrication. We Brazilians are passionate, and we are in love with—how do you say?—*tragic* frames of mind. Saudade is part of our national character. Saudade, I suspect, is why many of these people are here. They hunger for something, someone. What is it that you long for, Lee?"

"How did you?" But she shut off his question with a kiss. Her lips were damp, and unpleasantly cold, but the sensation pleased him. It had been years since he'd kissed anyone on the lips. He pulled her closer into him, seeking more warmth, and found none. Instead, to his alarm, he could taste bile coming up into his throat. He turned away, gagging. "I'm so sorry!" He'd experienced no seasickness since coming on board. He'd been inordinately proud of himself. To have it come now, at the most inopportune time, made him despair.

It took him some time to recover. At some point he was forced to his knees. When he could finally look up she was gone. Who could blame her? He'd embarrassed her as much as himself.

When he regained his feet he searched for her to apologize. The deck glistened where she had been standing. He heard the shush and scrape. He turned—one of those ubiquitous deck hands was cleaning up after him, avoiding his gaze. "Aren't you supposed to put out barriers when you mop? Someone might slip and fall!"

The little man looked terrified. "So sorry, so sorry!"

"I . . . I didn't mean to snap at you," Lee said, and walked away.

He wandered around looking for her, having no idea what he would say if he found her. He didn't want to make her uncomfortable, but she had kissed him, hadn't she?

He took the elevator down and walked up to the bow. Balcony after balcony piled up behind him—when he turned he saw a few people watching from above, one shouting drunkenly. With both feet planted Lee could feel the ship's engines throbbing inside him. He walked around the edge of the deck, paying particular attention to any women standing by the railing, until he'd made his way to the stern. Here he could see the wake of the ship, the furrows of water turned silver by the moon.

An opportune place, if he were so inclined, to leave the cruise and everything else behind. But how horrible to be alone in all this water. After a few hours you would beg to die.

Lee spent the next morning in bed, not quite able to pull himself out of dreams he could not remember. Even with the *Do Not Disturb* sign out there were numerous knocks on his door. Finally he woke himself up enough to yell "Read the sign!" He felt satisfied by the sounds of rapid retreat, but had he missed an opportunity to see the woman from last night? Somehow she had known his name, so it would be no surprise if she could find his door, or had he misunderstood all that?

He needed more sleep to drain any residual sense of unreality, but blasts of the ship's horn made that impossible. Defeated, he stared at his cabin walls. A series of prints conveyed an attitude of eroticism, while still far from explicit so that no one could complain—curves and blurry flesh-colored swatches of color, some lines hinting at a highly abstracted embrace. Highly abstracted embraces seemed the most he could hope for at this stage of his life.

These images recalled a series of Chagall prints Ann chose for their bedroom. He didn't know much about art. Their titles contained words like "lovers," "marriage," and "kiss." With clouds of color that spread across the lines of the forms, it was as if the passion those couples felt extended to everything they touched, everything they saw. It was too much, or at least he had thought so at the time. Now he envied their enthusiasm. The figures were so full of emotion they floated—they'd lost all sense of decorum or gravity.

He remembered those kisses—necks impossibly elongated, their swimming bodies in extremis as they wrapped around each other. Ann had loved them, and he had loved them more than he would say. But they promised so much— had anyone ever felt such passion in a normal marriage?

Yes, yes they had. Feelings he didn't have words for. After Ann passed away he took the prints down and stuck them in the back of a closet so he might forget they were there. When his girls asked what happened to the prints he said he wasn't sure. He had no idea what his life was now, but it wasn't about that anymore.

The kiss last night had been nothing like the kisses in those prints. But it still had been surprising, although not exactly pleasant.

When Lee finally left his cabin he encountered the ship's activities director, her fixed smile more predatory than friendly. From the beginning she'd made him feel bullied. "I'm so *glad* I was able to run into you. You haven't been sick, have you?"

"Out too late," he said, "I suppose having too much fun. You must have hundreds of people, don't you, to be concerned about?"

"All equally important. Tell me, how can I make sure *you* have the time of your life?"

The very phrase *the time of your life* depressed him. "I'm doing fine, easing into things. Relaxing. There's nothing wrong with that is there?"

"Of course not! But I'm sure we can do better. I know four lovely ladies eager for some male company at lunch."

He began his retreat. "Too much fun to have today, I'm afraid." He turned his back and practically ran.

"You'll leave empty-handed if you don't *make it happen!*" she shouted after him. He felt dizzy and struggled not to fall as the floor appeared, briefly, to melt.

Every afternoon the decks stank of suntan oil. Every lounge chair was full of barely-clothed flesh in various stages of destruction. He thought of Jonestown, the bodies darkening in the intense tropical heat.

These were not ugly people. They were just trying to enjoy their vacations. Lee believed there were no ugly people, but he himself didn't have the courage to lie about half-naked, not with his aging carcass. He scanned the faces looking for his mystery woman, even though she would seem out of place in a lounge chair in the sun.

"Aren't you going to say hello?" He recognized Sylvia's voice, but he couldn't find her in the sea of glistening skin, oversized sunglasses, and floppy sunhats. "Over here, in the red."

He walked over. She wore an old-fashioned-looking red two-piece suit. He thought she looked unusually sober. "You seem relaxed," he said.

"You probably think I look fat in this."

"I think . . . you look fine. Most of us aren't that slim, not at this age. We hold onto that memory of what we used to be too firmly. If you like what you're doing, that's what counts, isn't it?"

"I guess—I didn't expect you to be so enlightened. Most men aren't."

"I'm not enlightened. If I were, I would be dressed in swim trunks."

She laughed. "Will I see you at dinner later?"

"I don't really know. But enjoy the sun."

That hadn't been so difficult. Perhaps he knew what to say

to people after all. He continued to look at faces, struggling to remember the features of the woman from the night before. It wasn't a good feeling. No doubt she would be appalled if she knew he was searching. But he was just making himself seen. If she wished to approach him it was up to her.

He strolled through the restaurants, and stood at the back of a dance class. He looked for that yellow dress, but wouldn't she have changed by now? He hadn't behaved like this since high school.

He wondered what Ann would have thought of his behavior. Embarrassed for him, possibly, or sad. By sunset most of the chairs were empty. He should eat something, but he didn't think he could. He sat down. He should be writing his daughters, letting them know how he was doing, but what in the world would he say? *I've met someone*, perhaps. Both the truth and a lie.

Both the sea and the sky appeared the rumpled gray of an unmade bed. The horizon line had been almost completely erased. Staring too long into the blurring of borders made him ill.

"You miss her—she is all you can think about." The woman slipped into the next chair. Instead of looking at him she stared into that disorientating gray. Her dress, too, was gray this evening, or some shade of off-white.

"It's more complicated than that."

"You've lost your story, then," she replied. Today he could see that she wasn't a young woman. The skin of her neck was crepey, and there was loose flesh beneath her eyes. Perhaps she was his age after all.

"I just feel I should be doing something, but I don't know what to do." It made him feel unbearably sad to say this.

"You were in a story which worked for you for a very long time. But that story has ended, and yet you find you are still alive, and now you are in a different story you do not yet understand."

"So what am I supposed to do?"

"Live your life. Enjoy your vacation. Life may look quite differently when you return."

"But I don't seem to be very good at this."

"Take a walk with me," she said, standing up and grabbing his hand. "You can do that much." It seemed he didn't have a choice. She guided him along the deck until they reached a small door in the hull that said "Crew Only." She opened it and dragged him inside.

They were at an intersection of corridors. She took him through another door and down some metal stairs. He felt like a child being hand-led like this. The air was steamy. Her gray dress clung like excess skin.

These interior walls lacked the polish of the public areas. No upholstery or shiny white paint—the metal was dirty yellow with brown rust around the seams and rivets and bolts. There were distant echoes of harsh male argument and laughter, the rattle of machinery, metal banging against metal.

Another trip down another set of stairs—the paint completely worn off the grungy treads. They hadn't even bothered to mop up the dirt. Where were all those eager little uniformed men with their mops and smiles you saw on the passenger decks? The filth in the corners and along the edges had congealed into a black scum.

A muscular, shirtless man walked past them without a glance. Pressure was rising in Lee's head, a thrumming against his ear drums. He wondered if they were below water level now.

He wanted to ask her name—it was absurd he didn't know—but it didn't seem like the time. He should have insisted she reveal where they were going, but he couldn't make himself speak. Her hand was delicate, yet she gripped his so firmly it hurt. Sweat made her skin appear gelatinous. Sweat was running into his eyes. He struggled with his free hand to wipe his face.

The next level down was packed with equipment. A

wall of noise moved through him like a wave. His internal organs shook. Overhead were layers upon layers of pipes, cables, gears, gauges, valves. The corridor shrank until it was no more than a catwalk—on either side he could see more machinery and more shirtless men far below, so distant they appeared to be miniatures, or was it possible the cramped working space required dwarves?

The walls of the ship were weeping, rivulets oozing down the seams and gathering in depthless pools below. The air smothered him in the stench of decay.

A narrow ladder dropped into an even darker place—there was no light, no reflection. She made him trade positions and when he hesitated she nipped his cheek with teeth like ice. The blood ran down his face and when he tried to wipe it off she darted forward as if to kiss or bite but licked him instead. Her tongue felt expansive. "You need to go first," she whispered. She let go of his hand as he took the first step down, but when he hesitated—*What am I doing?*—she placed her bare foot on his shoulder—*When did she take off her shoes?*—and forced him down several more rungs. He surrendered and led the way into the jet-black mist.

At the bottom he couldn't see his feet on the floor, if it was a floor. It was something solid, but it felt less than stable. Before he could figure it out she jerked him off his feet. The blackness fragmented into hundreds of glistening bits, resembling butterflies or birds, but which might have been fish. They disappeared as suddenly as they had appeared.

Lee felt the damp on his face, but it didn't feel like sweat. Maybe he was crying. Certainly he felt barely controlled, fear and incredible sadness welling up with no words for any of it. He tried to think of his daughters and how sorry he was to leave them, but their faces broke down into incoherency. He sobbed, and glistening air bubbles propelled in front of him. He was deep underwater and should have been dead, drowning in excruciatingly slow motion.

She wrapped her arms around him, arms so flexible they might have been boneless. She wrapped those long tubes of skin around his head, her moist whispers ordering him to turn, rocking his head painfully.

A translucent shape came forward out of the nothing: huge eyes and skeletal head, teeth so long and sharp it couldn't close its mouth. Floating around it was an expanse of insubstantial rags, great sheets of peeled flesh unfolding, their bioluminescent edges pulsing slowly. They suddenly darted in Lee's direction. He screamed with no sound. Something caught in his mouth. He reached up and felt his teeth, several inches long and razor sharp. Something blurry went into one of his eyes. He reached up and slowly pulled it out. His eyes were cavernous holes where anything could enter.

He shook his head vigorously. All the loose skin of him, the torn flesh and ragged filaments of him, floated around his face. He looked down at his body and could find neither his arms nor his legs.

He turned to her then, her mouth so wide, her lips so swollen, so dark. *Saudade*, she said, *Saudade*, until she had him completely in her mouth.

Lee was suddenly awake, lying on his bed in the cabin. Water drained off him and onto the sheets, then onto the floor. Everything was wet and everything stank. The housekeepers were always so eager for something to do—he had plenty for them to clean today.

He glanced up at that terrible, banal artwork, and thought of those Chagall prints hidden away in the back of a closet at home. He could send a letter from the ship telling his daughters where the prints were, and that they could have them. Ann would have wanted them to have them. His message would get there before the ship returned to home port.

The intercom came alive and a lovely voice announced that all passengers were welcome to go ashore and identifying the day's exit points. Lee hadn't ventured off the ship at any of the ports of call so far, but he needed to, didn't he, if only to buy souvenirs for his girls? When they were little they'd loved souvenirs from his business trips. He'd arrive home and after all the hugs and kisses they'd gather around his giant suitcase on the bed as he opened it to reveal what he'd brought them—usually a little T-shirt or a stuffed animal with the city's name embroidered across the front. It had been this simple ritual that had always made such perfect sense and it had been wondrous.

He climbed out of the wet bed and stripped off his soggy clothing, leaving it on the floor for the staff. Brisk use of a couple of towels left him moderately dry. He found his best shirt and pants in the closet, a pair of dress shoes, clean socks and underwear. Nothing terribly fancy, but still, the best he had brought. Every bit of the carpet was damp and he had no dry place to sit. Water was even dripping off his desk chair. So he stood and balanced himself carefully against the wall, pulling on his clothes and trying not to let them touch the carpet for more than a second or two. It took a while but finally he was dressed. At the last moment he grabbed his good sports jacket off the hanger and left the room.

The water in these Caribbean ports was so clear you could see schools of fish travelling beneath the crystalline surfaces. But so far their perfection had not persuaded him. Lee felt there had to be something terribly wrong behind such movie-magical sets, and he had no interest in discovering exactly what.

But today's excursion was for his daughters. A crew member swiped his ID card and he walked down the gangway at a brisk clip, eager to get his errands done and then back on board. His pace fell awkwardly into step with the cacophonous melodies of the ubiquitous steel drums. It was quite the production—the musicians wore non-identical but similar yellow and orange tropical suits. Two dark-skinned dancers performed in complementing colors. The music wasn't exactly unpleasant, but there was too much of it and too much the same. Lee felt as if everyone was looking at him, but doubted that anyone had actually noticed at all.

The beach here was white enough to hurt the eyes. He wondered if the sand was hot to the touch, and remained on the wooden walk just in case. He felt as if he had stepped into a rich oil painting whose colors were almost too intense to bear. What was that style called? He wished he knew more of the proper names for things. Ann certainly had.

But for Lee this was like the worst kind of dreaming, the kind that came when you were running a high fever and you felt as if you were rotting from the inside out, as so many of these islands probably were, what with the fruit, the jungle, their heightened cycle of birth and death. Or had he imagined it all? He knew very little about these places. He didn't even know what island he was on. He hadn't bothered to check.

It didn't take long to find the shop he wanted, one offering native wood carvings—animals mostly, but a few religious icons, and some doll-sized figures with extraordinarily ugly faces, the kind of eccentric gift both his daughters loved. The figures looked more Polynesian than Latin American but that didn't matter. The clerk offered to box them up ready to mail—a shipping center was only a few doors away. Lee mailed them and headed back to the ship.

He chose not to tour the island. Maybe that was a mistake, but what could a casual visitor see anyway? He couldn't imagine an excursion that wouldn't depress him. He'd want to know what was on the other side of the barbed wire or behind the huts. He'd want to know what the tourists weren't allowed to see. He'd want to ask them how you lived on an island in the middle of the ocean. If you wanted to go somewhere where could you go? And none of this would answer the question of his aching.

He was tempted to find the woman again but knew he

shouldn't. Instead he returned to his cabin to write long letters to both his daughters. He wasn't surprised to find his cabin in pristine condition. That was what they did here— they cleaned up all your messes as if they'd never been. They erased your mistakes. It was a complete escape from life. Some people welcomed that.

He wrote his long rambling letters full of memories and feelings and good wishes and everything he could think of to say to the people he cared most about in the world. Exhausted, he signed "Dad" to each and crawled into bed. In the morning he would look the letters over carefully to make sure he hadn't said anything he shouldn't have, and after he was done he would drop them off to be mailed at the next port.

Lee woke up sometime in the middle of the night. He was shaking. He thought at first that the ship's horn had blown, that some disaster had occurred, but he waited there in bed and heard nothing more—no horn, no footsteps outside. He couldn't even hear the ocean, or feel its movement.

He got up and slipped into the same clothes he'd worn that morning. He even put on his sports jacket. It was likely to be cold.

He walked out onto the empty deck. There was no one at the railing, no one in any of the deck chairs. He walked by the closed shops and stared in at the mannequins, willing them to move. The lights in the restaurants and even in the casino were out, which seemed unlikely. The casino was open all the time.

The elevator wasn't working, so he took the steps up and down. He encountered no one on any of the decks he tried. He decided he wasn't going to get upset over this, and so he stopped looking. He could have knocked on random cabin doors, but of course he wouldn't do that. Let them sleep—it was the least he could do.

He went back up the stairs to the top deck of the ship.

There was a swimming pool, but no one was in it. It was so dark he couldn't even tell if there was water in the pool. He heard nothing.

Someone stood at the forward observation point by the telescopes. He walked up behind her. Of course it was her. She was peering into one of the eyepieces.

He stepped closer. "What do you see?"

She turned around slowly. "I have not been home in a very long time, and I've never seen it from this angle. Sometimes I believe I do not miss it, but actually I miss it very much. *Saudade*, of course. *Saudade*."

He stepped up beside her and looked out at the ocean: boundless, dark, and moving, although he couldn't hear the waves. But he could see no land ahead of them, or anywhere else.

"You should look through the telescope. It might satisfy your yearnings."

He didn't want to do that. But he rested his hand on top of the scope and gazed at her. She seemed different, but he couldn't quite see her face, even though they were very close together. Perhaps his eyes were going bad. Perhaps even if he looked through the telescope he would be unable to see what was right in front of him.

"Perhaps you would like a kiss first," she said, "for encouragement."

He didn't want to, but she came to him anyway. He closed his eyes when their lips met. She tasted of something he did not recognize. He felt his body beginning to lift, to float. Still their lips were locked together, their tongues barely touching. He could feel his neck beginning to stretch, and bend, and soon he was upside down, and floating out over and past the rail, and over the ocean.

But they were still kissing, they were still kissing. Until all his weight returned.

Sleepless

A car glides down the lane. The headlights melt the shadows, the darkness flowing into the gutters and into the drains. As soon as it passes the darkness flows out again and fills the neighborhood. My eyes struggle to readjust. I used to see better, but I can't remember exactly when.

The detective peers out at me from under the trees across the street. Maybe he thinks I can't see him. Or he knows I see him but doesn't care. You can't see into a person's heart just by looking. You can't know them from what they say. Most of our self-knowledge comes from the necessary lies we've told ourselves. If I could tell him anything that is what I would say.

My house has a crumbling deck up on the second floor, just above the garage facing the street. I always intended to replace it, but never have. I wouldn't let the children play there, although there probably was never any danger. The deck sits directly on the garage roof, so it isn't as if they could have fallen through. The railing needs repair, but it is still strong enough for most purposes. But they might have gotten splinters, or fallen and scraped themselves on the splitting boards. Children get hurt in all kinds of ways, both expected and unexpected. You can't protect them from everything. Protection in general, I've decided, is a problematic enterprise. You lose everything in the end.

It has been cloudy for several weeks, but no rain has come. Sometimes lightning passes from cloud to cloud as if the world were building up a charge. There is smoke in the air—several houses have burned, one just a few blocks over. They think it might have been lightning, but no one seems to know for sure. The sense of anticipation is draining, and some afternoons I am close to weeping. During the day the sky resembles bruised flesh. The vague illumination proves there is still a sun—it's hiding behind the clouds as if reluctant to appear. Just because I don't see the sun doesn't mean it isn't there. But very little light filters down to the houses below. Many people remain indoors, yet that doesn't explain so many absences, this sense that the city is emptying itself of human beings. There seemed to be more people around when I was younger.

Sometimes I suspect there has been a subtle shift in the laws of the physical world, some series of minute changes whose consequences become apparent only over time. But I've always had a poor grasp of science. Most things appear to happen for no reason. I can offer no theories, no explanations. I would ask Mary, but Mary is out. The empty house has nothing to say.

When I am alone in the house I find myself making noise in order to fill up the empty. I suspect the rest of the world feels the same. All these empty houses, empty people—sometimes they make a surprising amount of noise.

Middle of the night I am standing on the crumbling deck, leaning on the railing, searching the shadows for the detective. Sometimes he smokes, and I can see the nervous jitter of his lit cigarette. Otherwise he is hard to find. I have many questions, and aren't detectives supposed to have the answers? Sometimes they're reluctant to give up what they know, but I still have a little money left from the insurance. I am sleepless, and this has become my habit.

Every evening I make myself go to bed around ten or eleven (although it is hard to know for sure when you don't look at the clock), but then my eyes open again at two or three, and I am unable to go back to sleep. I have read that in centuries past this pattern of sleeping was not that uncommon—people slept in two shifts, with a period of middle-of-the-night wakefulness available for doing certain activities in the darkest part of the night. Sometimes I think this lost productive time is rightfully ours and modern life has stolen it from us. But it would only be useful if I returned to sleep. And it seems I never return to sleep.

I wander the house at night, travelling room to room. And yet I try not to disturb things. I've tried to preserve the house as it was. At least there is less to clean, less to straighten that way. I don't use most of the furniture anymore. And I eat over the sink, immediately hand-washing my plate and putting it away. I try to add nothing and take nothing away. But still I have to sit somewhere, and have designated particular chairs. I sit in these chairs and I listen to the air within this enclosed space, and I find hiding beneath the quiet the greatly reduced roar of the missing crowd, overcome with grief, confusion, and uncertainty.

Sometimes I will sit in an overstuffed chair until dawn or after, but lately I've been going out to the deck and standing, or leaning back in the battered lawn chair I carried up here years ago. Mary hated that, the shabbiness of it, and would always insist on the need to maintain appearances. But the neighbors have never complained.

It isn't as if I'm too alert to sleep. Everything I think or feel, everything I see comes filtered through a gauze of fatigue. I've never felt so tired in my life.

Tired, and yet infected with an odd sort of restlessness. It is as if the restlessness lives in another part of the house, and I am aware of it only because it makes the occasional noise, or steals some of the heat or oxygen I need to survive. So I have to be aware, and diligent, and that's what makes me wake up in the middle of the night. I feel that if I'm not careful enough something might eat me in my sleep. I would ask Mary to reassure me if Mary were here.

Some nights I stand out on the deck waiting for the rain.

It has to come sometime. The air feels heavy, as if at any moment it might tear, and leak. The dark shadows on the pavements resemble patches of damp, but are not.

The detective steps out from under the trees in front of my neighbor's house. His head is so dark I can't see the expression on his face. I don't know how long he's been hiding there, but I suspect it has been for some time. Has he been watching my house, or something else? Maybe he has been watching no one, and has his own activities to attend to in the middle of the night.

The figure of the detective is so still at times I think I am imagining things, and what I've mistaken for a person is merely a certain confluence of shadows. But then the figure moves again, just a step or two. Then it appears to pace.

Mary used to complain about my indecisiveness. You can put yourself and your loved ones in serious danger due to your lack of action. I come down from the deck, out the door, and I cross the street. If the detective in the shadows is surprised by this he doesn't betray it.

"Excuse me, can I help you?" I ask him, as bold as I've ever been in my life.

The detective steps into the available light. The streetlamp is at least half a block away, but the illumination from it yellows his skin. "Thank you," he says, "but I'm fine."

I point my finger at him in what I hope is a threatening gesture. "You were looking at my house."

The detective, his face a mask of unconcern, looks past my finger. "I was. Are you aware that your roof tiles are badly chipped? You're going to need a new roof."

I turn around and attempt to examine the roof. It is completely obscured by shadow, but I have no reason to doubt him. This region is prone to hail storms and very few roofs survive unscathed. "I see," I say, although I obviously cannot. "Are you pretending to be some sort of roofer, looking for business?"

"No. But hire somebody good. The scam artists are everywhere, and they prey on the elderly. Don't try to do it yourself, a man of your age."

A man of my age? I suddenly feel shaky. I glance at my hands to corroborate, but it's too dark to see if they're more crepey than expected. "What are you talking about? I'm not even forty yet."

The detective steps closer. His eyes are unnaturally open, and the way he moves them, scanning my face as if for clues, is unnerving. "I must have." He pauses. "Misjudged, perhaps."

I examine his clothing: comfortable shoes, but not tennis shoes. Dark narrow wale corduroys. A light blue shirt. And all neatly packaged inside a black rain coat. Unlike me, he could fit in anywhere. "What are you doing out here? I've already talked to the police. We've all talked to the police many times."

"And yet no one has been arrested," the detective replies.

This is true, but hardly surprising. In my experience very few mysteries are ever solved—they are simply forgotten until they raise their ugly heads again. "Do you think you can do better?"

The detective looks away. "I operate privately. When you operate privately, you don't always obey the rules." He stares at me. His eyes won't let go. "Don't you find that to be true?"

I shake uncontrollably. The ground vibrates, the detective and the house behind him warping until they are almost unrecognizable. I don't understand. We haven't had a quake this bad in years. I'm thinking I should warn Mary but Mary is out with the children. I fall to my knees and I scream at the ground. When the quaking doesn't respond I scream some more. But I've never been able to stop whatever is about to happen.

When the earthquake ceases I am staring at the house with the crumbling deck up on the second floor. His neighbors say he keeps his curtains closed and they almost never see him outside, except late at night when he paces the deck, watching. When I question them they're willing to tell me everything they know about him, but they know very little. People lie to themselves—it's built into their DNA.

I don't want to alarm them, but I believe he is far more dangerous than they can imagine. I want to help them, but for now all I can do is continue my investigations. I'll keep my eye on him, and use everything I know to try to understand his behavior. But very few mysteries are ever really solved. As a detective this is my greatest frustration.

During the course of this investigation I position myself near a different house every night. I have the time—I have very little home life left. I try diverse angles. I attempt to discover new perspectives. You have to maintain a fresh eye. You never know when a small detail is going to break a case wide open. Or break you, for that matter.

I never tell the residents I'm doing this—I don't want to alarm them. The last thing I need is their well-meaning interference. Better that they hold on to their illusions of safety than to worry about what's happening around them. I don't mind doing all the worrying for them—I have grown so used to apprehension it has become a kind of comfort zone.

I spend most of my time examining this street, and the streets surrounding, this entire section of town, for clues, for threats. Context is everything. I sleep very little and this gives me something to do when the hour is late and my house an uncomfortable prison for my thoughts.

I actually can't remember what they call this part of town. I had the name a few hours ago, but it periodically escapes me. So many details go into my head that sometimes they push other details out. Not that it matters in the end—names change, as do the people who live here. We live in a mobile society. Buildings are torn down and other buildings go up. Time is a process of constant revision. If you're lucky the worst memories disappear first and by the end you become an empty slate. Sometimes it hardly seems worth it to learn the names of things.

Most people make themselves unaware of the uncertainties which face them, or if aware, they have developed sufficient distractions so that they rarely think. The world would be intolerable otherwise.

It seems as if this case has gone on forever. I have put in thousands of hours, walked hundreds of miles. I have questioned the same people again and again. Now when they see me coming they lock their doors and pretend they're not home. Sometimes I wake up in the morning completely forgetting what I did the night before. It's frustrating, of course, but I'm not by nature an angry person. I tell people this before I interview them, but it does not elicit any new information.

Last night I set the alarm for eight A.M. but woke up at five following a series of dreams which I cannot remember. The fact that we frequently forget our dreams is an obvious evolutionary error. Even when we think we remember them I suspect those memories are generally the result of waking improvisation. Large areas of self-knowledge are unfairly denied us. The human mind is a mystery to itself.

I went back to bed and when the alarm went off at eight it jangled me so badly I thought I had gone temporarily blind. But I'd only closed my eyes. How could I forget closing my eyes?

I spend hours every day walking these streets, noticing, cataloguing. Some might call my focus obsessive. I normally resist taking notes where the public can see me, but the minute details of a community, especially a community in the midst of decline, can be overwhelming if not recorded immediately.

I prefer to walk because I miss too much when I drive. Walking slows the clock—in the time it takes to pass a building you can observe more precisely the specifics of its decay. But there is far too much territory to cover by walking alone. Suburban towns tend to be spread out, sometimes with expansive and poorly tended greenbelts (which can bear fruit during a systematic search for bodies) separating the neighborhoods. So when I grow fatigued I return to the place where I've parked my car. I usually leave it near some familiar landmark so I can find it easily. It's an older model, but I've taken good care of it. I don't want the pain involved in becoming used to another.

Every day I visit at least one of the sites where a victim has been discovered. This hasn't always been easy because the victims are seldom identified as such and because no one has hired me for the job. Many of these people are elderly and living in reduced circumstances and haven't the funds to hire a private detective. They count on the police, and although the police are required to file a report on these deaths they seem reluctant to admit that a crime has been committed. They refer to the statistics. Almost all the victims have been past a certain age and have felt poorly for some time. Most of them lived alone. But none of us feel as well as we used to, I think—it's that time of life. And doesn't everyone know by now that statistics lie?

I get no help from the authorities with my investigations. Much of the time they are dismissive, if not downright rude. Because I have no legal standing the coroner's office will not speak to me and the hospitals turn me away. As a result I almost never know the exact time of death or many of the circumstances. The victims' families are reluctant to speak to me so I have to rely on the neighbors, on rumor and innuendo.

Over the past few years many in the neighborhood have died or moved away. Younger families have moved into some of the houses but quite a few remain empty. Sometimes I will pass several houses in a row with their doors and windows boarded. The yards are overgrown with high weeds and when the wind blows the trash down the street it becomes trapped here with no one to remove it. There is a quiet here that does not invite interference. When I dwell too long at a crime scene I begin to understand the reasons behind law enforcement's lack of response. No one wants to come here. It has become hard to believe that human beings would choose this as a place to live.

I admit to taking a certain sort of comfort in desolation. It's an occupational hazard. The appearance, the feel of desolate places—it confirms some particular perceptions I have of the universe. It corrects any hopes I might harbor for safety and permanence.

Every week there has been some sort of fire. Very few of these incidents have been nearby, but I am convinced that this neighborhood will have its turn. As it is every evening brings with it the distant aroma of smoke. And in the darkest part of the night you can see the faraway lines of flame from an upstairs window or deck.

I catch a vague glimpse nearby of a figure resembling my suspect entering a house through the back door. There is only a dim suggestion of light coming from the windows so I have no idea if anyone is home or not. I feel I should hold back and continue watching, but I've been watching for months it seems, and without further consideration of the consequences I run into the back yard and follow him in.

Within a few steps I've gotten myself wedged between two walls of junk piled close to head height. The little bit of illumination in the room comes from two dim bulbs overhead surrounded by a cloud of frantic moths. I can only see the top layers of trash with any clarity: a large number of plastic shopping bags in varying degrees of fullness, empty packaging for anything from shaving supplies to eggs to small appliances, newspapers and magazines and other printed material, clothing and miscellaneous linen and toys and unrecognizable hardware and plastic parts. The age of these things varies greatly, although fresher-looking items appear to be on top, as if this were geological strata and I was down in a crevice trapped between layers of time.

A kind of trail meanders between the piles but I'm a little too wide for it. When I move my movements are transferred and the whole room appears to shake.

Ahead of me something rustles, then bolts into the next room. It might be some sort of pet or maybe a rat, but I suspect it's the killer, crouched down and hiding. I move along the trail as quickly as I can and I make it through the next doorway safely before things start sliding and debris strikes the back of my legs.

This room is larger than the last. I suppose it might have been a living room and dining room combination at some point, now filled almost to the ceiling with old furniture stacked one upon the other into confusing towers, a tangle of wooden legs, upholstered seats, upholstered backs, step stools and side tables and the spaces wedged with lamps and containers and boxes marked with "Aunt Delia" and "Mark" and "Cynthia" and maybe a half-dozen more names. And again a dim light bulb overhead and a constant flapping of moths like the beating of a hundred tiny hearts.

This is what happens when you cling too tightly to memory, I think. *There's no more room to move. There's no more room for anything else.*

I can hear the sounds of someone moving ahead of me, breathing raggedly, bumping into furniture, shifting things. I think about how the killer is making an easier passage for himself but also making an easier path for me. I can hear my own untidy breathing, sounding so loudly in the room against a background of beating moth wings, and I realize the killer must know that I am also in the house with him, and that there's no more reason for pretense, and all there is for me to do is to catch up with him and stop him if I can.

In the next room there is a bed, magazines and decaying

paperbacks piled all around it, higher than the bed so that they spill on to it, so that it's like a lake being filled in by the collapsing hills around it, and there in the center is the old man in the midst of his death rattle with the killer crouched over him, putting the pillow over his face and pushing down.

I scream and leap into the bed like a diver leaping into that vanishing lake but the killer eludes me. And now it's me straddling the gasping old man, his body beneath me like a pile of broken sticks, and it's my weight causing his suffering, making him sink into the bed.

I keep thinking *I'm not supposed to be here*. But now that I'm here I know what I need to do.

I stare at my hands. They are heavily scarred from all the struggling fingers which have tried to pry them from heaving shoulders, from heads moving side to side as the trembling mouths blast out their final *No's*, from throats convulsing with their last attempts to catch those fleeing breaths.

To let this one live would only prolong his miseries. There is an emptiness in his face from all that he has seen in his life. It's as if all character has been worn away. He is straining beneath me but is it more life he is hoping for or is it an end? With mercy I push and I push until he is done.

I begin to smell the smoke as I make my escape. The edge of my sleeve is on fire and I shake it with annoyance until the flames disappear. Has the detective set the house on fire to cover his crime? By the time I struggle out the back door the entire structure is involved and I begin to realize the detective may not have my best interests in mind.

I can't remember where I left my car. Usually I park it near some familiar landmark so I can find it later after I've been wandering the neighborhood on one of my missions. After an hour or so of walking I still can't find it and I consider that it may still be in the garage at home. I can visualize it hiding like a slumbering panther beneath my crumbling deck.

As I meander home I wonder how many of the houses I'm passing are empty, and how many contain one or more people hiding, peeking out of their windows, afraid to come out. And of course some of these houses contain the dead who haven't yet been discovered. I believe I used to know some of these people, but if pressed I couldn't name any of their names.

During the past few months I have visited most of these homes in some way, strolling by the windows for a quick peek inside, sometimes sitting behind a bush and listening for hours, occasionally entering if I think the house is unoccupied. If I am mistaken I apologize, or I do that difficult thing which must be done. In either case I take responsibility. I handle things, even when there is too much to handle.

Peeking into other people's lives, I discover what it is that haunts these places, the dreams unfulfilled, the lives which have run out of content, the unacceptable losses. I've tried to be a comfort to the elderly and infirm—in many cases my face is the last one they will ever see.

This is not what I wanted. It was never what I wanted. But there is a certain comfort in it just the same. All my anxieties have been verified. My own sense of desolation has not only been confirmed, but multiplied. It manifests in everything I see.

I go back into my house being careful not to disturb things. Ideally people should think it's empty. When the police inevitably break the door down they will conclude that no one has ever lived here.

Mary is still out, the kids are still out, and of course they will never return. Sometimes I think I'm still out there looking for them, even when I'm sitting up sleepless in my chair.

It was a terrible accident that took them away from me. Everyone says so, so it must be true. But life is full of accidents. Sometimes it seems that even a good life is just an accident that happened to go your way.

I sit on the deck as it falls apart around me. The stench of smoke is stronger, and seems to have found a permanent place in my head. I gaze across the street and wait for the detective to appear, but he is being playful tonight, and puts out only his shadow for me to see.

A Stay at the Shores

Carson was in no hurry to return home after the conference. He was single and lived by himself, without even the questionable comfort of pets. He was also between friendships, his last being a widower of similar age who died nine months before this trip. Perhaps his last companion, and perhaps the last person who might remember Carson had ever lived. The man had loved books, and listened to Carson as if he had important things to say. Losing this man's company was a blow whose seriousness he was just now beginning to comprehend. No one would be waiting for him; no one anticipated his return.

Perhaps if he had made more of a splash at the conference someone might recall him in a footnote somewhere. It was the only way he could imagine he might avoid complete oblivion.

It had been a small gathering devoted to transcendentalism. The paper he'd delivered on the sonnets of obscure transcendental poet Jones Very was received with profound indifference, but at least it was another credit for his CV. The college where he lectured was unimportant but his departmental chairman took great stock in such things.

Carson would have liked it if someone had said something nice about his paper. He would have considered it a small victory.

Professor Litton asked him to come for drinks afterward. He was surprised, and worried that perhaps he had unwittingly committed some sort of error. He hadn't thought

Litton even knew his name. "Sorry I missed it, Carson." The older man frowned. "That committee meeting always runs long. Was it a triumph?"

Carson shrugged. "At least I didn't stumble."

"Good, good. You're a professional now. How many of these have you been to?"

"This is my twelfth."

"Very good. I'm sure we'll want to draft you into the organizing committee eventually."

Litton went on to describe the committee's work, alluding to a long history of mysterious quarrels and ambiguous in-fighting. Although at first he listened for some opportunity for more visibility in the academic community, Carson's attention eventually wandered to the rest of the room, where older men in ill-fitting suits hunched drearily over their small glasses of colored liquid. These were his fellow transcendentalists, and not one of them displayed even a hint of a smile.

One fellow nearby appeared to be staring at him while clutching his drink white-knuckled. His eyes were brown stains floating on yellow pools.

"Carson? Did you hear my question?" Litton looked cross with him.

"I'm *so* sorry, Professor. My mind wandered but a moment. I've been quite tired lately. I'm never able to sleep at these things."

"Sleep brings clarity, Carson. One cannot investigate the spiritual aspects of nature through a fog of fatigue."

"You're quite right, of course."

"I was simply asking for confirmation that you are unmarried, that there is no one at home waiting for you?"

It unsettled him that the professor should ask about the very thing Carson had been contemplating so much of late. "I am. There's no one . . . at least for now."

"How are you planning to return home?"

"A bus to the airport, then a quick flight. Nothing terribly interesting."

"Quick seldom means interesting." The older man spread his hands. "Are you aware that there exists a rare opportunity to travel by ship from a historic port?"

"Well, no, I've never been on a boat. But we're miles inland here."

"There's a train to the coast. Infrequent, but direct."

"I've never traveled by train either."

"All the more reason! How old are you, if I may ask?"

"Sixty-three in a few months," Carson replied.

"Too old not to have tried. You *must* do this! Although I've never made the journey myself I hear it's a unique experience. Isn't that what we're all about at this conference, exploration?" Litton made an expansive gesture with his arms. Carson again glanced at the men and a handful of women gathered in the bar. No one here looked like explorers. "Survivors" was the word that came more readily to mind. "I'm told that it's the oldest continuously operating port in the nation. And yet so *little* is known about it really. Rumor has it that it was a port not only before the whites, but even before the Indians. I've heard vague stories about religious sects in the area as far back as the days of the Vikings. Currently it goes by The Shores, but it has had many, many names. Think of it! All that forgotten history—and boundless opportunities for original research. You could make a *name* for yourself, Carson."

Carson's train would get him into The Shores many hours before the ship's departure. Ample opportunity to ask around, find out if there were any threads worth pursuing. That was a blessing. He was a nervous traveler under the best of circumstances, and here he was attempting two unfamiliar forms of travel on the same journey. Carson had been unable to find the place on any internet maps, but he was able to purchase a train ticket with his cell phone and reserve a spot on the scheduled vessel. Litton's recommendation had felt like a challenge, perhaps a test, and although Carson disliked the fact that he'd been so easily persuaded, he did feel considerable excitement. He couldn't remember the last time he'd done anything that might be described as *unexpected*.

The train was surprisingly empty. He walked from one end to the other, soaking up the particular nuances of train travel, especially that unsteady passage from car to car as the floor beneath him shook. What if everything uncoupled at the very moment he stood between cars?

In total he counted seven other passengers, unless some were hiding in the bathrooms, and he encountered no staff at all. How could they afford to run such an under-utilized service? And when he examined their faces—those few not obscured by a pillow or blanket or hand—they looked as uncomfortable as he felt.

He would have liked to talk to someone, but with so few people on the train he might appear desperate. He returned to his original car and sat.

After the first few miles of typically urban, then suburban scenes, the view became primarily one of open countryside showing little variation. At first there were the usual traces of civilization: power lines and telephone lines, roadways with the occasional relatively slow-moving car, the infrequent bridge, and now and then a water tower or prefabricated metal shed.

According to the route map on display in the car The Shores existed at the end of a long appendix-like finger of land descending from the southern-most tip of the peninsula. The land now streaming by was almost featureless, populated by low bushes and the rare stunted tree, with no structures of any kind. Nor was there any evidence of roads, suggesting that rail was the only way to access the area. Except of course by boat, but so far he hadn't seen any boats. He should have been able to catch glimpses of the ocean on either side by now, but had not. Instead, after a hundred yards or so of barren land a thick, low-lying fog appeared which stretched away as far as he could see, eventually joining the low-lying clouds at the horizon to form an ethereal tube through which the train traveled to its unseen destination. The lower edges of this fog were dark and smoky, as if it had picked up some form of contamination.

Carson sat and gazed out the windows, wishing to nap but unable to. He was far too anxious. According to the route diagram the train should have reached their destination long ago, but perhaps the drawing wasn't to scale. He spent over two hours trying to make sense of it. After another hour passed he thought the journey's length defied logic, and outside the windows there was still this streaming sameness, with no indication of sea.

At last he detected differences in the low-lying plumes of fog, darker shapes and lighter shapes, forms advancing and receding, menacing approaches and sinister retreats. Eventually he could make out faces among the masses, and appendages that defied all expectation. Were these simply the imaginings of a mind with too little stimulus? Finally he had to look away, his heart thrumming inside his ears.

He'd certainly had these issues at home. Long periods of silent, solitary study sometimes led to waking dreams, illusions of a sort. Sometimes he practically invited them in, thinking them more stimulating, or somehow more truthful than the world of cold fact. Wasn't that what monks attempted to achieve? Breakthroughs into the unconscious? But they had a mission to find such things. Carson simply wanted to find some way to avoid insanity.

Eventually he couldn't just sit there anymore, and sprang up and started walking, even though at this point the train's speed made it difficult to do so safely. He staggered back through the cars, avoiding the more threatening faces until he found a young, depressed-looking woman who drew back at his approach. He sat down next to her, even though she looked terrified.

"I'm so sorry. I didn't mean to frighten you," he managed, trying neither to look too dangerous, nor too afraid. "But should this trip last so *long*? Look at that route diagram near the ceiling. We really should have arrived in less than half this time!"

She looked surprised, and then said, "I'm *so glad* you said that! I've been thinking the *exact same* thing!"

"Then you've never traveled this route before?"

"I've never traveled by train at all. A casual friend recommended it. A train, then a ship. I've never done either. She thought it might do me some good." He gazed at her, puzzled. "Sorry," she continued. "I lost my husband over a year ago. I'm still . . . adjusting."

Her response relaxed him a bit. But it didn't alter the *wrongness* he felt. They chatted for a few minutes about their lives and where they were from. She asked him what he did, and although she'd never heard of transcendentalism, she claimed to enjoy poetry. Her name was Denise, and she had been married for over ten years when her husband passed away. "This is my first big trip without him," she said. "Well, actually my first trip farther than the grocery store, since he died."

After that he no longer knew what to say, and sat there silently, watching the windows. In only the few minutes they'd been talking the fog had rolled in and completely filled the glass. It felt as if the train were picking up speed in a renewed hurry to find its destination. He jerked his head anxiously from one side's set of windows to the other's. A stretch of windows suddenly darkened, and on another window several black, parallel streaks appeared, followed by a shove that violently rocked the car.

Denise screamed and clutched his arm. Instinctively he

placed his other hand on top of hers. He felt embarrassed. He didn't know what he would say if she objected. "Sometimes when I've been by myself for a long time I think I make things up," she said with apparent urgency. "I imagine terrible things are watching me. But even that's better than believing I am completely alone."

They remained like that until the fog began to clear and the train slowed down.

He wasn't sure what he'd expected. A resort atmosphere, he supposed, milling crowds and beach umbrellas and lots of people in bathing suits. The Shores was none of that. A cluster of heavily weathered buildings—warping gray boards and pitted paint—ran from the small train station down to a larger structure which appeared to be just as weathered, but sported a wraparound deck and windows all around the first floor, and two more stories of darkened windows above. There were a few old deck chairs scattered on the surrounding sand. With not a soul in sight, except those who'd just left the train, The Shores appeared to be some sort of abandoned compound.

Still no sign of an actual ocean. The fog had greatly retreated, but still apparently obscured the water.

He noticed that Denise was far ahead of him with the others. He felt a surprising sense of loss. He'd allowed himself to hope, he supposed, but he had no idea what he might have hoped for. He walked faster, trying to catch up.

The sign above the door said *The Shores—Restaurant and Office*. Inside all Carson could see was a restaurant of mostly empty tables. The other passengers sat scattered about. He was suddenly starving, and found a table, walking right past the one containing Denise. He tried to catch her attention but she was too busy studying the menu. He grabbed a table by the window. The menu was a small, typewritten sheet, listing a half-dozen or so items, two of which were egg dishes. The rest were seafood, but weren't described specifically, instead using phrases like "catch of the day" and "Chef's seafood special," and "Mariner's Pot Luck."

"May I take your order?" The woman was in her fifties, perhaps, black hair gray-streaked, with a plain, clearly bored face. She wore a blood-red apron with matching shoes.

"Um. The Chef's seafood special I suppose." She turned. "Oh, where do I catch the ship, when it arrives?"

She turned around, looking at him somewhat puzzled. "Well, whenever it happens, it'll happen there at the end of the sand." He glanced out the window. "You can't see the pier because of the fog. But whenever that rolls out, and whenever the tide comes in, well then you'll be able to leave, but not before. Why, are you in a hurry?"

"No, I suppose not. Not really. Oh, is there someone about who could perhaps answer some questions about the history . . ." But she had already gone.

He was gazing out the window again—the fog appeared to be breaking, but he wasn't sure what was being revealed underneath—when the voice came from behind him. "So, have you been here before?"

Carson twisted in his chair. He thought he recognized the man from his gray and green clothing. He'd been one of those trying to sleep on the train, his face buried in a pillow. "No, first time. I'd like to know more about it—can you tell me something?"

"Not really, my first time too." The man sat down next to him. "Looks like it's seen better days, though. I hear there was some kind of scandal, a religious conflict, a cult, something, a few years back. Maybe that hurt business. I just didn't have anything better to do. A train ride followed by a boat ride." He threw his hands into the air. "Whoopee!"

People were looking. Carson felt embarrassed. "That was it? You didn't hear something that attracted you?"

"I had nothing else to do. I live alone. I've been alone a long time. You?"

"I have . . . friends, activities. Too much to choose from, really." Carson looked down at his hands. He owed this stranger nothing. "Maybe one of the other passengers has been here before, or knows some of the history."

The man looked around. "Nope, I've asked. We're *all* first-timers. A couple of people have heard rumors, gossip. I wouldn't put too much stock in that sort of thing. Don't worry about it. Relax. Enjoy your trip. I'm going to try to, at least." He stood up and left.

Carson's food arrived. It was a large plate. A small circular patty of pale flesh lay in the center. "I ordered fish," he told the waitress.

"And fish you got. A local variety. You've probably never seen it before."

"What kind?"

"Oh, you wouldn't recognize it. Like I said, a local variety. The rest of the world, I think they've forgotten about this little fish." She left.

Carson lifted the meat with his fork. It rose as one solid piece. Underneath there was a pale, flattened fin, and what resembled the remnants of a small leg. He lowered the patty back onto the plate. Then he looked out the window again.

The fog had completely disappeared. But there was no ocean. The shore appeared to drop steeply away at the edge of the sand into a broad and deep basin stained a variety of colors. He might have been mistaken, but he thought he saw movement in the basin. A long pier of black wood projected out over the basin, supported on similarly black, spindly legs.

He stood up to get a better look. Around him the others were noticing this as well, standing up, some of them pressing their faces against the windows. At a nearby table the passenger who had spoken to him earlier was sitting, crying, and digging into the flesh of his palm with a fork. "I knew it. I knew it," he mumbled.

Denise came up beside him. "I really don't understand," she said, "how there could be a ship arriving."

The waitress arrived again, this time with a grubby-looking older man in a stained apron. "Can I help you folks?"

"There's no ocean," Denise said, her voice rising. "How could that be? We all paid for passage on a ship!"

"Well, it's the tide, ma'am. You've heard of tides, haven't you?"

"Of course I know what a *tide* is! But there's *no ocean* out there! No way for a ship to come in today, or any other day! What *is* this?"

"You know we used to have brochures that explained all this. I don't know what happened to them. It's an *attraction*! It's what's so unique about The Shores! The tide goes out, but sometimes it doesn't come back in for a while. Not for *days* sometimes. Sometimes not for *weeks*. Sometimes it's so long you forget there ever was an ocean here. That's part of the attraction, of course. It's never been explained, or if there was an explanation it's been lost."

Carson walked up to the man in the dirty apron. He didn't mean to be threatening, although he didn't mind if he *looked* threatening. "That's *impossible*. Tides don't *work* that way! There should be a change, what, every twelve hours or so? Besides, we bought tickets for a specific date and time!"

"It should say *approximate* on your tickets. Approximate. It's the best we can do. Uncertainty is part of the *experience*. At one time folks *appreciated* that. We have male and female dorms upstairs. You're welcome to stay as long as necessary. It's included in the price of your ticket. Meals, too. You don't have to pay extra for anything while you're waiting for your ride."

"I want to get back on the train," Denise said. "I feel like I've been lied to. I'll just take the train back to where I got on. I don't care about a refund. I just want to get out of here."

"I'm sorry, ma'am. But that just isn't possible. The train has already left."

The passengers sat quietly, some of them, although a couple laughed nervously. The man he'd spoken to earlier stared out the window at the nonexistent ocean. Surely, they weren't giving up this quickly? Carson decided to speak up. "Where did all the water go then, when the tide went out? I'm sorry, but you're not making any sense."

"It's an inexplicable phenomenon, sir," the fellow said, trying to look bold. "A natural wonder we may never understand and can only appreciate. Some say that volcanic action has created caverns beneath the ocean floor where the water stays until forced back into our basin here. Hell, there are even a few who claim a giant creature unlike any the planet has seen before sleeps in one of those caverns. Periodically he swallows the tide and only returns it when he's in the proper mood. Some folks say he's some sort of god, and in times past, he did have his share of worshippers." The man chuckled, but no one was smiling. "I'm not much of a church-goer, myself."

"Why sell tickets to a trip you cannot promise with any precision?"

The man paused and glanced at the waitress. "I don't make those decisions sir. I'm only an employee."

By the time the man in the dirty apron had finished his explanations, or attempted explanations, none of the new arrivals were talking. It was getting late, already much later than the scheduled departure of their theoretical ship. The sun had fallen low in the sky, turning the empty ocean basin an unnervingly red color. Carson couldn't deal with it anymore and retired upstairs, looking for a place to sleep in the men's dorm.

He was surprised to find the dorm already filled almost to capacity with slumbering forms, with only a few empty cots available. The light was dim—a few small lamps at the corners of the room provided a weak, brownish illumination. Heavy curtains blocked the windows.

Carson walked quietly to a cot and sat down. He slipped off his shoes, one of them falling and making a soft thud. The fellow in the cot next to him sat up suddenly and stared at him. "Has the ship arrived? Has it come?" the man asked groggily.

"No. Sorry. No, I'm new. There's no ship. The tide's still ... out. I'm afraid we won't be departing today."

"No ship, no ship at all? You're saying there's no ocean?" The man shook his head, rubbed his eyes.

"No. I'm sorry." Carson stared at the man. His clothes were dirty. His beard was matted, sketchy. He stank terribly. "How long have you been waiting?"

"A few days. Weeks, maybe? Although it could be months? But it's okay—they feed you, they give you a place to sleep. No extra charge. It's free. It's always been free." He looked sharply at Carson, eyes wide open. "You're new, aren't you?"

"Yes I am."

"Well, you'll find out soon enough how it is. You become unsure about what you are seeing, what you are hearing. Every night you listen to the sounds the world makes, and you just aren't sure what they mean anymore. You'll see, or maybe it'll be different for you. Maybe."

The next morning Carson woke up to an almost empty dorm. The restaurant was full, but largely quiet. No one was talking. There must have been a hundred of them or more: men and women, no children.

And outside the restaurant, no ocean. He could see several people aimlessly wandering the beach. He thought he saw a few out in the basin: gesticulating, arguing. But it was too far away. He couldn't tell for sure.

After the meal he took a walk with Denise. They didn't say anything, but it seemed to be taken for granted that they would walk together. They wandered among the old buildings leading up to the train station. Most were unfurnished, but a few had the occasional broken table or chair inside. There was water damage everywhere, as if one day when the tide came in it had come much farther in than anticipated.

Carson was looking into the space between two buildings when he thought he saw a familiar figure passing by the other side. He couldn't recall their name at the moment, but it was someone he once knew very well, someone who had been quite important to him. How was it that a person could lose touch like that, that you could lose track of them completely, and even when you find them again you discover you have lost their name? He shouted and ran down the narrow passageway but could find no one. There were still people down on the beach, but no one else walked among the buildings.

Later that day Denise swore she had seen a woman she had once known very well. A neighbor or a schoolmate, perhaps even a distant relative. Carson helped her search but they could find no further sign of the woman. Before the evening meal they were sure they could hear the sounds of the ocean. They followed the sound to a narrow, deep hole in the ground. They got down on their knees. When they put their ears near the hole the ocean came through loud and clear.

"That must be the caverns down there," Denise whispered. "Can you imagine? That's where the ocean has gone." Then she reached over and pulled Carson's face to hers and began kissing him. It was wonderful, but then she stopped, and wouldn't talk to him about it again.

That night the dorm wasn't as full as it had been before. Carson wondered where the others had gone. The ship hadn't arrived, and the train had not come that day. He wondered if the others were still out on the beach, or in the basin, arguing.

This continued for several days. He was tired of waiting for the ship, and realized there was no guarantee it would even take you where you wanted to go, assuming you even knew where you wanted to go. He considered the serious possibility that people who took the ship might never be heard from again, and even their names would be lost. Sometimes Carson tried to get on the train when it dropped off new passengers (there were more and more of them almost every day), but the train doors wouldn't open for him. He watched others try with the same results.

Life settled into a comfortable pattern of the expected. Denise still took walks with him, but she never kissed him again.

Carson had become accustomed to life in the dorm. It wasn't that much different from life at home, except he had many fewer personal possessions, a blessing in some ways. He retreated there every afternoon, sometimes for hours at a time. There were always two or three men sleeping—some seemed never to leave their beds—but no one bothered him.

Just as at home, Carson would lie there and gaze at the ceiling or the walls, and what he saw, he thought, was some reflection of him. Just as at home, he would attempt to identify every sound he heard—some so subtle they were likely no more than a change in ambient air pressure—and he would imagine who, or what, had made them.

It wasn't at all surprising to him when he eventually made contact with that ancient god sleeping in the caverns many miles below, who held the missing ocean somewhere inside its massive form.

What he saw against the dark wall might have been the creature's eye, or whatever the creature itself saw when it gazed into its own mind. The abject solitude and the knowledge that even if they found companionship after all these years, entrance into the final darkness could only be done alone.

He walked out of the dorm, too restless to sleep. He ignored the people who called to him. He ignored even Denise's voice when it rose above the continuous din. He avoided the outstretched hands both of the ones he knew and the ones he'd never met before. He wandered down into the absence of ocean, and found the ones who now made their homes there, who prayed both to the missing sea and to the god who had taken it all away.

And weeks later, when the ocean finally came roaring in, Carson was waiting by the railroad tracks. With his ear to the ground he could hear the train's distant approach, even over the screams of the drowning, and the hoarse enthusiasm of the others as they imagined their salvation was finally at hand.

When the ship did arrive, all sleek and swollen and clamoring with bells, Carson still waited for the train. Even as the ramp was lowered and all those ragged passengers finally boarded, Carson remained, listening to the ground, and anticipating the train.

And at last when it looked as if he'd made a miscalculation, the ship's speakers pleading for any final boarders, the train arrived, and the newcomers began to stream out. He had but a moment to reflect on how arbitrary it was, how unjust, that these late arrivals could simply walk up that ramp into the ship without suffering what so many had been forced to endure.

Maybe this is what they all really wanted. He understood the attraction of letting history swallow you completely and without trace. He supposed it was only his arrogance that kept him from joining them on that voyage to nowhere.

As one of the last passengers left the train Carson shouldered himself inside, jamming a shovel into the door to keep it open just a little while longer. The passengers looked alarmed, and began to run. "I'd think about staying on the train!" he shouted, even though he didn't really expect any of them to listen. The shovel handle snapped and the door slammed closed.

The inside of the train car was cold, and Carson snuggled into himself to stay warm. Through the train's metal walls he could hear the distant horn of the ship signaling its departure.

He didn't know how long he'd have to wait, but he hoped it wasn't too long.

As for the ship, wherever it was headed, Carson knew it could be no place good.

Reflections in Black

Randall left work early again, feeling ill. Nothing definitive, a general fatigue, a general *malaise*—that was the word, although he'd never used it before. If he'd stayed in his chair another minute it would have required an army to get him out. He didn't know where he belonged, but he didn't belong *there*.

The bus was unusually crowded for the time of day. He wondered if there might be a concert or some such event. He found a seat quickly and hunched forward, trying to shut out the pack. But there were just too many of them, jostling about, not exactly noisy, but murmuring. That constant murmur. And they smelled: rank body odor and cigarettes, and things left out in the rain. But it had been a dry fall, so that stench had to be from something else.

He glanced around. Had they all been fighting? Their faces were discolored, bruised. That fellow's nose had gone scarlet, swollen. The woman next to him appeared caked in blue, turning black around her eyes. Another woman's lipstick smeared from both ends of her lips, as if a razor had widened her mouth. Some of their clothing was torn. He studied the women, seeking exposed flesh. It was an old habit, but he didn't mean any harm. He simply liked women. Was that an exposed breast or an elbow? He felt vaguely ashamed, but he looked anyway. Another word he'd never used occurred to him: *voyeur*.

Their outfits were unusually colorful, some of the clothing beyond outlandish. They were in costume, he suddenly realized, but they'd been wearing their costumes too long, and now their costumes stank, and their makeup had deteriorated.

Halloween wasn't until tomorrow—were people partying early? He'd never liked the holiday himself. It seemed such a sad and desperate celebration, poking at your fears for some supposed fun.

"Paula!" A female's voice from the back of the bus. Maybe an objection. Maybe a warning. Randall couldn't get the tone, the intent, or even the age of the speaker from just a single word. He turned around in his seat to see if he could tell who had said her name. Maybe, he thought, he might even see Paula herself. Would he even recognize her after so many years? He'd certainly had plenty of practice trying to imagine her older face, her body. Of course it was unlikely to be her, but what did they say? A small world.

His cell went off. One ring. He looked at the screen. "Not Available" was all it said.

"Paula!" He jerked his head up, looking for the speaker. No one looked at him. No one looked eager to speak. Each huddled to him- or herself, nursing their poorly disguised injuries, murmuring softly.

He'd always thought of her as the one who got away, although arguably he never had her in the first place. She'd been pleasant enough, and consented to his kisses. But never further, no matter how he'd suggested it, although he'd never been that direct. They'd gone to dinners and movies and he'd felt cowed by her quiet beauty. She was taller than him, and had that beautiful voice, especially when she laughed, or whispered into his ear. Those were early college days and he had lacked confidence. He never told her how he felt, and he had no idea how she felt about him. It was ridiculous to be thinking about her now, but someone had said her name, and he hadn't had sex in a long time. If he could find that person he would tell them to shut up.

His cell went off again. "Not Available" flashed on the

screen. He answered anyway. There was nothing but static on the line, and perhaps under that a distorted murmuring.

At his stop he pushed his way through the stinking crowd. Everything he touched left his hands feeling greasy. Climbing off he looked back to see if anyone watched him as the bus pulled away. It was hard to tell. The one face turned in his direction appeared to be sleeping.

As he walked home it occurred to him how the homeless huddled under steps and in alleys appeared to be in costume, but for them it was constant and involuntary. But he was romanticizing things again—it had always been his problem. After the breakup Miranda said he'd always expected too much—he had too much imagination—that was why they'd ended up hating each other. She'd been the last of many.

Randall had been furious at that comment. It was as if Miranda had broken the rules—it was over, she had no reason to say anything. That night he'd tried to track Paula down. Maybe she was still unattached. Of course it was just a fantasy that they might reconnect, but such things did happen in the real world.

But he couldn't find a "Paula Jenks" on any of the social media. A general internet search turned up very few possibilities of the right age. Maybe she married and had a new last name. Women were difficult that way—it made it more complicated to track them down. The websites wanted a credit card number to delve further. It felt a bit too desperate to pursue things that far, however. He would have felt like some sort of stalker. So Randall had let it go.

He felt deflated as soon as he entered his apartment. He hated the familiarity of it. No matter how much he rearranged things it always felt the same, and nothing at all like where he should live. Perhaps if he had more room, or even a house, he could turn his environment into some sort of sanctuary. But that required more money, and although he was in a job he couldn't stand, he couldn't imagine another.

He went into the dingy bathroom and washed his face. In the dim light his reflection looked darkened, bruised, and mottled as if make-up had been applied to unsuccessfully hide the damage. He was only forty, but aging poorly. Tomorrow he would wear dark glasses for his commute. He thought he had a pair large enough to disguise things.

Revelers outside his windows were breaking things. What had gotten into people? If it was this bad the night before Halloween, what could he expect on the actual night? He vaguely remembered a name for this night from when he was a kid. "Malice Night" or "Prank Night"? No, *Mischief Night* was what they had called it, but he didn't remember it being anything like this.

He thought he'd successfully put Paula out of his mind until he'd heard her name on the bus. It seemed possible the experience had ruined him. A month after he'd given up searching for her he'd been drinking and thought he'd try again. Who cared how it looked? Maybe Paula would be pleased to hear from him. Maybe she'd been thinking of him too. He chose one of those "lost loves" websites and entered his credit card information. He felt relieved that he didn't have to talk to a live person. The website just asked him a series of questions and he typed in all he could remember. He remembered she was a year younger, so he knew the year she was born, and he remembered she had lived in Georgia all her life, so she had probably been born there as well. He knew where her mother had lived—he couldn't remember the exact address, but he thought he might recognize it if he saw it. He might have even visited Paula there, or had he?

He'd been excited when her social security number came up. There were flashing screens and "progress" bars—all for show he presumed—with intermittent results. Randall had been much less excited when a married name came up, "Paula Duncan." Husband named Frank and an address where both of them lived. Then after an agonizing period of more so-called "processing," there was an obituary notice for Paula Duncan from a mortuary in the town where Frank and Paula Duncan lived. A vague disappointment consumed him. He did some more checking with the social security number he had. In one of the online records that number came up "deceased."

And that was that. The service charged his credit card and didn't even offer condolences. Why should it? He hadn't been the husband. It made him feel vaguely dirty, as if he'd been peeping through the bedroom window of Mr. and Mrs. Frank Duncan.

Randall couldn't say he was heartbroken. He was saddened, certainly, to think someone so vibrant, so beautiful, someone he might have *loved* was gone. But he hadn't seen Paula in years. It had been merely a pitiful fantasy.

Then today happened. Whoever the Paula had been on the bus she hadn't been *his* Paula, and he needed to stop thinking *his*, because she never had been.

Randall's cell phone rang. He picked it up off the coffee table, expecting to see "Not Available" again. But this time the screen said "Paula Jenks." He frantically hit the button and fumbled it to his ear. "Hello?"

No one spoke. There was a hollow, liquid sort of background noise, a soft echoing effect, as if the phone were at the bottom of a well. "Hello?"

A clicking noise. Then, "Hello, is this Randall?" He didn't recognize the voice, and as had become his habit when dealing with telephone solicitors and scammers, he avoided saying 'yes.' "This is Randall."

"Randall, this is Alice Jenks. Paula's mother."

"Oh. Oh, Mrs. Jenks. I'm sorry. I heard . . ."

"The reason I'm calling is because Paula has been trying to get in touch with you."

His eyes filled with tears. "I'm sorry. I heard that Paula died. I'm just so relieved . . ."

"Died? Who would say such a thing?"

He could tell her the truth, but it was embarrassing. He couldn't think of a way to say it without sounding creepy. "I'm sorry, it was on social media. You know how that goes, rumors and half-truths. Obviously it was a different Paula."

"Well, I don't have the internet, but I know how people are."

"Could I speak to Paula?"

There was a pause, with more liquid clicking. Randall thought they'd lost the connection. "I'm afraid not. She's lying down, feeling poorly I'm afraid, poor dear. She's been trying and trying to contact you, with no luck at all. She became quite worked up over it, actually. I told her to rest. But I had to promise I would make the attempt for her. If I hadn't I didn't think she would fall asleep."

"How did she try to contact me? I've moved a few times, but I've always left a forwarding address. And I have email, social media . . ."

"Oh, my daughter doesn't own a computer. I believe she may have written you a few times over the years and you never answered. She gave me this phone number. She wrote it on this pad by the phone, several times in fact. The same number, but several times so she wouldn't forget. But she couldn't reach you."

"I didn't get her letters. If I had gotten one of her letters I absolutely would have written her back. And I don't have any phone messages from her."

"Oh, I don't think she would have left a message. She hates speaking to those machines. But Randall, she would absolutely love to see you, she really would. She's been in poor health for years, but I think seeing you would make all the difference."

Would it be rude to ask what was wrong with Paula? He wasn't sure, and he didn't want this woman to think it would make some crucial difference to him. "Of course I can come sometime. Where do you live?"

"Might you come right away? She feels so badly, I frankly worry about her. Could you come for Halloween? She dreads the holiday, all those costumes and masks, that morbid preoccupation. We're in the same house, a few miles from the old campus. Are you very far away?"

"Not at all. Give me the address. I have to take care of a few things, but I'll be there tomorrow night."

He was at least twenty hours away by car, probably more, and he didn't own an automobile. Randall left a phone message for his boss telling him he was much sicker than he thought. He threw some clothes into a bag and left the apartment.

The rental was much too high but he had little choice. He hadn't driven in a while, but his initial nervousness passed once he got out of the city and onto the highway. He kept his cell phone on, lying on the passenger seat beside him. He expected the woman to call back, confessing that it had all been some tasteless Mischief Night prank, but she never did.

Once he crossed over into Maryland he could see that a large number of people were out—teenagers mostly, running around in the dark, yelling and breaking things, screaming in pain or excitement. At one point he had to veer around two figures in clown suits in the middle of the road. He couldn't be sure, but his impression was they had been copulating. They howled as he passed.

He'd never liked driving at night. As it was he had no idea if he would make it to Paula's house by Halloween night, or what it might mean if he didn't. Perhaps nothing, or perhaps everything. Timing mattered in life, and his timing had always been mediocre at best. He was bound to lose his job, but it certainly wouldn't break his heart.

Paula would be much older than the woman he remembered, the woman he might have loved, but then so was he. She probably still had the eyes, those high cheekbones, that beautiful voice. He hoped she still had the smile.

Randall's night vision wasn't what it used to be. That was clear now that he was out here, the lights from the oncoming cars stabbing his eyes. The reflections off his windshield felt dangerous, confusing.

It nagged at him that he was travelling all this way without actually having talked to Paula. Her mother had sounded sincere, but here he was driving hundreds of miles with no sleep because of a phone call from a woman he might or might not have met.

About 2 A.M. in a rural area beyond Richmond he ran over something. He didn't see it until he was about to hit it, and he still had no idea what it was. A mound of clothes, seemingly, but there was hair, or fur, in a streak along the top. And it screamed when he ran over it.

He stopped a few yards ahead of the object and glanced in his rearview mirror. He couldn't see very much with his tail lights, but whatever it was, it didn't appear to be moving. The responsible thing to do, of course, was to walk back there and check. What if that was a human being?

But he hesitated. He hadn't seen any other vehicles the past half hour or so. The area was poorly lit, and although there was a building just off the roadway, some sort of maintenance shed, it was dark, and there were no other structures in view, no one to call out to if he needed help.

He grabbed his cell phone. No bars, but a 9-1-1 call might still go through. Something flashed by the car. He looked up. Several dancing ragged figures—perhaps they were meant to be scarecrows—shouted at him nonsensically.

Something slapped his driver's side window. He stared into the bloody red face. "Watch where you're driving!" it shouted, moving its lips in exaggerated fashion. What he thought was blood was actually some sort of paint, garish and dripping. He drove the car slowly through a growing crowd of garishly-dressed revelers, who sprawled on and off the hood, daring him to hurt one of them. He was tempted to hit the gas pedal a few times, but what if he actually hurt someone? He would be charged—he might even go to prison. This went on for two or three miles before, seemingly bored, they let him go.

After a few more hours his cell phone rang. He jumped, almost running off the road. Paula's name flashed on the screen. When he picked it up her mother got straight to the point. "So are you coming?"

"Yes, yes. Like I said, I'm coming. It might just take me a while."

"I just wanted to make sure. She's been asking."

"Tell her I'll be there. But I have to hang up now."

"All right, but please come." She hung up. They were up late, but then so was he. He wasn't sure why, but he felt as if she thought he'd somehow wronged Paula. But it was such a long time ago, and they'd been so young, babies practically.

He made a few wrong turns and became lost more than once. He drove part of the next day in the completely wrong direction. He was going to be late, he supposed, but was now too tired to care. By the next evening, Halloween night, he stopped paying attention to all the people in disguise. It seemed somehow normal, as if they were at last displaying their true selves, however deplorable. Once or twice someone spat at the car, or struck it with something. Randall didn't stop.

Somewhere in Alabama both headlights went out. Randall was so tired he almost didn't notice, and when he did realize he simply stared straight ahead, counting on the moonlight and occasional streetlight and the luminous paint on the edges of the road to show him the way. Eventually they came back on as suddenly as they had gone out.

It began to rain about an hour from his destination. Randall turned the wipers on, but they weren't making good contact with the windshield and left a thin skim of water after each swipe of the blades. He had to lean over the steering wheel and gaze intently through a confusing array of fragmented street lights in order to stay safely on the road. Eventually the rain let up as he entered a series of narrow neighborhood streets. Leaves were down everywhere, making a dark and nasty mess in the gutters. Water pooled in spots on the uneven pavement, shimmering with yellowish reflections. The only signs of trick-or-treaters were some scattered candy wrappers and a few soggy remnants of costume, scarves, gloves, random bits of cloth, and what looked to be a cheap mask torn in half, dropped in the hurry to get home.

He pulled up in front of the address a little past eleven. He sat for a few minutes, thinking it looked vaguely familiar. He remembered coming here with Paula, but he wasn't positive it actually happened. The house was a typical Victorian: sash windows, stained glass, and a finial on the roof, a canted bay window in front, geometric tiled walk and a round tower at one corner. It was hard to tell how big it was, or even the exact color. Tall unkempt evergreen bushes and trees hugging it so closely kept it dark and secretive, in contrast to the neighboring properties and their denuded trees. He'd barely been aware of the change of seasons when he left the city. Here it appeared full-blown, almost past.

He hadn't yet decided what to say to her. He trotted up the walk before he could lose his nerve. Several windows were lit, so he assumed they were waiting for him.

The door opened before he could ring the bell. A woman's pale face: could this be Paula, aged so harshly? No, surely too old and too short.

"I presume you're Randall?" Her voice surprised him with its strength. She sounded almost angry.

"Yes. I'm sorry it's so late, but I got here as soon as I could."

"It will do."

She guided him through a short hall and into some sort of sitting room. Although there were lights on in the house the rooms were dim. Perhaps the darkness of the wallpaper and the excessive décor were too much to overcome. This room was relatively tidy except for tall stacks of women's magazines piled sloppily by each chair. There were a number of pictures on the side tables. All of them were of Paula around the age Randall had known her, but none newer than that.

"Paula will be joining you soon. She requires a little time to get ready."

"Do you have a more recent photograph of her somewhere?" Maybe it was rude to ask so quickly, but that's what was on his mind.

"My daughter doesn't like to get her picture taken. I approve of that. I've always thought there was too much vanity in the world."

He sat down in a chair by the window. It was low, and he had bad knees. He worried that it might be a struggle to get out of it. "I think you're right. I hate getting my picture taken myself. I don't, usually. I think the last time was when I renewed my license."

"My daughter doesn't drive. She doesn't feel the need to."

"I see." Although he didn't, really. The Paula he'd known had loved touring around, driving to new places.

The old woman sat down and stared at him with an expression that was almost a smile but not quite. Calculated interest, perhaps. Because of the lowness of his chair he had to look up at her. He felt as if he were under observation.

"It's been years since you've seen my daughter. Have you thought about her very much?"

He squirmed. "Yes, yes I have. I have many fond memories. And sometimes I wondered how she was doing."

"And yet you never called."

"I . . . think I called. I'm pretty sure I tried. But you know how it is. People move around, their lives get complicated. Before you know it years have passed."

"My daughter has never moved. She has been here all these years." Paula's mother leaned forward slightly. Randall had the uneasy feeling she might leap on him and he wouldn't be able to get out of the chair in time.

"I'm s-sorry," he said. "I should have tried harder."

"You became involved in your own concerns, your own . . . passions. I imagine you only thought of her when you were between women, when your appetites made you remember how beautiful she was. That is often the way with you men, I think."

Surely it was more complicated than that, Randall thought. He really had cared for her. But he thought about the timing she suggested, and saw the truth in it. But still he said, "No. It wasn't like that. I never stopped caring for her. Please, can I see her now?"

She didn't answer right away. She turned her head and raised an eyebrow, as if listening for something. There was another open door on the other side of the room leading somewhere else in the house. Randall leaned slightly and tried to look through it. It was a hallway, and very dark, but he thought he saw a glimmer of something, and movement.

"She'll be down soon, I promise." He straightened up quickly, unaccountably nervous that she had seen him looking. "She just wants to look her best for you. She was always a pretty girl, but the years, they do things to the best of us, and shallow people, they sometimes judge us harshly."

"She was always beautiful. I'm sure she still is. A few wrinkles, a few extra pounds—that doesn't bother me, I promise. Look at me, I'm not perfect."

"No, you are not," she replied. He guessed she wasn't going to let him get away with anything. "You have to look past the surface to see the person inside. Tell me, if I were able to look inside you, Randall, what would I see?"

"I . . . I don't know how to answer that." But some words came readily to mind. *Petty, bitter, impatient, disappointed.* So he was dishonest as well. "I guess you'd be disappointed."

"Only if I had misjudged you, Randall. Only then." She

turned her head and looked back through the entrance hall from which they'd entered this room. "I see it is only a few minutes before midnight." Had there been a clock in the hall? He certainly hadn't seen one. "Do you like Halloween, Randall? Are you familiar with its customs?"

"I dressed up and went trick-or-treating as a child. I guess I haven't thought much about it since then. I was never into scary stuff. I never could understand why anyone would want to be scared, frankly."

"For some, it is evidence that they are still alive. You are alive, aren't you Randall?"

He forced out an awkward laugh. In truth, he felt as if he could hardly breathe in this house. "As far, as far as I know." The forced laugh he repeated made him feel a bit crazed.

"You are a lucky man, certainly. The approaching hour provides us with a unique opportunity." She smiled widely, exposing several broken and missing teeth. "There is a traditional Halloween ritual. I recall it very well from when I was a young woman of marrying age. I remember being so eager to participate in this ritual, as were many of my friends. Do you want to hear about it?"

Of course he didn't want to hear about it, but he couldn't imagine saying no with her looking at him like that. "Of course. Please tell me."

"It's quite a lot of fun, actually. When you're young you're always wondering what is going to happen to you, what you might be in for in your life. More so than when you're older, I think. When you're older you already know what's going to happen to you."

"I guess. I guess that's true."

"Very good. We are on the same page, then, Randall. The ritual is simply this. At midnight on Halloween a young man or young woman turns off all the lights and stares into a mirror. Eventually, according to this ritual, you will see the face of your future spouse standing behind you, looking over your shoulder. Isn't that *delightful*? Doesn't that sound like *fun*?"

"I guess. I guess I can see how that would be fun, if you were young enough."

"Oh, don't be such a stick in the mud, Randall! Do you think my lovely daughter would be interested in a stick in the mud? Play along, why don't you? It's something to do until she comes down. And let's just say you see *her* face in the mirror, looking over your shoulder. Think of her reaction if you told her that! It would likely make her very pleased, don't you think?"

"It might." It was an interesting idea. It gave him something to open with when he finally saw Paula. And he could tell her anything—it didn't matter what he actually saw in the mirror. He didn't expect to see anything. But he could tell Paula he saw her in the mirror, and how beautiful she was, but not nearly as beautiful as she was actually standing there in front of him. "I'll do it. Where's the mirror?"

"We only have the one. In this entire house, only the one mirror. It's hanging on the wall at the end of that hall." She gestured to that other open door and the darkness beyond. "But you must hurry. It's almost midnight. Soon it will be too late."

Randall struggled out of his chair with some effort. It felt as if the air in the room was so heavy he could hardly move against it. He staggered a bit as he made his way to the open door. "Could you turn the light on in there? I can hardly see."

"Oh, but Randall," she said sternly behind him. "Weren't you listening? The lights have to be out, or the game won't work at all!"

Game, ritual, he wished she would make up her mind. He peered down the hall, his eyes struggling to adjust. There was that slight glimmer again. It must be the mirror, he thought. But no signs of movement. "Okay. Okay."

He stepped forward a few steps. The lights in the sitting

room went off behind him. "Hurry!" she said from the dark. Her voice rose. "There isn't much time!"

He quickened his pace. The glimmer at the end of the hall appeared to change. Of course, he thought, because of his own movement. There was a sound behind him. Was the old woman following him in? He stared into the darkness, trying to concentrate, attempting to force his eyes to adjust.

"One more thing," she said behind him, but her voice had subtly changed. "*Voyeur.*" Had he understood what she said? "If the viewer were destined to die before getting married, he or she would see something else entirely." Her voice was completely different now, completely changed, reminding him of that voice he had heard, and been captivated by, that beautiful voice so many years ago.

"Midnight," the voice said.

He was looking into the darkness so determinedly his head was splitting. But at last he was beginning to see his reflection in the black, his features distorted, melting, disappearing in patches, moving, rotating. A woman's face rushed out of the darkness behind him and stopped above his shoulder. Paula was as beautiful as ever, unaged, until she too began to distort, the flesh melting from her bones, until that moment when they were exactly alike, two naked skulls, staring.

Whatever You Want

The Christmas season was impossible to escape, gobbling up more of the calendar with each trip of the world around the sun. This year Trish was appalled to find Christmas aisles in the big box stores just days after the last "Trick or Treat!" of Halloween.

Little Bean was all of three now, but thanks to television able to recognize the holiday for the first time. She'd chattered on and on about "Santy Claws," one of the few clear phrases Trish was able to pick out of a stream of moist gibberish as Little B roamed their small apartment in unrepressed delight... and rage, if Trish ever said *no*. Anger or joy, Little Bean always seemed to be screaming.

Every mother Trish knew said, "Mine did the same thing. They grow out of it." Trish made an effort to believe them. "Don't take it personally." She tried to believe that too, even under a barrage of *I hate you!*s.

"Well, you asked for this." That's what her mother told her. Actually, she hadn't asked for this, not the deadening sameness of motherhood, the isolation of the single mom at the playground, the loss of a future she could now only imagine. Little Bean's dad was supposed to be doing this with her, but he'd wised up, skipped town. She wondered what kind of Christmas *he* was having.

It wasn't that Trish *hadn't* wanted a child. The truth was she just didn't know. And then she had one. And that child would cry and cry as if desperately wanting something she wasn't getting, but Trish had no idea what it was. Was it because Trish secretly hated breastfeeding? Found it painful and somewhat disgusting, her child chewing on her like that? Was it because she'd never wanted to do this, at least not by herself?

Trish had a fleeting notion that one day Little Bean would suddenly start speaking, confessing that she could have told her mother what she had wanted at any time. She just hadn't cared to.

Little Bean wasn't the only person Trish had to please. She had her mother and father, grandparents, friends (at least the few that were left—a bunch had bolted once they realized Trish with a kid was far less fun than Trish without). She had sworn she wasn't going to wait until the last minute to shop, but here she was—Christmas Eve—frantically looking for a parking spot with her child screaming in the back seat.

She drove past the big malls. Their parking lots were full, cars prowling the lanes opportunistically, following shoppers walking out of stores with their arms full. She remembered an old mall farther out, scheduled to be torn down, but remaining open until the end of the holiday. Maybe she'd find unusual things there for the people on her list. They'd be impressed, especially with her having a difficult kid to take care of. It was already late afternoon. Another heavy snow waited in the night. The streets were flooded in steel gray fog.

The road out was poorly lit, with few houses along the way. The last rays of the setting sun made the distant woods appear on fire. An arc of tree limbs protruding from a snow-bank resembled a partially buried giant spider.

Once past the worn-out WELCOME TO THE MALL sign, construction barriers guided her through the main level of the old shopping complex. Orange cones and plastic webbing blocked everything. She descended a curved road to the basement level, parking crookedly between piles of debris, but so had everyone else. She got out and lifted B from her car seat. Her daughter thankfully was sound asleep. Trish remembered a vast amusement hall on this level. Now the windows were empty and greased.

A dark furry shape in the middle of the sidewalk turned out to be the burnt remains of a Christmas tree, a few soot-blackened balls dangling from its skeletal limbs. She was already feeling discouraged about finding anything good here, but she was running out of time. Too late to shop anywhere else, she was on a mission to find and buy.

Beneath broken concrete the ground moaned as if collapse were imminent. Some cracked exterior steps led to the main level. As darkness filled the risers the steps appeared to float in midair. B weighed almost nothing. When she got to the top she checked the blanket to make sure her daughter was still there. The child's face was pale, but her lips moved, as if whispering secrets Trish was not meant to hear.

Only a few weary-looking shoppers stared into the dimly-lit windows. An older man staggered past her, his overloaded bags hanging down and brushing the snowy sidewalk. His red Christmas sweater bore a giant white clown's face—big googly eyes over the nipples and a misshapen red nose, a wide crooked smile like a rip across the belly. He didn't appear to notice she was there.

There was a manger scene in a display window. Someone had replaced the baby Jesus with a dirty doll's head. The other figures were hunched with filth and looked less-than-human, their tiny faces dismayed. Skinny melting candles on either side leaned with dangerous possibility. A pile of rags on the sidewalk nearby stretched forth a hand clutching a can. The mouth splutter that followed might have been "please!" She gave the genderless arm a wide berth, sure it was a scam. She wanted to think the best of people but she was never up to the task.

A pile of dirty snow was studded with black stones, a waterlogged scarf. It might have just been the remains of a good shoveling, but Trish thought she could make out a face.

Dark figures hurried past the mall entrance. Some of them actually ran. "In a hurry for disappointment," she'd often heard her father say.

B stirred as they went through the doors. She thrust her blonde head out of the blanket looking startled. She began to cry, then stopped as she looked around.

"Down," she said, and Trish lowered her to the floor. She clutched three fingers of her mother's hand. Trish felt relieved. Maybe the kid would behave—she needed at least one thing to go right today.

"Toys?" B said weakly, as if afraid of the word.

"No toys today, Bean," Trish replied. "Santa will bring you some tomorrow. We can't be selfish every day—today we shop for other people."

"Santy Claws!"

"That's right, Bean," she replied, distracted. From this angle it was difficult to read the names of the stores. She had no choice but to go down each aisle and find some place still in business.

"Santy!" B cried again, and broke away, running straight ahead into shadows and dim light.

Trish stared for a moment, and then shouted, "Bean! Come back here!" She ran into the murkiness after her, furious. She had absolutely no control over the kid.

They were in some kind of central space, poorly lit, and half of it was blocked off where demolition had already begun. Trish was vaguely aware of a few shoppers circling the area, going in and out of shop doors that opened onto this space. Some were blackened silhouettes, like ambulatory fire victims.

Trish didn't even see the line of children until she ran into the tail end of it, and Bean, waiting with the others. She grabbed onto her little girl and started to pull her away.

"No, Santy!" Bean screamed, squirming.

"Can I help?" The voice was nearby and below her. Trish

looked around. A very short old woman in an elf's cap much too big for her head stared up at her.

"I—there's not enough time." Trish was flushed, angry. "There are presents I just *have* to get."

"Leave her here and you can shop. We'll take care of her. She'll visit Santa Claus, and you'll get your shopping done unencumbered."

"Santa Claus?" Trish gazed up the line to its beginning. There was the big chair holding an old man swallowed up by a voluminous red suit. He appeared to be asleep as a small child chattered into his face. Santa's beard was long, but not very full. Large patches appeared to be missing, and that child, leaning so close to the old man, was eating them?

"But I can't just *leave* her here. *Can* I?" She looked back up at Santa. The next child in line crawled up into his unpromising lap. The old man startled, straightening up so quickly the child almost fell. The large reindeer nearby suddenly came to life—someone in costume—and jumped forward, but Santa had already steadied the child with his knobby hands.

"Don't you just *hate* Christmas? I know I do," the elf woman said. "People are *terrible*, and the little brats, aren't they just the *worst* this time of year?" The old woman's grin displayed many missing teeth.

"I . . . well, yes, sometimes." Trish looked down at B, whose eyes were fixed on Santa. "There's just never enough time. And it's not like I get to do anything fun, anything *I* want to do. It's really not fair."

"Do you know what your little girl wants for Christmas?" A new voice, another woman's. Trish turned and was appalled by the towering height of the figure. It was the costumed reindeer from Santa's side—how did she get here so fast? The reindeer suit had brown arms and legs and an enormous white bib covering the torso, a large grotesquely friendly reindeer head with wide-set eyes staring at some distant point in space.

"Everything, everything she sees on TV. She jumps up and

down and goes crazy over every single toy commercial. She wants it all." Trish hated the way she sounded, but it was the truth.

"Don't we all," the little old woman said.

"That makes it easy," the voice inside the giant reindeer head replied. "I'll just have Santa tell her she'll get whatever she wants."

"Whatever she wants," Trish repeated. "Well, isn't that great. I'd just settle for getting what I deserve."

"Sometimes it's the same thing, don't you think? Go shop. We'll take care of her. Everything will turn out as it should. I promise. On my oath as a reindeer!"

Trish glanced at Bean, still transfixed, shuffling ahead with the other children. No other parents to be seen. She wouldn't even notice her absence. Her daughter was so self-contained—she cared nothing for Trish at all. "I'll hurry," she said, and turned away.

"Wait!" It was the old woman. Trish turned back around. "What do *you* want for Christmas? We'll put in a word for you with the old man. Anything."

But Trish had no time to think. "Just tell him whatever I want, whatever I deserve." She rushed off, relieved to have a few minutes of shopping time by herself. Bean's dad probably wasn't shopping—he probably wasn't even celebrating Christmas. He was probably just sitting in front of his TV drinking. Maybe that was sad, but Trish envied him.

The first place she went into was an antique shop, apparently, and the items—a messy clutter of metal and wood, paper and cloth—were poorly displayed. Of course they were *all* going out of business, so a handsome display no longer mattered. And it also didn't matter what she got the relatives, did it? Whatever she got them, Trish knew they would just politely nod—what was the point in trying to please them? She should just do all her shopping here.

A grubby artificial Christmas tree stood just inside the

door of the shop. It appeared to have been repaired many times, branches taped or wrapped in graying string. A tiny bird's skull hung from one branch. Other items on the tree were so mossy with dust they were impossible to identify. Others were identifiable, but as inappropriate as the bird's skull—a kitchen whisk, dental floss, a comb—mixed with such traditional decorations as a ceramic angel, an antique star, some lovely blue and green globes.

Trish turned and glanced back at the distant Santa line, still moving slowly. She thought she recognized Bean's yellow jumper. With no sales clerk in sight she ventured deeper into the store.

Several collapsing cartons of grubby ornaments filled one table. The hand-lettered sign read "Seconds." She picked through a few, afraid to dig too deeply in case something nasty lay underneath. Each ornament was distorted in some way—imperfect spheres, lopsided egg shapes—irregular and shifting coloration. The softer ones resembled diseased organs.

An assortment of Jesus dolls—folk art—were gathered in a bin. They all looked like bad Jesuses to her. A box labeled "Fire Sale" was full of unidentifiable blackened things, all with hooks to hang from a tree.

In the central part of the store stuffed rats hung from a line stretched overhead. Most wore Santa hats.

"I had a bunch left over from Halloween, but it's the red caps what make them festive, dunnit you think?"

A thin man with a very wide grin peered down at her. His hair was black and slicked back and had rolls of dust—her mother called them woolies—decorating it here and there.

"Very . . . clever," she replied.

"Can I help you find what you want?" he asked.

"I'm not sure I know."

"Maybe, maybe not," he said. "Most of us actually do—we're just too afraid to say. We'll be closing soon, by the way."

Trish glanced away, uncomfortable. "I just need a few

things, and then I have to go retrieve my daughter. She's visiting Santa."

"Are you sure? They haven't had a Santa in years." He moved a little closer. She could smell the oil in his hair. How could he not know? Santa was set up practically right outside his store.

Trish felt she should leave, but stopped herself. She'd be done in just a few minutes, and then she and the B could go home. "Well, they must have changed their minds. I have to hurry along." She went deeper into the shop, away from him and his greasy, dust-laden hair. She picked up a dusty old brooch for her mother—she could clean it, and she'd get one of those defective ornaments for her father. They never liked anything she gave them anyway. And this, this would let them know exactly how she felt about this horrible holiday. Maybe they would stop expecting her to come—what a relief that would be.

But she still needed something for her sister, the cousins, and whoever else she'd probably forgotten. At the back of the store was a stack of Victorian Christmas cards. She began thumbing through them quickly, seeking something that might actually impress.

The first card to catch her eye bore a picture of an unhappy-looking man in stocks being tormented by a jester. "Happy Christmas to You!" it proclaimed. In the next, a seriously wintry scene of ice and snow, a man was being mauled by an angry polar bear. On another there was some sort of bifurcated root thing with a human head wearing a top hat and monocle. A root branch stuck out like an arm, clutching a heart-shaped object with the message "A Merry Christmas to You." She held on to these—she didn't really understand them, but they still perfectly expressed everything she was feeling.

On one card a snowman had turned sinister and was threatening a little boy. And here were two dead birds, their feet pointing stiffly upwards—"Merry Christmas and Happy New Year!" Then another, "May Christmas Be Merry," with a frog dancing with a hideous black beetle as a giant fly held aloft a golden ring. They were all suitably unpleasant. What a wonderful, wonderful shop!

On another card a hideous goat creature with long black fur, twisted horns, and a forked tongue threatened a tub full of babies with a giant fork. Was he really planning to skewer them? Maybe this one was too much. She would give it to her father.

"That be Krampus," the skinny clerk croaked at her elbow.

"Wha-at?" He'd scared her so badly she felt dizzy.

"Krampus. He's the opposite of the Santa Claus. He's the other one, the one what punishes the children who misbehaved during the year. Tortures them, I reckon. I've got loads of Krampus gear, if you're interested."

"No!" she cried. "What a terrible idea! Who'd want to invent such a thing?" Guiltily, she dropped the cards. She glanced at her fingertips—they were filthy. She quickly rubbed them on her sleeve.

"They invented him to protect the kiddies, I reckon. Keep them from getting into trouble. Sometimes you have to scare those little ones, just to make them behave. They can be like little animals, if you don't."

"No, no you don't!" she cried, and started for the door.

"Sometimes the truth is a scary thing."

She turned and stared at him. "What's that?"

"She needs something she's not getting, but the hateful creature won't tell you what it is. You didn't sign up for this, now did you? You didn't ask for this. This is not what you wanted at all." The clerk's face had gone dark, as had most of the shop.

"I have to go," Trish said, crying. "I have to pick her up."

"But it's too late for all that now," the clerk said, invisible, just a rough voice issuing from the dark. "You already made your choice. They're shutting us down. They're tearing down the mall."

"Who are *they-ey*?" Again the quake in her voice, the awful evidence that she was terrified.

"Why the ones what make the holidays. The ones what make the malls and then tears them all down. The ones what know all the rules in the rule books, but refuse to tell you what they are. The ones what takes the kiddies and does what needs to be done."

Trish ran from the store. "B—Bean!" She shouted at the dark. All light was gone except for a thin line of silver overhead illuminating a narrow shaft of bright dust. Or was it snow?

She wandered around in the thickening black calling her daughter's name, running into things, tripping over what might have been loose tiles or ceiling debris. Once she touched what she was sure were antlers, and begged Santa's assistant for help. But there was no answer. Feeling further down she realized it was just a head with nothing inside.

Eventually the dark ahead of her lightened into shadow, and then lightened again into an amber mist. She stumbled forward into a field where the mall used to be—after they tore it all down. The grass and the tall weeds were whitening gradually under a silencing fall of snow. There the distant trees whose edges still showed a glimmer of flame. There the collapsing haystacks and the broken fences. And then among the naked trees the worn and battered chair and the withered old man dressed in faded red hunched over a yellow bundle in his lap. He appeared to be mumbling something. Or was that just Trish, mumbling to herself?

"Please," she said, like that beggar she'd encountered earlier. "Please, there's been a misunderstanding."

He looked up at her, his beard torn apart, the surrounding skin raw and bleeding. He held the yellow bundle up. "No," he said. "You were asked what you wanted."

"But I don't *know* what I wanted! I never have!"

She rushed forward and yanked the bundle from his arms, holding it tightly against her chest as she ran.

She didn't look until later, when she had her child back safely in her car. She wept and apologized, and she promised all she would do to make up for her mistake. But the twisted and weathered log inside the bundle remained silent, although Trish could just make out the beginnings of a nose, and the lines of a delicate mouth, if she stared long enough into the cracked wood.

Ladybird, Ladybird

Patty sat by his bed for hours working crossword puzzles. She'd avoided them for years. Now she relished the small, hard-won successes, and the occasional solution resulting in a cascade of triumph. She never realized she knew so many words, or had such a passion for learning new ones.

"Four down. The end of the day. *Eventide*. I think my grandmother was the only person I ever heard use it in actual conversation, but it's a nice word, don't you think? You might have liked my grandmother. She had your sense of humor; but she was kinder the way she used it."

Carl said nothing of course. He was asleep, or unconscious. Patty wasn't sure which, or if there was a difference. *Asleep* sounded more pleasant.

One of the older nurses came in. Dottie. She was the one who kept her hair dyed deep black, pulled back so severely it appeared to hurt her face. But Patty had decided it was the only way the poor woman knew to express an unspoken grief.

"You like the crosswords, don't you? Seems like you're working on them every time I come in. I tried once or twice, but they're too hard for me."

Patty finished filling in eighteen across. *Sorrows*. What Longfellow says every man has in secret, which the world knows not. She looked up. "Sorry, didn't mean to be rude. But if I don't write the word down immediately, I'm afraid my mind will wander away from it. *He* says my mind goes flying away to Never Never Land every chance it gets."

"Peter Pan, right?"

"That's right! See, you could do crosswords. It's hard at first, then as you do more you get into the swing of it. You never really know what you know until you write it down. That's why I keep a diary. For words I suddenly remember, or something important I somehow forgot. Carl didn't know about Never Never Land until I made him watch the movie with me. He hated it, but at least he learned about Peter Pan."

The nurse went to Carl's bed and checked the bag of cream-colored TPN and the line going into his chest. Carl stopped eating a few days before Thanksgiving, yet he insisted Patty cook a full holiday meal just for the two of them. She made a couple of different Jell-O dishes thinking maybe he could at least eat those, but all he had was half a glass of weak tea with no lemon. She could tell the smell of the food made him ill, but he insisted on sitting there watching her eat. She even ate some of the turkey, which she'd never much cared for, because it was his favorite. She had to throw it all out when he went into the hospital three days later.

"I'm not sure this intravenous feeding is doing him any good." Dottie said it softly to herself, but it was obvious Patty was meant to hear. Dottie probably wasn't supposed to say that, but it was something Carl's doctors had already discussed with her, so what did it matter? He wouldn't live to see Christmas, but Patty had known months before the doctors discovered the cancer was back. Carl acted as if he had years and she wasn't about to tell him otherwise. But she knew. Just as she'd known her grandmother was dying before anyone else.

Patty turned her face to the window, now understanding a bird was coming. When it arrived, she smiled and gave it a quick nod. It turned its head sideways, staring at her, then nodded back.

"Is that a crow?" Dottie had stepped closer to the window for a better look.

"Different species. It's a blackbird. Don't you love the Beatles' song?" Patty started to hum it, then stopped abruptly. "Crows are bigger, about the size of a pigeon. And cleverer. Have you ever seen a raven? Almost twice as big as a crow, chicken-sized."

"Like in that poem by Poe," Dottie said.

"That's right! See, you have everything you need to be good at crossword puzzles!" Dottie smiled, and Patty felt a sudden buoyancy making the fingers on her left hand flutter. It was the first time in the weeks they'd been at the hospital she'd made the old nurse smile.

The nurse went back to her regular checks and Patty continued to work on her puzzle. As she sometimes did, she thought of a nursery rhyme to help herself think, "ladybird, ladybird, fly away home."

"What's that?"

Patty looked up and grinned. "It's an old children's rhyme, ladybird, ladybird, fly away home? It just popped into my head. I didn't realize I said it out loud."

"I thought it was ladybug."

"The Brits call them ladybirds. They're supposed to be lucky. We call them ladybugs, same thing."

"They don't look anything like birds."

Patty laughed. "No, they don't, do they? But I still like the way it sounds. Some of the British call them ladycows, and they certainly don't resemble cows. No wait, it must be the spots! I never realized before. Each cow has a different pattern of spots. That's how you can tell them apart. I mean the cows, not the ladybugs, but I believe the number of spots on the ladybugs help tell you what species they are. I guess I should read up on that." The nurse appeared to be staring at her. "I'm sorry—I don't know why I'm blabbing like this. You'd think I hadn't had anyone to talk to in years!" Patty felt the tears building in her eyes and she looked down at her puzzle.

"That's all right, honey. You just know *so many* things."

Patty kept staring at the magazine, but she couldn't stop the smile. "I do. I really do."

More birds had gathered outside the window, some hovering a few feet away and others weighing down the branches of the nearby trees. Patty wasn't sure if she could make them go away or not, but she was afraid Dottie would be alarmed if she noticed how many there were. She gazed intently at the ones on the windowsill and blinked her eyes several times. The birds seemed suddenly agitated, but she detected no other change.

"How long have you folks been married?"

"A little over forty years. He's been a big chunk of my life."

Dottie turned and looked at her. "Really? You don't look that old."

Patty felt herself blush. "Why thank you. I'll be sixty-nine next month."

"Well—" Dottie reached up to touch a dark curl hanging from her forehead. "You don't look it."

"Easy living, I suppose."

Dottie was rearranging and fluffing up the pillows beneath Carl's head. "Do you think he would do the same for you?"

Patty shifted her chair around to partially block the window. "I don't know what you mean," although it wasn't entirely true.

"I mean if you were to switch places, and it was you in this bed, would he sit there day after day, watching, waiting?"

"I'm not sure I can answer. I've never been able to read minds."

Dottie looked at her curiously. "Don't get me wrong. When a spouse falls dangerously ill, the other one is usually right there where you are, asking questions, sounding hopeful, doing little favors. But when the partner doesn't show it's usually the man."

Patty smiled at Carl, nodding. "Well I guess now we'll never know."

"We women are the caregivers, aren't we?" Dottie looked grim as she tugged and smoothed the sheets, none too gently Patty thought.

"That's certainly part of what we are."

"When you spend your money, do you get an equal vote?"

"I do all the household shopping. I tell him how much I need, and I decide how to spend it. He never interferes." Patty maintained her smile, but she could feel it faltering.

"And the big things? Cars, boats, home improvements?"

"We don't have a boat." Dottie frowned at her. "Okay, he makes the money, so I guess he feels he should have a bigger say, on *some* items."

"I should mind my own business," Dottie replied. "But like I said, you obviously *know* so many things."

Patty wasn't offended, but she was embarrassed. She thought of all those times Carl had come home with a purchase, and said it was a surprise, and showed it to her, and it was obviously just for him. She never objected. She asked him questions, and enjoyed listening to him, how interested he was in what he had brought home, how passionately he would speak of his research into the purchase, and his detailed vision of how they might use it, none of which he had shared with her beforehand. These were among the longest conversations they ever had.

And there *had* been a boat. He changed his mind after a week and took it back.

"Do you have any kids?"

Again, Patty smiled. "We lost him when he was two."

"Oh. I'm so sorry." Dottie didn't ask how, and Patty didn't volunteer. She thought of pointing out how many couples divorce after the death of a child but did not. Carl had not done well with it and could not speak of what had happened. She had not done well with it either. But still they had stayed together, and she had taken care of her husband, who in his inability to examine his loss was much like a child.

The nurse left the room, and Patty went back to her crossword. "Ladybird, ladybird, fly away home," she recited, then realized the terrible rest of it. "Your house is on fire; your children shall burn!"

Well, he hadn't burned, and the darkness of that thought shocked her. He'd choked on a medicine bottle cap one of them must have left in his crib. She honestly didn't know which of them had been so careless. For the rest of that day, and for months afterward, it certainly felt as if their house were on fire.

As she did most nights, Patty stayed late, even though there seemed no need and she grew weary of sitting there, trying to distract herself with another puzzle, not wanting to see whatever she might see when she raised her head. Still, it was better than going home alone. And Christmas was but a few days away. She kept her long winter coat and her purse in a chair beside her. She was always ready to leave.

When something did happen, Patty couldn't help but lift her eyes. Sometimes Carl would make his own milky twin, which would rise from the pillow leaving the other Carl lying there. Sometimes the twin would look at Patty and sometimes not, before falling back into Carl. Sometimes an alarm would go off, but monitor alarms and IV pump alarms were always going off, and none seemed to trigger much urgency. For the nurses they must have become an annoying sort of background disturbance and easy to ignore.

Each time Patty felt a certain lightness, an upwelling making her want to leave her chair, but then the normal would return and she stayed put, waiting for everything to make sense again. But when had the normal ever made sense? She didn't believe in spirits. She didn't believe in much of anything.

After the first few evenings Patty never stayed the night again. She'd gotten a stiff neck from drowsing in the chair, her head propped against some pillows, and something about the resulting angle made everything unresolved.

Each night Patty would say goodnight to Carl and pause for a moment to give him the opportunity to say it in return. From here she would walk the halls as witness to moments of unaccountable change, to the suggestion of an arm raised from an empty bed, and once a silent exchange of conversation from within a perplexity of shadow. Once home she was alone in an empty house without even that.

Tonight, she felt compelled to linger. She stood up and pulled on her coat, buttoning it tightly because she sensed the deep cold on the other side of the window. She picked up her purse and waited, watching Carl's face as he began to struggle for breath, a violent shudder in his chest as if something were fighting for escape. His features transformed with a pale confusion, and she found she could not remember what her husband had looked like before.

Patty walked briskly out of his room ahead of the alarms, found the door to the second-floor patio a short distance away, and went outside. She stood there, waiting, watching the roof and the sides of the building and the black sky beyond. Soft puffs of steam and stray trails of smoke drifted out of various pipes and chimneys, and she wondered if she would be able to tell the difference, if there was any chance she would know when her husband left the building, or if there would be any trace at all, or even if that was remotely how it worked.

What she was not prepared for was the way she began to rise, how her chest had swollen with such feeling she could not quite *parse*, a word she had not used since high school English.

Soon she was high above the building, far above the tallest trees, and it amused her to think if someone saw her right now, they'd think the wind had stolen some poor woman's coat.

When she finally perceived that last trace of him, in rapid retreat from a life wed to her and everything they had known, Patty knew she was expected to follow, assumed to somehow keep up. *Fly away home*, she thought, and went in a different direction.

For All His Eyes Can See

Peter wakes up in the darkness in an empty bed. He's knocked the sheets off again, and he lies there naked, imagining that he has been prepared for surgery. He doesn't know what they can do for him, but he needs someone to do something. But even in dream and imagination the doctors never come. Finally, fully awake, he remembers he is in Clarice's bed.

Clarice is gone, but she is usually gone when he wakes up, no matter when he wakes up. Every night she ventures out across the seas of trash and ruin that surround the old warehouses, staying away for hours, and sometimes all night, eventually dragging back old tires, obsolete electronics, broken umbrellas, someone's torn clothing, unidentifiable bits of fire-blasted metal, whatever might interest her for whatever reason. Sometimes she brings back something for him: an old knife blade, a twisted bit of wreckage, and the remains of an accident. Of course these items aren't really for him. They're for him to look at and to report on what he sees: the wear and the corruption along the edges, the occult blood and the microscopic bits of flesh, the hidden evidence of reality's decay which his human eyes should be unable to see, but which do. For this is his talent, his secret advantage which is really no advantage at all. And—he doesn't delude himself on this point—it's the only reason Clarice is interested in him—his eye for degeneration.

But still, she has *chosen* him. After his years of solitude, someone has chosen him. And in doing so has allowed him to feel what he imagines other people must feel.

"She's using you, you know? She's the kind—uses you up and then throws you away. I'm not sure for what—you ain't that pretty. I can't stand looking at those eyes of yours for more than five seconds. Like two wasp nests in plastic bags. Just telling it like it is."

That was Billy, who mined the piles of trash several streets over at the lower end of Main. Billy had advice for everyone, on any subject. Peter, who has no advice, always listened, even though these things were not news to him. Where Clarice is concerned he entertains no illusions. He just no longer cares. "How do you know these things, Billy?"

"Experience. Experience. You may be smart and older— what are you now? Fifty?—but you have no knowledge of romance, Peter."

This was a true statement, but Peter still didn't like hearing it. Not that he wanted Billy to go away. Before Clarice, Billy was about the only person Peter spoke to every day.

Billy has been gone for months. No one seems to know what happened to him. That's not that unusual in this time of displacement; sometimes entire blocks disappear over a few days. The people too. They die or they move away or some other thing that Peter doesn't understand. And Peter has to try to forget one more thing no longer part of this world.

Peter eventually falls back asleep, thinking of Billy, and all the other people he used to know but doesn't anymore. He dreams about clouds boiling black across the sky, and the earth churning noisily below.

Hours later he wakes up again, with light cutting through the cracked warehouse windows high above the bed. This has become the best part of Peter's day, waking up in Clarice's room, the sun striking her bits and pieces in unexpected ways, making even the most unpromising among them glow.

Out one corner of the windows he sees a blackened and fire-twisted skeleton of rods and wires. For a long time he couldn't figure out what this was, then finally recognized it as a TV aerial mounted on the roof of the burned-out building next door. He has not watched a television in a very long time, and has no idea if there are still broadcasts. Some parts of the city still have random bursts of electricity. He has been in Abby's trade shop when the lights glimmered on for a few minutes before going out again, so like a little magic trick, a cheap illusion, and the cruelest thing he has seen in months.

He tries to touch everything in Clarice's room as he leaves it. He never knows if he will be able to return or not, or if Clarice will disappear before he comes back, so he is trying to build a replica of this room in his memory he can visit whenever he wants. He knows the touching is a risk—she is very particular how she places things. Objects are arranged as they might be in a museum, for display, with nothing completely obscuring the thing behind it. Glass and metal and plastic and wood. Knob and dial and armature and casing. So many different styles of screw heads and nail heads and brads and markings both ornamentive and functional in design. Peter has no idea what the meaning of any of this might be, or if there is any meaning to be had. But Clarice collects them here for a reason, even though he doubts he will ever know that reason.

Outside Clarice's room the walls of the warehouse are festooned with water damage and rust deposits, and a pervasive dark liquid decay that bleeds out from the underlying structural members. The bedroom used to be an office in a corner of the second floor. The rest of the floor is open, although now full of the junk museum Clarice has collected. Some of these articles look too big for two people to carry. Some appear too big for six. In one corner lie the picked-over remains of a large truck. Its metal carcass is much too large for the freight elevator. Peter has made up several stories to explain its presence here, but is unable to settle on the one that satisfies.

Part of a bridge trestle leans in another corner. Nearer the center of the floor are the blasted shells of old gas pumps, the tail section of a plane, a detached (and twisted) fire escape, a shattered cast iron fireplace, a cluster of traffic lights, a burned bed, amalgamated piles of computers, TVs, and other electronics.

Angular shadows chase each other through the interior. Peter is inclined to imagine that they are the shadows of angels' wings, but he knows better. Outside the high windows the world has broken into sharp edges.

"Look at this. Tell me." He remembers how Clarice had been that day, tall and so slender she had no profile—he couldn't even see her the way she was wrapped in gray, there by the scorched posts of the burned bed. She'd discovered him in the street outside the warehouse that very morning. He'd been scavenging for food among the debris, something he did for hours every day, but never before so close to these old warehouses. Every scrounger he knew said they were dangerous, but no one wanted to say why.

But his findings had been pitiful lately, and actual starvation was beginning to feel like a very real possibility. If he didn't find food soon, or something he could trade for food, he was likely to starve. So a little risk was necessary. Besides, you never knew if a scrounger might be lying to you in order to protect a horde or preserve an advantage. The truth was it had always been hard to live, even before everything blew up. Especially if you didn't like looking at people, and seeing what was in their eyes. Back then you had to talk to people behind desks, and those people could get you a bed, a shower, or a little food, or they could deny you, make you jump through hoops. And all that for some temporary repair, because nothing ever was fixed, not as far as Peter could see. Now all the desks had been blown up along with everything else. At least no one was making promises they couldn't keep.

"Go on, touch it. I know that you want to." That's the way she'd said it, like she knew everything. Like it was some kind of sex thing. Of course Peter knew she didn't understand everything—otherwise she wouldn't need him to look.

She'd just turned up while he was searching through the trash that day. He didn't know how long she'd been standing there. She might have been standing there for hours. Or just dropped in out of the sky. In any case he hadn't heard anything, or seen anything, before he saw the gleam of her. So tall and perfect and bright. And him too shy to really look at her, or not wanting to, afraid of what he might see.

She'd asked him to come upstairs, said she had things for him. He hadn't wanted to, but he did it anyway, because she'd asked him. She said there was something different about him. Of course she meant his eyes, although she'd never come right out and said so.

"Let me just put this in your hand. You tell me what you see."

He'd been shy, and looked down. But she got it into his hand somehow. It was an old metal bedspring, burned and corroded. It felt rough and repulsive against his skin, the way bits of it flaked off and stained his fingers a rich dark brown, like mud, or shit. Under normal circumstances—with anyone but Clarice—he might have answered with something obvious, like "it's an old bedspring."

But even that first time he knew that wasn't what Clarice was asking for. And that he shouldn't mess around with her. She was as serious as a heart attack, and wouldn't appreciate a joke either good or bad. So he did then what he does every day. He focuses, and if the conditions are right, and there is sufficient light, he can see the edges of things, or rather how so many things lose their edge over time.

The spring has smoke in it, and fire, and that faint trail of disintegration all things have on them as the world and everything in it dissolves into nothing. And it has flesh, or the ghost of flesh, and there's something of a woman's life in this, and her death, and that's how he knows a woman died in the bed this spring was once a part of. And it was no accident. Nothing about this metal spring is accidental.

He tells Clarice all this in his stumbling way. The words tumble and roll and drop out of his mouth. And Clarice grows warm, and he loves it when Clarice is warm. And that was when and how she first took him in.

He takes the broken stairs down to the first floor of the warehouse, which is impassable; there is so much old stuff, so much destruction jammed into it. There's only a clear path to the front door, which he takes, and breaks out into the too-bright day.

"Is she up there?"

The voice is dry and torn to pieces. Peter looks around for Diaz, discovers that he has crawled behind the industrial waste bin a few yards away. No agency empties that bin anymore, but the contents are always being recycled. Now and then Clarice adds something she's tired of looking at. Peter wonders if she might get tired of looking at him.

"No. She's gone."

Diaz slides out from behind the bin on his battered creeper board. He owns a wheelchair. Peter has actually seen Diaz in it a couple of times. But he seems to prefer this thing like what a mechanic uses to slide underneath cars. Or used to use. There probably still are mechanics somewhere, working on cars, but Peter hasn't seen any for a very long time. Diaz is good with the creeper, though—he moves fast as a rat across the broken pavement. "Good, we can talk then," and he slides Peter's way.

Diaz has many angles to his body, like some broken thing that has fallen out of the sky. Peter is amazed this fallen angel is able to move as well as he does. But it only requires a cursory glance for Peter to know that Diaz isn't long for this world—the tumors decorating Diaz's interior are like a brilliant constellation in Peter's eyes.

Diaz hasn't said anything more, and lies there patiently

looking up at Peter, as if waiting for the answer to some question. "What did you want to talk about?" Peter asks.

"Some of us just wanted to know what she does with you up there every night, if she's keeping you under—what's the word—duress?"

"Some of us? Who's still around? I haven't seen anyone in weeks."

"A few of us still hang on. Excuse me, but I don't think I should be saying who. She's treating you well? You're looking fat."

Peter self-consciously pinches one side of his belly, finds a little bit of a roll there. Clarice does feed him well—she always has food. "She shares," he says. "She's a generous person."

"Generous, or dangerous?"

"I don't feel in any danger. People just fear what they don't understand. It's always been that way. More so now, maybe, with so much taken away."

"Stuff is still being taken away. People are still disappearing. You know anything about that?"

"She's harmless. She's been good to me. I can't remember the last time anyone was good to me. My folks weren't even good to me. She *chose* me—can you imagine? I've never been chosen before. Now I'm getting fat and people are jealous they weren't chosen, that's all. It's an old story."

Diaz spits into the rubble and begins creeping away. "You don't see it. She chose people before. At least three or four that I know of. Do you see them anywhere? Because I sure don't."

Diaz spreads himself out and scurries faster until he is around the edge of the bin. Like a crab, or some kind of insect. Diaz seems clearly afraid of him. Peter doesn't understand—he had never hurt anyone, never done anything.

As far as he knows Clarice hasn't either. He doesn't know why people say these things, except for their fear and suspicion. But they shouldn't make up tales—that's what is dangerous. Peter has looked at Clarice hundreds of times and never seen anything, and doesn't Peter see everything?

What does she do with him every night? As if he would tell them. Most nights she feeds him something, and then she asks him to look at something and tell her what he sees. Sometimes he sees nothing. Sometimes it would appear he can see more than he has words for. She shines lights into his eyes and does other things to them he doesn't understand. Sometimes she asks him to look at her and say what he sees. He thinks this last request is some kind of test, because it would seem he can't see anything. He can't see her at all. He could never describe her because he's never actually seen her. So instead he gives her a compliment. He says the food she gave him was very good. Or he says she makes him feel safe, or she makes him feel useful. And that must be the right thing to do because she never punishes him for it. She punishes him for other things but not for that.

Some nights she tells him poetry, speaks it right out as if she knows it by heart. Goethe and Emily Dickinson, and others whose names come to him in the dark.

> *She died—this was the way she died;*
> *And when her breath was done,*
> *Took up her simple wardrobe*
> *And started for the sun.*

And,

> *and finally, insane for the light,*
> *you are the butterfly and you are gone.*

And,

to die and so to grow,
you are only a troubled guest
on the dark earth.

He cannot remember who had written what—he has never been clever that way. But he remembers the lines—she says them over and over until they've become part of the fabric of his thoughts. She says she is preparing him, but she never tells him for what. She says that life will not always be this way, but she never tells him why.

He stays out all day wandering the seas of trash, the forests of cars, the hollowed-out buildings, wandering further and further with each hour. She tells him this is his job now. She tells him this is what she wants him to do. He needs to see as much as his eyes can see. He needs to train them, she says, but for what she does not reveal.

By the end of the day his eyes are frequently raw and irritated. Sometimes he sees haloes, and shadows, and fleeting things which are a little bit of both. Sometimes the surfaces of his eyes feel like layers of transparency, as if they might crack and flake, dropping lustrous leaves on his face, his shirt.

But for all his eyes can see he wonders if sometimes he is missing things. Sometimes shadows move which should not be moving. Sometimes everything just flows and he can't tell whether it is disintegration or transformation or both. Bits of the world are taken away and he never sees them again.

After hours wandering through an interminable field of rubbish he discovers a burrow in the layers of cloth and paper and cardboard and warped and tortured metal. It's like a wasp's nest, he thinks, as he stares down into the dark oval hole which he assumes is its entrance. Surrounding the opening is furniture collapsed and covered by sheets and brightly-colored spreads. He knows enough not to peek beneath them. Anyone living here is unlikely to welcome visitors, and he has no desire today to see anyone dead. There is activity deep inside the rubble, but he won't go down that hole, not even for her.

He travels a little beyond, into an area where there are discernible streets and some buildings still standing, so that at least there is some skeletal impression of neighborhoods. He looks for people and although there is the occasional distant gesture out of the corner of his eye he finds none. He gazes around at the assorted neglect beneath the late afternoon sun, the greasy patina of a worn-out and exhausted world.

He has suspected for some time that he is not in the best of health. He has developed a rash of some sort that has left the flesh on parts of his arms looking like a crumbling mess of old wallpaper, the skin lifting in numerous places, puzzle pieces flaking off into wings and rising in the ash-flecked air. The dark lines between the pieces gape wider, like his despair. He wonders idly if he will still be human if he loses all his skin.

The world flutters around the edges. Something beats at his left eye. It might be his eyelid, spasming its objections, or his abused retina beginning to detach. Blindness suddenly seems an actual possibility and he wonders if Clarice will have nothing to do with him once he cannot see.

In the distance he can see pieces of cloud peeling off and diving, their silver bellies flashing in the sun as the darker parts of them spread open into expansive wings. They drop swiftly into the ground below, sometimes rising up again with struggling figures in their grasp. He tries to follow their flight paths but there is too much distraction. Here and there the clouds burst open and curtains of fire rain down, but he is almost convinced that the effect comes from his eyes suddenly seeing through the clouds and witnessing the madness taking place beyond. A sudden explosion burns across his vision, seeming to dissolve the clouds and rupturing through to a backdrop of black space shimmering with gestures of violet luminescence.

He drops his head, unwilling to see any more, and again

there are the familiar shells of buildings, the vague lines of the streets, the chewed up and no longer necessary material of the human-made world.

A black bird approximately six feet tall is pushing a grocery cart down the vague passageway between two buildings in front of him. For some reason he decides the bird is female, although he isn't sure of what type, possibly a raven. The wheels of her cart wobble and squeak, and their nervous activity appears to be infectious because she keeps jerking her head from side to side, almost looking back at him, but not quite. Even though her eyes are enormous, like inky globes, and mounted on opposite sides of her head, so she wouldn't have to turn her head that far to see him. She has a long stiff tail that bobs as she walks, the edge of it kicking up the loose wreckage and spraying it back on him.

Creatures keep falling out of her feathers and scurrying away, hiding under crushed cars and fallen bits of wall. After some review he decides they are giant lice.

In another few jittery minutes she picks up speed, takes wing, dangling the cart beneath her. Some of her scavenged groceries fall to the pavement below, but she appears not to notice, or care.

Suddenly a human woman comes running at him through the ruins, waving her hands and screaming for his attention. Her head thrashes wildly about, and as it comes around he can see the tiny black wings fluttering through her hair and digging into the back of her scalp, feeding. Between their wings and beneath their claws he can see blood and her glistening white skull. She attempts to clutch his arm but there is nothing he can do for her, nothing he can do. He can only see.

To his relief a bit of the sky comes down and carries him away.

"Peter, Peter, pumpkin eater . . ." Clarice's voice floats high above him. He looks for her, and sees that he is back in her bedroom, with something flying high above him, although he cannot quite see what it is. He can only feel its gravity.

He twists his head around. He can only see the skeletal remains of things, or rather their dusty outlines in the air. The transparency of everything assaults him.

"I'm afraid your eyes don't operate in the conventional way anymore. They've become their potential, my darling, as they were always meant to be."

He thrashes about, but she has pinned him somehow to the bed. Out of the corner of his eyes he can see the piercings, but there is no flesh to speak of, or at least he can't see it. There is only pain.

"You will be all right, if you want to be. If you want to be you can be perfectly fine. We just need what your eyes can see. It's simply one of the last steps. Everything every one of you has been, it's all properly recorded now. But you can still live on—it will just seem very different, I suspect."

She comes closer, and for the first time he can make some sense of her. A form with the form ripped away. An empty breath. An invisible frame where the dust adheres. And two terribly, terribly gluttonous eyes.

"I've trained them of course, so these, these are *mine*."

She pries them out almost simultaneously, with surprisingly little pain. He tries to blink the distortion away, but then realizes she's also taken the lids.

And yet how would he know? His body begins its revolt, convulsing as if to purge what is entering it through his empty eye sockets: the sights and the vistas, the terrible beyonds. Because his eyes had not been the instruments—they had been the filters meant to keep it all out.

Heterocera

The rules for distinguishing moths from butterflies are not well established. Claire had been reading about these lovelies for weeks, hoping to better understand them, but a lack of understanding appeared to be the norm. The reason they were drawn to artificial light (*positive phototaxis*) was still unknown. Most were nocturnal, but not all. She wondered what might have seduced these evening creatures to show themselves during the day, like ghosts lingering after sunrise. Most moth adults do not eat at all. Having chased so many from closets, she was surprised by this. Apparently, their children did all the damage.

Claire's child was a blessing. She was so sorry Alice discovered her father that way. Her husband snored, so they'd kept separate bedrooms, lying together only for sex, which hadn't interested her in a while. She much preferred the holding afterward. He'd lain down for a nap and never got up again. Claire found him with his mouth open and struggled to get it closed, afraid the moths might crawl in. Maybe they did when she wasn't watching.

Why had Claire covered him with all those coats? Alice had the right to ask. He'd been wearing his old clothes, and she thought he would hate it if his daughter's last memory of him was in those rags. So, she went into his closet looking for something nicer.

The clothes bar was overloaded; he hadn't thrown anything out in years. She'd started with the coats, piling them on top of him. It didn't seem inappropriate at the time. In their younger days when they were too poor to pay the heating bill they'd put a layer of coats on the bed at night. It was so deliciously cozy they laughed until they fell asleep.

By the time she reached his collection of pants, the moths gathered on the closet's back wall distracted her. They'd looked like little wedges of bark. When she touched them, they either flew away or their dead bodies dropped to the floor. Then she had a mess she had to clean up.

She first tried scooping them up with her hands. But they did that thing butterfly and moth wings do, the colorful scales turning to a powder that got all over her hands. She hated the sensation. What would happen if she kept rubbing their wings? Would all the color come off, leaving her with a pile of transparent bugs? Or would they disappear entirely, that delicate powder having disguised their essentially spiritual nature?

Finally, she went downstairs to get a broom, and that's when she lost some time. This happened occasionally, but never for this long. It seemed a few hours at most, but Alice, who later discovered her father's bare foot protruding from under the coats, said it must have been days.

"We'll tell them you and I were away on a trip. When we returned we discovered Dad's body on the bed."

Claire was shocked. "Sweetheart, didn't we teach you better than to lie?"

Her daughter grabbed her hand and gave her a sad smile. "Mom, I'm afraid the police will make a big deal out of it. I don't know, but a judge could put you in a home. I don't want to take the chance. I can't lose *both* of you." Alice frowned. "You do know Dad is dead, don't you?"

"Of course. Of course I know." Claire was suddenly terrified.

Alice called the police and her husband's body was taken away. They asked few questions and her daughter answered every one. No one asked Claire anything. She might as well have been hanging in the back of her husband's closet.

That night her daughter slept in the guest room. The next morning Alice went grocery shopping and filled the cabinets and refrigerator with food. The amount of food alarmed Claire. How could she possibly eat it all? Then Alice reminded her she would be there to help.

"Mom, I have to go back to my place and move everything out. It'll just be a couple of days, three at most. You'll be okay here by yourself, won't you? Then I'll come back and move my stuff in."

"*All* of it?"

Alice laughed. "I don't own that much. You have plenty of space. I'll hire a cleaning service to tidy up the house before I move in. We'll kill all these *bugs*. You'll love it."

"*Bugs?*"

"What are they, moths? They're *everywhere*. You have an *infestation*. We'll get rid of them."

Claire looked around. Dead moths littered the floor. No, some of their wings were moving. Moths clung to the wallpaper. Several beat at the lamp fixture overhead, trying to reach the light inside.

"We can keep a few lovelies, can't we?"

"Mom, no. They're *vermin*. They'll eat your clothes." She thought to correct her—it was their children, of course—but said nothing. It made her sad to hear Alice talk that way.

That night she sat on her husband's empty bed. Things had happened so quickly—no, she could no longer trust that was true, it could have been weeks—but she hadn't thought that much about him. When had she become so callous? But you get to be a certain age—and she certainly had—you expect terrible events to happen, you imagine them in excruciating detail, so when they do happen there seems to be little left to feel.

Roger would have understood. He understood most things. And he loved Alice, but he wouldn't have approved her moving back home. Your children develop their own lives and they drop you as a frame of reference. They have their own closets and they eat elsewhere.

Something crawled out of the trim of Roger's closet door. Followed by another something and something else entirely. They took wing and floated like stray thoughts above her head.

She opened the closet. She'd never finished going through his clothes, and now the moths were crawling and flying everywhere. She grabbed a few garments and tossed them on the floor of the bedroom, then grabbed some more. They were heavy and made her arms hurt, but eventually she got them all out.

A large moth hung on the back wall. She couldn't tell if it was alive or dead, but she was afraid to touch it. It was *so big*, and in the pattern on its thorax she could see Roger's face.

She turned to go, thinking she would call Alice—surely she had her daughter's number—when the moth enveloped her. Claire gasped for air, but he held her until she calmed down. He whispered to her words he hadn't said in years, and then they glided toward the window.

Before they could fly they had to break through the glass. But even though there were so many sharp pieces, she didn't feel any pain.

Sleepover

Tina gazed through the glass door as the surge swept the base of the hill—darkening, thickening, behaving unlike any water she'd ever seen. It was more than water, more than mud, taking apart their neighborhood and carrying it away. The hurricane hovered somewhere northward, stalled and feeding the deluge. *This is what happens when the planet hates us.*

She'd been there several hours, thinking it her role to witness. They couldn't get out yet. The kids were safely upstairs, maybe sleeping, probably still mad. For some reason they blamed her and Michelle for all this. But that was adulthood—when the kids were miserable it was your fault. You were the powers that be, even when you were as helpless as they.

At first light everything had been still, Elm Street looking like a street even though underwater. But as the morning wore on things began to move, swirls and eddies appeared, borders were lost. Bits of trees, houses, cars, and everything else rushed by.

"Is that the Thompson house? It looks like that blue paint they so liked." Michelle pointed over her shoulder.

She didn't want to say, but said it anyway. "Pieces of it. But maybe they're from the garage. Their garage was closest to the street, and it was the same color. Hopefully just the garage."

"I talked to Amy's mom, so all the parents are updated. She's scared. But I promised we're taking good care of Amy. I reminded her that we live on this tall hill, way, way above the flood. We may lose power, but we've got plenty of blankets, and a full pantry."

More sky-blue pieces of the Thompsons' life swirled past. They were now three days into what was supposed to be an overnight sleepover. "Is Janet's dad still determined to drive his boat over here?"

"I think I got him to understand how crazy that would be. He told me to keep her calm. Like I wouldn't." Michelle hugged her from behind. Tina leaned into her, although she wasn't feeling it. "Great timing for a sleepover, huh? I almost wish we had a less popular kid."

Michelle squeezed tighter. "No way to know Sue's birth-day and Hurricane Zeke would arrive at the same time."

She stepped out of Michelle's embrace. "Sorry. I can't relax until this is over. Did they calm down? They were so *fiercely angry* with us, even Suze."

"I think they were *praying* earlier. It was very sweet, but it made me sad. They were all cross-legged in a circle, holding hands, mumbling something. Even Sue."

Tina shook her head. "*Suze*? She doesn't pray."

"We told her she could choose any religion."

"Have you seen her be religious before?"

"I think it's the situation. Isn't Janet's family pretty reli-gious? She appeared to be leading them."

Tina heard a loud crack and turned just as a large tree limb fell. "Are they asleep at least?"

"Most I think. All that mad wore them out. They were scared, poor babies. Sometimes scared comes out as anger."

"They *interrogated* us. Why don't we have solar, why do we drive such a big car, do we recycle . . ."

"Well, at least we recycle."

"*Of course* we do. We *care* about the environment." Tina couldn't be sure, but she thought the water might be higher up their hillside. She thought she could see more bushes before.

She didn't see the birdfeeder. Had they hauled it away? She wasn't sure. They'd always intended to—it was cracked. This area had been sinking since the twenties. Flooding had gotten a little worse every year. Decades of oil development—that's what she'd read. Who knew anything except what they'd read or been told? The driveway around back, the steps, and the foundation were all severely cracked. They were surely safe up here, but much awfulness was possible once you couldn't trust the ground beneath your feet or the sky above your head.

"Is my dad coming?" The little girl in the doorway had an expansive coiffure of black curls spilling in random directions. Janet's tiny face was damp and intense. She smelled unwashed, like a furry beast.

Michelle walked over and caressed her cheek. "It's too dangerous, sweetheart. Try to get some sleep. Before you know it the sun will come out and your dad will be here to take you home."

"So, the storm is still happening? The water is getting higher?"

"It *is*, honey." Tina wasn't sure if the child could see the flooding from her vantage point, but she stepped in front of the door. She felt foolish. "But it will stop soon."

"Why so many hurricanes? Why is the weather always worse?"

When Tina didn't answer Michelle said, "It's *complicated.* I don't know if anyone really understands the reasons, or exactly what to do. It's bigger than our little lives. But we're *trying.*"

Janet stared, her nose shadowed, dark like an animal's, her eyes wet and burning white. She made a soft grunting noise. "You *a-dults.* You don't really know *anything,* do you? Just how to break things." She disappeared upstairs.

"Do you *believe* this kid?" Michelle laughed.

Something crashed into the side of the house. The lights

went out. Both women ran to the door. Several limbs from the giant tree in the side yard draped the porch. The trunk had partially crushed the roof. Tina unlatched the door.

"What are you doing?" Michelle grabbed her arm.

"The gas meter is on that side. I need to make sure the line isn't damaged." Tina ran onto the porch, down the steps and around the side. She started pulling branches out of the way. After a few seconds Michelle was working beside her. The meter was yards away. Tina was suddenly aware that above them the girls' shiny faces stared down from the black dormer windows.

Branches lashed her arms and cheeks. Finally Tina could see that the meter was okay, but part of the wall had collapsed. She grabbed Michelle's hand as they struggled back to the porch steps.

She could see all the girls in the dim interior crowded behind the door. Somber and wide-eyed, their Sue stood next to Janet. It started raining again. Tina could feel the wind pushing her off balance. Michelle raced up the steps and tried the door. She pulled on the handle, twisted it and pulled on it again. She started beating on the frame. "Let us in!"

Tina walked up and stood beside her. The children's hair appeared wet, their faces streaming. But they hadn't been outside. They were breathing hard, panting. The whites of their eyes gleamed. It matched the shine coming off their exposed teeth.

"What's happening here?" Michelle was shouting into her face. "I don't understand what's going on!"

Tina didn't want to be uncharitable, but she understood what Janet meant. Her wife sounded stupid. It was both frightening and embarrassing.

"They're not going to let us in," she told her. "They've chosen another side."

Torn

"The mind is its own place, and in itself can make a
heaven of hell, a hell of heaven."

John Milton, *Paradise Lost*

I.

Turning and turning in the widening gyre
The falcon cannot hear the falconer;
Things fall apart; the centre cannot hold;
Mere anarchy is loosed upon the world
—*The Second Coming*, William Butler Yeats

Taylor had time for an instantaneous impression as he
drove through the railing and plunged into the trees
below. After several failed suicide attempts, how ironic that
he would die in an accident, and utilizing a method he would
never have chosen, as he was singularly terrified of heights.
That his death would involve an automobile came as no real
revelation—he'd always been a distracted driver.

At least his father had predeceased him and would have no
opportunity to express his complete lack of surprise.

There was a fraction of a moment when he was aware of
rapid descent parallel to a tall tree. A once-in-a-lifetime view.
Then an explosion of land and his private Big Bang.

But he did not land, or so it seemed. Or perhaps he did land
but landing was no longer relevant.

He was standing behind the screen door of his childhood home. It wasn't a memory—nothing so present could

be memory, even though he had experienced this particular vision many times before. But always before it had been encapsulated in dream, and once or twice in drug-induced hallucination. But now, now it was so terribly NOW. And he was no longer a child, or at least not *just* a child. He was far more completely himself than he ever had been.

He was standing inside the house, on one side of the screen door, afraid to step out onto the front porch, as if that rusty mesh offered protection from what was happening beyond. But he'd always known that most protection was paper-thin.

Beyond his front porch the sky was turning, revolving, constantly unwrapping itself. A spinning, widening gyre. Someone was whispering into his ear, telling him the Yeats poem as if it were a secret he'd never heard before. The voice was harsh and familiar—his father's own gnarled, country twang. He felt sick to death. His world was falling apart. The center could not hold. It was pure anarchy hunting him down and finding him at last.

And at that center, staring through him, was the eye. He couldn't get a clear glimpse of it—there were too many clouds in the way—and yet he knew it was there. God's eye or something even more fundamental than God. Witness to his endless fall.

This turning did not take place exactly at the center of his view, but slightly to the left, and up, a spot so painfully specific he felt he might point to it at any time, wherever he stood in the world. And that exactness made it seem all the more terrible. In college, at his most vulnerable, he had speculated that this location corresponded to some exact weakness in his physical brain, some fault where a future stroke might occur. But of course his many doctors had never taken this notion seriously. He'd spent much of his college time going in and out of mental hospitals. He always felt lucky when people listened to his perceptions at all.

As the sky spun, its influence widened, and more and more

of everything was drawn into chaos. Anarchy. Everything was turning. It was a hurricane, or a tornado laid on its side, a mad god's snake, its tail whipping back and forth across the distant countryside, tearing up everything he could see. He needed to find shelter, but where do you shelter when everything is tearing itself apart?

The human mind has little patience with vagaries and complexities. Even when everything wears a fuzzy edge of strangeness, a burning halo of insanity, the human mind will simplify. Nameless fears become something more concrete and recognizable. Options are diminished. And when you run, you choose a single direction.

And so all his terror was reduced to the sure knowledge that a tornado had arrived, the largest tornado anyone had ever experienced, and Taylor had to find shelter. Every wailing siren told him this. That hoarse booming voice filled him with terror even as it warned him away from terror—*the falcon cannot hear! The falcon cannot hear!*—the danger was still real and profound. He could see the wind-flattened trees. He could feel the pressure escalating inside his head. He could see the distant telephone poles uprooted and thrown like toys. His fatal crash a distant memory, his crumpled car discarded like some obsolete vessel for his panicked spirit, Taylor ran across the open field in search of shelter: some ditch, some hole that would protect him from the rage eating everything in its path.

"Don't run from me, boy!" the roaring wind shouted with his father's voice, but Taylor ran even harder, sure that if it caught him he would lose far more than his life.

And there up ahead, in some shadowed depression in the grass, lay his escape. He couldn't tell how wide the opening was, simply that it must be wide enough.

He reached down and slid the circular hatch aside. The wind grabbed the splintered disk and tore it away.

The inside of the hole was ridged. He supported himself

with hands and feet as he eased himself slowly down into the darkness, the wind snarling overhead.

"I told you not to run from me, boy!" The rage poured down and twisted all around him, binding him in anger. The roaring voice tumbled him loose, and he spun his way down thinking, *I'm in the devil's own throat! Daddy has swallowed me alive!*

He shut himself down. It was relatively easy to do—these weren't his physical eyes anymore, this wasn't his physical body. This was his recollected self, plummeting through the wrath he'd lived in most of his life.

He recalled struggling through countless nights with no hope of reprieve, holding on to women who felt sorry for him, but who finally let him go when he became too much. He was worse than an animal—even the smallest animals didn't feel sorry for themselves as they fought through their isolated journeys. Death brought a kind of honesty to the fight; everyone who ever lived had to make their passage into death alone.

The quiet consumed him. His body held only itself. His hands could not massage the loneliness from his flesh. The only way he understood to fill the silence was by shouting. At least in this place he could vocalize what he felt—no one alive wanted to hear his screams.

He was sucked spinning down the long and twisted throat of the devil. The passage widened the deeper he fell, the pattern of its ridges changing from horizontal to vertical to diagonal to spiraling waves of force which latched on to him and began to pull him apart. The pain of it forced his mouth open and then he could hear the tornado within, turning rapidly, heating up, and creating a hell that burnt him from the inside out. His skin split from chest to groin, skin flaps peeling away, flagging back and forth as he desperately tried to grab them and close himself up.

The ground reached up and slapped him. *Boy, don't be such a pussy!* It was his own mouth speaking, the devil having taken control of his speech. He gagged on the shame that spilled from his own lips.

Wake up! Wake up! You're late!

Taylor stretched out and felt the edges of his childhood bed. His feet hung over the end of the mattress. His hands felt clumsy and swollen as he pushed himself up and out of the covers. He'd had the bed since he was nine years old—a steer head carved into the headboard, six-guns carved into the foot. It wouldn't be until college that he slept in a bed that actually fit him. The comforter was oversized and spilled off onto the floor on all sides—he'd bought that with his own money his junior year. It had a crazy, Picasso-like pattern. At the time he'd thought it was pretty adult.

He wasn't sure how he'd gotten here. Had Jennifer thrown him out again? No, he hadn't seen her in a couple of years. *Grow up!* That was the last thing she'd said to him. He'd gambled away the rent money that time, but it wasn't the worst thing he ever did. She should have kicked him out a half-dozen times before, for his anger if nothing else. Not that he'd ever directed the anger at her, exactly. His targets had been himself, and the world, his stuff. He had a habit of breaking things, taking a hammer to them, sometimes an axe. And sometimes her things got mixed in with his things. She should have thrown him out long before she did—she deserved someone better.

Charlotte? Brenda? Who had he been living with? Taylor couldn't remember. He must have been drunk, maybe for a long time—that's why he'd ended up back here with his dad. He shuddered. It must have been really bad for him, to have come back here. But at least that memory of driving off the cliff, of being torn apart in the devil's throat, that had just been a crazy dream. So he was alive, and he could still make up for things.

Then he heard the bellowing below the floor, the roar in

his head, and knew it was a lie. He wasn't okay at all. No more chances left.

But why here, now, in this tiny, crowded room? He couldn't remember ever throwing anything away. Once he finally had something, he wanted to hold on to it. Large boxes of toys—mostly action figures with their various alternate-world accessories—were jammed cheek-to-cheek beneath the north-facing windows, split and spilling their guts onto the copiously stained brown carpet.

He swung his feet around and sat on the edge of the bed, gazing at the figures. They made him smile. He never left them the way they came, right out of the package. He'd mix up the males and the females, and add in the animal sets, the dinosaurs and the military figures. Sometimes the parts would easily snap into the other bodies, but most of the time he had to saw them apart, remove arms and legs, decapitate them, then glue them onto bodies never intended for them. He had a whole army of military guys with elephant heads, bull heads, rhino heads, and he would imagine that was how those soldiers would look if you could see into their souls. He put a dress or hot pants on the rhino man and they fit perfectly. Rhino man was his favorite. All he did all day was stomp around and rage. Anything he felt got turned and twisted inside him until it came back out as absolute fury.

Only a suggestion of sunlight ever made it through the windows. He'd illuminated the room with matching mustang lamps—one on top of his battered chest of drawers, the other on an inverted cardboard box beside his bed for reading. He leaned sideways and reached under the bed—the mixed stacks of comic books and pornography were still there. There were also centerfolds on the walls—busty women with big round thighs who actually frightened more than they aroused. And the dozens of World War II posters—Nazis and Japanese and GIs heavily equipped and intricately uniformed. Of course he'd been born twenty years after the war, but it was the most interesting thing he and his friends ever talked about. Men were always going to war. It was imperative.

As a boy, Taylor could think of nothing worse than a Nazi, but he'd envied their sense of style, and their unity. They were like a gang of brothers with evil intent.

So, are you coming down to breakfast or do I have to drag you?

The floor spoke to him three times daily: breakfast, dinner, and shut the hell up and go to bed. The last came even when he'd been perfectly quiet for hours. Maybe the old man could hear him think.

Taylor looked at his arms and legs—he was still an adult man. Would his father see him the same way, or would he see him as a boy? He was anxious to find out. If the old man started anything then he would obliterate him, or at least try. After all, he was a grown-up adult man—what could that sack of shit do to him now?

"About time. Everything's cold, but I guess that's on you."

The figure at the sink wore a greasy white T-shirt and brown leather shorts which left the bottom of his butt cheeks uncovered. Sticking out of the front of the shorts was a large codpiece studded with numerous rusty barbs. The chest and belly were huge and barrel-like. The head was that of a pink rhinoceros capped with thinning black hair. Two large yellow tusks protruded from the corners of the gnarled mouth. "Sit down. If you're late for school I'll kick your ass." His father's unmistakable voice.

Taylor sat and watched as his father slathered both their plates with blackened, crusty eggs and stiff twists of bacon. A thick slap of baked beans followed. There were already two glasses of buttermilk on the table to wash it all down.

The pink rhino didn't bother with the rickety kitchen chairs. It grunted, squatted, farted, and shoveled the food into its albino gullet. Less than a minute later it straightened up, turned and exited the kitchen, throwing a "Get to school!" back over its shoulder. Taylor wasn't sure if the rhino had actually looked at him or not. He wasn't afraid exactly, but he had no desire to stay. He went into the living room. It had a stillness about it, and a foul stench that he recognized instantly: fried foods and unwashed clothing, unbathed male bodies, garbage that should have been taken out weeks ago. Just as he remembered—no wonder his mother had left them both. He could feel the anger building inside. He walked out the front door and pulled it shut. It made a hoarse sucking sound as the rotting frame absorbed it.

The neighbors' houses were still recognizable. The Campbells, with their yellow gingerbread trim and flower boxes under every window. The Hills, their back and side yard full of cars and appliances in various states of disassembly. The Thurmans, with their ancient gold RV that as far as he knew had never left the driveway. He'd spent more of his waking hours in these houses than in his own. They probably felt sorry for him—none of them had kids. Bless them; they got him through high school.

But there was a quiet about the neighborhood that bothered him. He held his breath. He kept looking at the houses: their frayed edges, missing roof tiles, the occasional scorch mark on siding. All the flower boxes were empty, the autos and appliances layered in dust. The stench of rotting meat filled the air.

He went up to a window at the Campbells' house, leaned into the glass, and saw that the insides of the house had collapsed into the first floor. Large areas of the roof were missing, the sun illuminating the ruins. There was no sign of the Campbells; he hoped they hadn't been here whenever this occurred. He felt strangely responsible, which made no sense. He'd thrown many tantrums as a child, but he'd never hurt anyone.

The Hills were missing the back of their home. There was very little debris in the backyard, although much of what was there was red-stained. It might be blood; he had no intention of getting close enough to find out. Taylor thought he saw their living room couch in the alley about a hundred yards down.

He'd focused so much on the Thurmans' gold RV he hadn't even noticed that their house was no longer there. He wandered out into the street. From this vantage the level of damage became obvious. Most of the houses had gaps, chunks taken away, the bits distributed into the road and onto other properties. Every few lots there was a large empty space, and it would take him a second, but then he would remember a house had been there, and sometimes he would recall the name of the people who'd lived in it. And yet this didn't feel like normal storm damage. There was a crispness to the debris, a kind of selectiveness, as if some thought had gone into who deserved more, who deserved less, what should be destroyed, and how the debris should be placed. Judgment appeared to have been involved. But the agent was ultimately mysterious. You could blame God, or you could blame the devil. In the end it didn't matter—you were still screwed.

Of course some of these neighbors had made him angry, just as he had angered them. He'd been a troubled child, a destructive child. Sometimes when he'd tantrumed he'd had no awareness of what he was doing.

In the distance a series of dark clouds corkscrewed out of the sky, drilling into neighborhoods then spinning away again. *You better run, boy!* The voice vibrated in his skull, passed through his bones and shook the ground beneath him. But he felt glued to the pavement. Another dark funnel whirled into a house a block away. He could see the people spilling from that one as it was lifted from the ground and pulled apart by massive unseen hands.

He saw the occupants land, and bounce, and get up again. They had the resilience of ants. Falling pieces of house landed on them, smashed them into the ground, but they oozed boneless from under the wreckage and scattered again. He saw other figures searching through the remains of the neighborhood, drifting in and out of the broken homes, carrying their trophies aloft. They were broad-shouldered, big-bellied piles of flesh with huge shovel-like hands. They vaguely resembled what his father had become: rhinos, or hippos, up on two legs and raging. They wore torn shorts and T-shirts, but a few had added bits from police or military uniforms to their wardrobes—a shirt, a collar, a gun belt (with or without gun), pants or partial pants, the occasional military cap. Patches were sewn on at various places—some appeared handmade and bore Nazi insignia. Several of them wore wide belts below their bellies or around their necks, studded with a variety of shiny metal bits. Some had codpieces similar to his father's, in a range of sizes, ornamented with nails, rusty hardware, or bits of glass. They moved awkwardly, straddle-legged, as if upright was not their natural posture. They made these thunderous, obnoxious guttural noises which might have been laughter, or were at least celebratory in nature. Most had less distorted heads, but still appeared far from human. Some bore a resemblance to cows, elephants, bulldogs, bison, pigs.

When he'd been a kid playing with his action figures, his armies had been ruthless. Whenever they'd found a lone straggler they'd shown him no mercy.

Two of the creatures noticed him and waved at the others. The voice inside his head came to life again. *You can't run from us all!* They galloped towards him, the group gathering numbers as it progressed, determined, muscling aside any debris in the way. He stood frozen, confused at first. Then his limbs felt on fire. He turned and ran.

The streets were so crowded with the shattered remains of buildings and vehicles that swift progress was impossible. Taylor would run for a few yards and then have to stop and move some piece of wreckage or figure a detour around it. He glanced back sporadically, reasoning that those chasing him would be facing the same difficulties, but the swollen male caricatures were adept at vaulting over the piles of rubble, bursting through the wreckage, sometimes using these maneuvers as leverage to increase their speed. They would catch up to him in no time.

The twisters were also relentless, multiplying, piercing the overcast sky, drilling through rooftops, spinning across fields, tearing out clumps of trees, whipping ponds into a muddy froth. He'd been lucky enough to avoid them, but the numbers of near-misses were mounting. Towering formations of spinning earth and rubble rumbled across the ground at shocking speed, veering dizzyingly close before separating and taking out nearby structures. He ran as fast and as erratically as he could, just in case there was intelligence behind their movements. Like so many things in his life, it felt deliberate and personal.

His pursuers largely ignored this weather, even when one of their number was scooped up and tossed away. Several were torn apart like stuffed toys. But these figures made no effort to avoid the worst, as if knowing their fates were inevitable.

The largest tornado yet dropped between him and the mob. It turned sideways, tail whipping in broad strokes side to side. The creatures kept running straight into the worst of it, like rats jumping into a fan, with similar results. When the tornado finally dissipated none of his pursuers were standing.

He walked cautiously through the next several blocks in case they appeared again, scanning the ruins on either side. Ahead lay more destruction. The nearby neighborhoods had been well-chewed, the entire landscape one enormous garbage dump. Why exhaust himself when everything he saw was so unpromising? What did he have to gain? But if the choice were to lie down in this or walk ahead, he'd rather keep moving.

That's when the bus arrived.

When he was a little kid, waiting for the yellow school bus was the official beginning of every school day, and the first test of his almost nonexistent coping skills. It was a rickety, beat-up thing, always stalling, driven by an old guy who was always angry (years later he was fired—the rumors were he'd done something to a child). But the back of the bus was worse—that's where the big guys sat, the boys who really ran the bus, who pulled down your pants, twisted your nipples, held you down and farted in your face. And the bus driver—most days he just watched.

Taylor saw it coming—it would have been impossible to miss with the racket it made. It was squat and short, a low-ceilinged vehicle designed for few passengers, a sick yellow with brown rust spots, like an overripe metal banana, the front of the hood bashed and torn as if something had been nibbling on it. A ladder-like bike rack had been welded over that damage, sticking out about a foot on either side. It reminded Taylor of the cow-catchers they used to mount on the front of train engines.

The bus rattled to a stop and the side door squeaked open. The driver—a grizzled old man with rheumy eyes and swollen cheekbones—sat contained inside a rough construction of mismatched bars and grates pieced together into a cage. "Jump in," he croaked. His gums bled, his beard crusty and rusty-looking—several teeth yanked, or broken out.

Taylor peered inside. The limited seating was a hodge-podge: an upholstered bench, a screwed-down dining room chair, and a couple of collapsing overstuffed chairs. He looked back at the driver, who gazed at him with droopy, feverish eyes. The fellow wore a dog collar, leather harness with no shirt underneath, and an abbreviated pair of red shorts. His torso was layered in sweaty gray and white hair accented with the occasional brown drip. A plastic tube ran from his flattened groin into a foul-looking jug between his sandaled feet. One ankle was shackled to his chair, and one wrist was wired to the steering wheel. "Why would I want to do that?" Taylor asked, taking a step away from the bus.

"I don't care one way or the other. I just do what the man downstairs tells me to do." He glanced at his groin and grinned.

"Thanks anyway." Taylor turned away.

"'Cept you can't get nowhere 'less you take this bus! You ought to know that!"

"How do you know where I want to go?"

The driver blinked, rubbed the side of his face against his tethered arm. He shook his head. "Don't matter. This bus is the only way you're gonna get there." He snarled and spat blood through the cage. Taylor ducked sideways. He gazed down the street, at the destruction everywhere, the empty lots, the road nearly obscured for long stretches under a sea of trash. He stepped on board, choosing a pudgy green chair with collapsing sides which looked vaguely comfortable. The bus started up again with a grind and a lurch.

The vehicle rolled out slowly, wheels and internals protesting, responding with shudders and metallic screams as the driver pushed it along, banging his free hand on the wheel, throwing his head back and making his own high-pitched squawks as if mocking the machinery. "Come on you mother whore, you sonofabitch!"

Taylor wondered why he'd gotten in. The old guy was obviously insane. But then, why not? The fellow appeared to know how things worked here. After a couple of blocks the bus settled into a quieter rhythm. A half block more and it suddenly rocketed away, roaring down the jammed street faster than Taylor would have imagined possible. The driver appeared to know how to strike the wreckage with the bike rack bumper precisely so that the bus was able to clear most of the obstacles with little delay, although now and then he apparently decided a head-on approach was called for, and piles of twisted metal and tangled wood either disintegrated on impact or were bulldozed out of the way, the driver screaming at the straining engine until hoarse.

After a couple of hours they passed into an area of burning. It was difficult to determine what, exactly, was burning. High-reaching tongues of flame traveled the landscape with ease, gathering in spots and flaring even higher with an angry intensity. In some spots it appeared to be the very ground that was on fire, with flames reaching thirty or forty feet high even without the apparent benefit of fuel.

Taylor felt a stirring of confusing emotion that brought tears to his eyes. This really was Hell, wasn't it? He remembered, he'd been nine or ten when he started setting fires. He usually did it when he was angry, dropping lit matches into a trashcan, or putting a cigarette lighter to one edge of a curtain, just to see what it would do. When the flames multiplied he felt released. Then suddenly there was the panic as things went out of control. The first time he'd tried to pee out the flames, and almost caught his pecker on fire.

Taylor saw several fires erupt spontaneously from empty stretches of ground, the flames spouting upwards into geysers of fire. He anxiously glanced at the driver, wondering if he could steer them to safety if one of those geysers manifested nearby.

At first the fires were mostly soundless after that first whoosh of creation. Then there was the soft rippling sound as the flames whipped and danced. And then the flames sounded like people weeping, consumed by regret. Then they'd subside for awhile, lying down, simmering, before reaching up with the plasticity of flesh, flowing over into the bodies and appendages of a highly animated blaze.

"This must all be feeling right familiar to you by now." The driver turned his head part way around. He was grinning, as if this were all some huge, inappropriate joke.

"I don't understand. Why would it be?"

"Well, this here, this is what you've always been afraid of, isn't it? This is the destination that's scared us all, I reckon. That place where you can't even trust the ground right under your feet. That quaky, washed away, blown away ground. It breaks right under you, and then what are you supposed to do? Where are you supposed to go? How do you get away from a wind that falls out of the sky like the very hand of God and snatches you away from this world? What do you do when everything you depend on goes up in flames?"

Now they entered a neighborhood of taller structures, ruined buildings, most of them burning, toppling, and belching out ink-black smoke. It might have been the downtown of any city he'd lived in over the years. Every few minutes a side of one of the taller buildings would shear off and slide into the streets below. Colossal clouds of dark dust rose up, jeweled with thousands of burning embers. The nearest collapses created a constant rain of gravel onto the bus roof, although the driver appeared unconcerned.

Other structures fractured horizontally, and several buildings suddenly went sideways as if shoved by huge invisible hands. Many had been decapitated, flames rising skyward from their tops like guttering candles. Taylor looked for victims, but there was too much dust to see clearly enough.

Taylor thought he recognized several buildings—a grocery store from the old neighborhood, a comic shop, a restaurant where he'd taken a girlfriend—but they hadn't been located in the same city, had they? "They make movies about this kind of thing," he said. "They make money by scaring the daylights out of people."

The driver laughed. "But folks wouldn't be frightened by these things if the idea hadn't already been in their heads. What, are you saying this doesn't frighten you?"

"God, no. I'd just always hoped—I made myself think—that wherever I stayed—that those buildings would be stronger than this. That there really was nothing to be afraid of. That the danger was in my imagination."

"We always hope, don't we? When maybe we should just build things better."

They were deeper into the city now. A row of buildings beside them abruptly collapsed into fire and ash, the insides gutted so there was nothing left to hold them up. "But how can you live without a little hope?" Taylor could barely catch his breath. The hot smoke seared his eyes, heated the air he labored to suck into his lungs.

"You can't count on hope, not that we all don't try. We hope we'll have enough food to eat. We hope we won't die soon. We hope that person we love will love us back. We hope we'll have enough money to retire on. We think hope is magic, when all it is, is some desperate prayer with nothing solid behind it. Hope is pure bullshit!"

They drove past a small cluster of smoking buildings. The fires were gone, but the ruins were still changing, the surfaces shifting through a range of transforming deteriorations in shades of green and brown and gray.

"The best you can hope for," the driver continued, "is to die before your loved ones die. Die while you still have a place in this world. I waited too long—I should have killed myself. Now I reckon they'll make me do this for eternity."

The driver turned around in his seat. Taylor hopelessly clutched the arms of his chair as the bus veered out of control. The old man pulled back his gums revealing short, sharp tusks that grew visibly longer as Taylor watched. "See, they keep growing back, no matter how often they yank them out of me. They can't be stopped! If I wasn't inside this cage I'd be eating your face off by now!"

The bus swung dangerously close to a crumbling concrete barrier before the driver whipped around and corrected. He pointed at another thick grouping of improbably tall buildings, mostly obscured by haze, rising high into the clouds. "I used to work in one of those office buildings over there, a lifetime ago. I couldn't tell you which one, even if they were still all in one piece. Twenty-six years of moving papers from one place to the other, before we had computers. After that it was pushing buttons all day and sending the numbers where somebody said they ought to be. Pushed around a lot of numbers that way. I couldn't tell you why it was important, but people said it was. I thought it was hell, if you'll excuse the expression. Least you avoided that, I bet—young man like you."

The comment was like a slap in the face. At that moment boredom seemed a luxury Taylor could only crave. He'd never completed college, never lasted in any job more than a few months—he was lost his temper or felt insulted and walked off, or was fired. Never finished anything, never built anything, really, in his life. No wonder women left him.

"Where are you boy? You think you can hide from me? You wait; you just wait till I get my hands on you!" The voice repeated itself, again and again.

Taylor thought his father's voice was just in his own head, the way it scrambled his thoughts and shook his body. But now the bus was shaking visibly as well, weaving all over the road. The driver stopped and turned around. "That one belong to you?" Taylor nodded. "My sympathies." They waited until the voice stopped reiterating the old familiar threat. When they started again the driver appeared sleepy, then slumped over the wheel as he maneuvered the bus slowly around the burning debris that had fallen into the street.

"A man lives long enough, he loses too many friends," he muttered thickly. "And with each one gone, you lose a small piece of memory, and with that a small piece of brain. And if you're chained to your chair all day like I am, and not moving, well, the blanks accumulate." He peered over his shoulder at Taylor, and suddenly looked stricken, as if he'd forgotten something. He turned back around and continued the slow creep down the pavement. "I think I'm a little lost. I'm supposed to take you somewhere—I'm always delivering new folk to their appropriate places you know, their final destinations, not that I know that much about it, but for the life of me I can't remember where you're supposed to go. I fall into this blank space, and it's like I'm not even here anymore. And the world gets really quiet for a while, because there doesn't seem to be anyone else here. You stay here long enough, you'll get to be the same way."

The bus turned a corner and began a steady glide down a wide curve of highway alongside a row of ancient apartment buildings. Everything was on fire, and Taylor was sure the driver had fallen asleep. As the bus floated into the apex of the curve, the buildings began falling into the roadway behind them. "Wake up! Wake up!" Taylor shouted, but the driver didn't stir. Taylor flashed to a time he'd been with his dad, and his dad had been drinking, and they were going off the road. The bus picked up speed. Hot bits of ash and gravel peppered the windshield and the front hood. Several larger falling bits slapped the side of the bus and tumbled away.

Taylor watched through the back window as the last building poured itself flaming across the road, the final stretch of glowing wall striking the rear bumper sidelong and pushing the bus forward with a lurch.

"But nothing lasts forever, right?" the driver suddenly continued, his head upright and his gnarled hands clutching the wheel. "Not the memory and for sure not the original thing you remembered. We men take it the hardest. We don't know what to do with ourselves. We run out of whatever we used to do, and we go crazy trying to find something else to take its place."

Idle hands are the devil's playthings. Taylor's grandfather used to say that. It took him a while to figure out that the old man had been talking about Taylor's dad. Come to think of it, Taylor's worst troubles happened when he had nothing to do. That left him alone with his own thoughts—a place he didn't want to be. His girlfriends always seemed to have these contented inner lives—he could see it in their eyes. Taylor did not.

The driver whipped his head around angrily. "See these?" He opened his mouth and shook his head from side to side. Pink saliva flew everywhere. "These holes were where my tusks used to be! They yanked them out because they were too dangerous. Why was I born with them, I say, if I wasn't meant to use them?"

Taylor said nothing. Despite the driver's cage and chains, this was not someone he wished to provoke. They drove on in silence for a while until they were well beyond the ruined city. Smoke still issued from the occasional hole or fissure in the ground, but he saw no more standing structures, or flames.

He did see stragglers, however. Men or women, it was difficult to tell. Many of them were still burning. Some had fiery heads which made them look like great melting candles. Others had torsos that glowed from the organs boiling inside. Others had arms or legs that flaked off gradually into smoking ash and embers as they walked, and yet they continued to move.

Taylor tried not to look at them, but he couldn't help himself. He wanted to see if he knew any of them, but their faces were unrecognizable—they could have been anyone. *This is what happens*, he thought, *to people who fail to connect. Their faces wear off, or burn off in our memory.* Now that he was dead, is this the way he would be remembered? All those women he'd loved, or tried to love, would he just become this faceless moving shape in their memories? He'd failed to make a lasting impression, failed to have an effect, and so would be eternally anonymous.

Suddenly a shadowy form was beating the window looking in at them. Taylor thought it was a woman, even though most of the chest had burned away.

"I think she wants you," the old driver said in a husky, mirthful tone. The phlegmatic quality in his voice sounded more disgusting, more suggestive than usual. "Oh I've been around, I know these things. You're not a virgin, are you? I used to have lots of good sex, great sex. I knew how to do it right. Make no mistake."

Taylor looked again at the ashen sculpture beating on the glass—where the eyes should have been, where the mouth. Maybe someone he had known, maybe had made love to, and then forgotten. The form eventually fell into nothing. There were others who came also, to gaze, to try to get into the bus, to raise their burning limbs in greeting or in despair. And they all fell into nothing. And Taylor could see still others in the distance, all walking in the same direction, all falling into nothing, and there were always others to take their place. Was he bound to join them?

As if in answer, the driver said matter-of-factly, "The world's becoming all used up. Just like me. I'm just one big old used-to-be. And someday you will be too."

They climbed a small rise in the desolate landscape and began another barely detectable descent. A short distance away was another city, an older place of stone buildings and walls and the occasional tower, but nothing very tall, nothing that couldn't have been erected with some craft and manual power.

Closer in Taylor could see a broad two-story building ahead of the rest, and out in front of that building were several of those musclebound men with their thick animal heads and exaggerated codpieces—once so harmless, even innocent when they'd been action figures in his childhood playtime, when he'd made them embrace each other in stiff homoerotic poses which he'd called vicious combat but which as he now recalled them suggested so much more.

The bus stopped in front of them. "Well, this is where I was told to take you." The driver pulled a lever and the damaged door screamed as it opened. "Not that you're anything special. I'm always taking fellows like you here. Hell, this is where they brought me."

II.

"You are of your father the devil, and you want to do the desires of your
father. He was a murderer from the beginning, and does not stand in
the truth because there is no truth in him. Whenever he speaks a lie,
he speaks from his own nature, for he is a liar and the father of lies."
—John 8:44

The hybrid men surrounded him with no air of urgency.
In fact they looked bored. He supposed there was no need,
given their size, and the fact he had no place to run. They
didn't even grab him—they simply enclosed him with their
mountainous, top-heavy bodies, and walked toward the towering double-doors. Their guns were drawn and ready, looking like toys in their shovel-sized palms. Their arms were so
grotesquely swollen that their range of motion was severely
impaired. It occurred to him they walked like toys. He tried
not to touch them. Their skin was slimed in an oil-like sweat
that stank like dead fish.

Periodically one would turn his gigantic animal head
and gaze down at Taylor contemptuously, as if disgusted to
escort a creature of such insignificance. This one's features
were a cross between those of a pig and an elephant, the snout
repulsively flexible, and the large flappy ears crawling with
parasites. The eyes were angry, bead-like and trapped inside
deep folds of acromegalic flesh.

Their clothing was similar to what he'd seen earlier on similar creatures and on his father: bits of military outfits, leather
shorts, bindings, too-small shirt or none. There were modest
gestures toward conformity: a variety of similar patches at
seemingly random locations.

He avoided looking at their codpieces, which in practice
meant he couldn't stop staring at them. They were huge and
vaguely lopsided, decorated with a variety of sharp metal bits,

protruding razor blades, and jagged glass. He could detect the faint outline of a supporting framework: wire ribs and a spine used to make the appendage larger, stiffer, and stronger. A name was scribbled on each in bright pink lipstick: Ted, Clarence, Leon, Hugo. And each came to a sharp point, like a horn.

Up close, the windowless building resembled a fortress, the walls thick, made out of polished stone blocks fit so snugly together they'd be impossible to climb. Riflemen peered down from crenellated battlements. Three towers rose above the entrance, the center one sporting a flag atop a long pole.

Taylor blinked. It was the Marx Medieval High-walled Castle Playset made huge. He'd had one when he was nine.

The doors swung out. Eight tired-looking old men chained to iron rings embedded on the interior sides of the doors pushed them open. Once inside Taylor twisted around to watch those poor souls struggle to drag the heavy doors closed again. Two resembled those elderly fellows who'd lived at the end of their block. His dad had called them "those two old queers." Another might have been the janitor at his elementary school. Another could have been his grandfather's twin—he'd died in that awful nursing home. His father had been dismissive of all of them. Taylor remembered never wanting to grow old, if it meant that kind of disrespect.

The entrance hall was wide and dark and stank of urine and animal musk. Dirty straw was mashed between rough paving stones on the floor. An abundance of animal heads decorated the dusty brick walls. His father had taken him to a restaurant—when? Maybe his senior year. It had had animal heads like these on the walls—you could eat buffalo or elk or something even more exotic and majestic. Taylor had barely been able to take a single bite of his meal, and his dad had raged all the way home about the money wasted.

On one side red-stained punching bags hung from the rafters, casually being worked over by muscled men in similar abbreviated and tattered uniforms. The men appeared to be of two types, the bald ones, and the ones with full heads of bushy black hair. Several pig-like animals with thick tusks waddled among them. Although Taylor had never seen one, he assumed they were boars. Taylor actually knew less about boxing than he did about boars, despite his father's efforts to teach him.

A tall curtain of thick rope lengths studded with fist-sized knots led into the next room, which was brighter, with several skylights cut into the timber and plaster ceiling. Taylor had fallen off similar ropes in high school gym class—he still had an odd turn in his left thumb as a result. His father had been too drunk to take him to the ER, and in any case thought the injury too minor.

The room was jammed with tables holding guns, car parts, and old power tools in various conditions. More old men were chained to the tables, apparently charged with repairing this equipment. Taylor didn't understand much of what he was seeing—despite his father's impatient efforts he'd never had much aptitude for mechanical things. A team of nurses went table to table administrating meds to the old men and providing first aid. One of the men looked up and Taylor locked eyes with him. The whites were bloodshot, the pupils unengaged.

The next room was crowded with naked men his age and younger. He was helpless as guards stripped him of his clothing. One guard kept his huge hand on Taylor's face, preventing him from objecting.

The young men avoided eye contact, instead looking at the floor or at the high walls paneled in dark wood and decorated with animal skins. Three guards prowled the crowd leading huge mastiffs. They wore masks carved into a shark's head, an alligator's mouth, and a ram's skull. For some this was the last straw as they broke down weeping on the floor, curled up with faces buried in their hands.

The fellow next to him—a pale, seemingly colorless creature—touched his arm, and then led him over to a narrow horizontal slit in the wall. The fellow motioned, encouraging him to look.

A crowd of women waited in the courtyard below: older women mostly, with a few younger, but none of them children, crowded into one corner, blocked from escaping by guards on horseback. The horses were barely controlled, lifting and churning their front legs in the air. The riders whipped them steadily, the air full of slaps and explosive snorts. "Our mothers," the fellow whispered. "Our wives, our girlfriends. Perhaps your mother is down there as well?"

"My mother left years ago," Taylor said, and felt the burn and shame of resentment. For all he knew these women deserved their treatment. He immediately regretted the thought.

There was a raised platform at one end of the room bearing a massive chair. A monster with a bullish head and a six-foot span of horns entered the room and collapsed into the seat looking bored. He was like a caricature of masculinity, wearing a black uniform shirt festooned with badges and a snakeskin harness, along with the customary leather shorts and massive codpiece, except his was bright red and tipped with a polished silver point.

The monster's head drooped as if the weight of his horns was more than he could bear. The bull man kept staring at his large hands, examining his nails. The entire room was focused on him. He straightened and scanned the crowd, his giant head moving slowly through its arc as if to imprint every last face.

Abruptly the bull man's head dropped back. His mouth spasmed open, and he struggled with his massive tongue, as if not sure where to put it, finally allowing it to loll out and off to the side. Then with great effort he bellowed, his eyes bugging out and his cheeks vibrating. The sound was desperate and agonized, and Taylor could only imagine some mishap in a slaughterhouse producing anything comparable. Before the sound had completely faded the bull sucked in more air and produced another bellow even louder and more pain-filled than the one before.

The bellows continued their fraught rhythm as the room exploded into a chaos of activity. The guards moved in from the walls, herding the naked young men through a set of blue curtains into the next room. All looked panicked, except perhaps for Taylor's pale companion, who was watching the guards on the edges of the crowd. "Make sure you're chosen by one of the smaller ones," he said. "At least then you might have a fighting chance." At that point Taylor had no idea what he meant. He tried to stay calm.

Then he caught a glimpse of a familiar figure: the greasy white T-shirt, the brown leather shorts, the rusty studded codpiece. His father flipped his limp black hair off his pink rhinoceros head and snarled through yellowing tusks, "I told you I'd find you, boy!" Taylor pushed past his pale companion to the other side of the room, putting some distance, and bodies, between him and his father.

The chamber was hot, illuminated by a red pulsing glow whose source he could not determine. The beast men grabbed the young naked men, bending them over, and plowed their codpieces deep into the young men's backsides. These young men were howling and screaming for help, but the guards were screaming and hollering themselves—in celebration or mockery—as if at a sporting event.

"Got you now!" his father barked into his ear. Taylor could feel the rough hands on his hips before he was jerked backwards into dizzying pain.

For a few moments all sound was reduced to his father's coarse grunting behind him.

Taylor dropped to the floor and his father, off-balance, fell on top of him. Taylor kicked one heel back into his father's scrotum, squirmed around on the damp and bloody floor and managed to jab his right thumb into his father's fierce dark eye. He pushed and slid away, just out of reach of the swollen arms. Then Taylor jumped forward, his legs scissoring as he churned his way through the crowd. Bodies went down around him, and then a hand grabbed his wrist. It was that pale man pulling him along, climbing over backs and stepping on heads, until the boards covering a window shattered, and the two tumbled onto the hard-packed road below.

They were standing in the remnants of a roadway separating the fortress from a neighborhood of damaged homes. His new pale friend led him inside one of these houses so they could find some clothes. They could hardly move through the packed debris—at any moment he expected some interior avalanche to crush them. Had these people never thrown anything away? He counted ten televisions from a variety of eras, more than a dozen toasters, at least sixteen radios, closets full of toys, old newspapers and magazines. The hell of physical objects triggered a memory of his grandmother's house, and how they'd found her dead beneath a mound of dirty clothes and mold-encrusted food packages.

They extricated themselves and Taylor's companion led him through a maze of streets. He had no idea how this man knew where to go, but he seemed confident (which Taylor was not) and so he followed. In any case why would Taylor care where they went, as long as he could avoid more pain? They wandered through the city beyond the fortress of the beast men, a blur of walls and roofs, doors and windows constantly changing shape, size, and location. He eventually realized they were walking through a city in the process of destroying itself. He didn't know how else to understand it.

Walls fractured and collapsed. Wood and fabric burnt themselves black, then white, then disappeared entirely. They were not harmed by the falling debris, but it fell close enough that he was shaken by the impact and made uncomfortable by the heat. Their clothing burned from their bodies and their skin shimmered red. Taylor felt as if his molten flesh were losing its shape and slipping from the bone. He could not breathe in the smoke-filled air, closing his eyes and waiting for an end, and yet still walking, compelled to move forward. When they came out of the smoke there was the city again, completely different and yet still much the same, undamaged, until that vivid slow-motion movie of destruction began again. The only constant was the mountain of trash heaped just beyond the northern limits of the city, constantly fed, constantly burning. There was no safe place, anywhere, and so they continued walking.

"You can't get rid of them, these cities, can you? At least it requires a very long time," his companion said. "Not like people—we're getting rid of people all the time. We want the world to stop and pay notice when one of us dies, but the world is incapable of listening. It's as if the cities are the predominant life forms on this planet, and we humans their occasional dream."

The dead lay everywhere. There were so many of them and they had no convenient place to be. They were stacked yards deep against the walls. They lay like colorful lumps in the paths. Some moved their fingers or hands or stuck out their tongues, simply to maintain the habit of moving, and because there was no room for larger movements. Others lay motionless, and pretended to be ground, or pavement, or random debris. His companion crouched down and examined a few of them, prodding their bodies with his fingers, but they pretended not to notice him. "They believe their previous lives were like a dream a stone dreams when it dreams it is alive."

Taylor did not want to step on the dead but he really had no choice. The further they walked the greater the numbers of dead. Eventually the dead covered every inch of earth. After a while he learned the proper gait to use so that efficient progress was possible. After a while there was nothing to it, it seemed. It was as if he had been walking on the dead all of his life.

It wasn't right that the dead be rubble, that once-soft flesh should become such rough material, that the bodies which had embraced and loved and nurtured children, and that the precious children themselves should become waste, should become dumb substance. It was an assault of imagery he would never forget. And yet this was the simple truth of the physical world, and there was nothing to be done about it.

By the time they reached the end of the valley a starless night had fallen. They climbed out of all that darkness and continued on their way. Taylor discovered that this elementary transition lifted his spirits some, even though it was still quite dark, with the only illumination coming from the fiery lakes and pits dotting the landscape, and the flaming winds which wound their way at random, and had to be run from to avoid being burned. Every moment seemed heavy with uncertainty.

He still knew nothing about his companion except that, for some reason, the fellow had taken an interest in him, and had tried to protect him. It made Taylor a bit suspicious, but he really couldn't think of anything this pale little man had to gain in fooling him. Taylor had given himself up to pure instinct, and his instincts told him this was a very good man.

Taylor hadn't had much time to consider things deeply since his car went through the railing a lifetime ago. The expression made him suppress a giggle. But "deathtime" was a silly concoction, and there was nothing to laugh at here. None of this was what he had expected, and yet there wasn't much unexpected about any of it—it was all as familiar as the inside of his own head.

They began climbing a gentle ridge. It was still too dark to make out any details, but he could feel the shifting gravity in his body as they progressed. Suddenly he bumped into something, and that something fluttered against him as if to grab on, but for some reason was not able to. He pushed away from the thing, and it made a muffled sound of distress, and from the way it shuffled this way and that, seemed to be attempting to find him again. He moved away quickly, not wanting it to touch him, although he wasn't sure why. Perhaps he simply didn't want to be touched by something he couldn't see. And then he ran into something else similar, at least it felt like something similar, which also tried to grab him unsuccessfully, until he got away.

Then the moon slipped from behind the clouds. They were surrounded by a group of human-like forms which were almost completely encased in some kind of membrane. Their hands had broken through, and fluttered and flapped at their sides, but with limited movement since their arms above the elbows were still bound to their bodies by the membrane. Their feet and lower legs were similarly exposed, but their knees were still encased so only a minimal amount of shuffling was possible.

They stood about, unable to touch each other. Now and then they made awkward attempts at hugging themselves with varying degrees of success, depending on the length of their exposed arms. They appeared to be blind. Taylor wondered if they even realized that others of their kind were nearby.

Behind those figures and filling the rise were the skeletons of numerous houses, only a few timbers and beams still standing, a part of a wall, a fragment of a window, here and there an isolated door still standing incongruously shut with no wall to either side. A desolate, twilight city. He wondered if these figures had once lived in those houses. He wondered if they still did.

"It's skin," his companion announced. Taylor turned, watching in alarm as the man poked at a figure with his forefinger. The thing reacted by swinging its truncated arms, to slap or grab it was hard to say. "It's their own skin. It's overgrown their bodies. Well, except for these few bits."

"They can't make contact," Taylor said. "It must be hell for them." And once he'd said this his emotions overcame him and he began to weep. He fell to his knees in front of one of them and tried to think of something he could do. He reached out his hand thinking maybe he could touch the figure and comfort it somehow, but his companion grabbed that hand and pulled it away.

"You mustn't touch," his companion shouted, "unless you want to spend eternity the same way! Their isolation spreads to everyone who touches them. The best you can do is leave them alone with their misery."

"But what if I belong here?" Taylor said. "This is *me*, don't you see? It perfectly describes me. I could never make contact, no matter how much people tried to help me." But the companion had moved on, and was now trotting up the ridge. "Wait! Are we just going to leave?"

The pale man turned. "We can't help them, and we can't stay here. You have to keep moving, if you want to be able to move at all. Everyone has their own kind of hell. For some it's all tears and woe and confusion, drowning in vomit and other foul bodily fluids, or thrown into a molten pit after being hacked and dismembered, and hell consuming their souls. Eternal judgment and damnation and all that.

"For others, it's horrific pain and suffering as their bodies fail them. Like your uncle, remember? Many of us, we suffer because of someone else's politics, someone else's *enlighten-ment*. The witch hunts? A rampage of murderous guilt raging across the world, all to eradicate the odd ones, the suspicious ones, the ones they did not understand. Belief may be the most destructive force in the universe. I'm sorry they can't touch each other. But for most of us, in my experience, hell is other people. I do not believe it is your destiny to stop here."

Taylor wanted to ask him how he knew about his uncle, or his destiny. But then the voice came. *"Don't let me catch you!"* his father's voice boomed from the darkness behind them, rumbling up and pushing Taylor until he fell down. He'd always wondered why monsters sometimes eschewed surprise and warned their victims ahead of their appearance. Taylor scrambled to his feet. "I don't deserve this!"

"No, it's not the hell you deserved. It's the hell you imagined," his companion said. "And it appears that your father is an important feature in this particular hell. We must keep moving."

As they continued Taylor noticed how the bright hole in the sky became gradually larger the further they traveled, eventually becoming so large they apparently stepped through it, because now they were in bright daylight, and the dark world where they had been was now that black hole in the sky, right *there*.

They were walking across a vast and seemingly featureless plain, except for that small jagged crack running roughly parallel to their path, streaming with water. The water was clear at first, but gradually became darker, becoming blue, and purple, iridescent, and then shading off into reds, and deeper reds, until Taylor saw how pinkish the sand was becoming where they were walking, and how thick and bloodlike the stream.

A severed arm floated by, and then what might have been a leg, missing its foot. And then an empty torso, its rib cage yawning. Then an entire body, with too large a mouth. Other bodies floated by, gutted, all of them screaming silently.

Taylor was overcome by what he saw, and fell to his knees, and then on to his side. When he was a child and things became too much for him he would curl up under the covers and pretend he was somewhere else. Was that even possible here? He imagined himself in a still place, resting. But he was still burning inside, the fire threatening to consume him.

He became aware of a woman standing over him. Her skin was slightly milky, almost transparent. How had she gotten there? He had an image of threads of skin growing out of his feet which twined and thickened and slowly sculpted themselves until they became this full-grown woman. She bent over him, reaching down into his flesh and touching the fire, latching on to it, and jerking it out of him.

Taylor said, "I don't know your name."

"It's Tiresias," she replied. It was the voice of his pale companion.

"But you were a man."

She shrugged. "I was a woman for seven years. I even married and had children. I cursed the universe for it at first, but I'd always wanted to know more about the world, and what better way than in the body of another sex? Once I became a woman, I realized I'd missed an entire universe of being. You use your senses differently. Even the flow and fire of the earth begins to make a different kind of sense.

"Now I have died, and sometimes I am a man, and sometimes I am a woman. And now you're dead. Tell me, do you prefer being alive, or do you prefer being dead?"

"Alive, of course. Anything but *this*. I lived my entire life full of fear, but still it was much better than this. Are you saying I have a choice? Are you saying I can go back?"

She looked at him sadly. "You had a great many choices in life. But I'm afraid in death there is only the one."

She pointed at a specific spot in the air above him. It swiftly became a bright red burning hole hovering directly over his heart. The hole started spinning, growing larger, turning and sucking bits of the world through its fiery opening.

Taylor began to float, and then he too was drawn through the hole with the rest of the world as if he were trapped inside a slowly spinning tornado. The floor of a womb stretched out beneath him, littered with bodies, and beyond that the mouth of hell, mumbling obscenities. But he was seeing that mouth from the wrong side, he realized. He was inside his hell, hoping for a glimpse of what lay on the other side.

The hell mouth opened and vomited him out.

He'd fallen onto hard ground again. Ahead of him the earth rapidly curved away into night. *Just a bit further*, the companion spoke inside his head. Taylor looked around and saw no one. *You're almost there.*

Taylor walked down the curve of the earth until he'd reached the end of the world. An immense sinkhole lay there, so broad he could only imagine its end. He walked up to the very edge of it. He was terrified—he couldn't believe he was actually standing this close to such perilous, such improbable emptiness.

Taylor could feel his stomach drop, as if his heart, his bowels, had been pulled right out of him. The emptiness of it had a weight, and that weight was pulling him irresistibly toward the unseeable bottom of the abyss. How could you lead a normal life knowing such emptiness existed? How could you keep from throwing yourself in?

Then abruptly he was falling upward, and then down into the eternal dark of the hole. Once he began his descent, the gravitational forces surrounding him became visible as soft gray and white lines, twisting and twirling around him as they snared him and dragged him deeper into the whirlpool of dark. Unable to bear the darkness he closed his eyes and found himself floating inside his mother and dreaming of a life outside.

He tried to contain himself, but the flaps of skin covering his torso simply would not stay closed.

At the bottom he passed through another hole, and then onto the ice below, a frozen lake of blood and guilt, and the ability to feel, or care, deadened.

Taylor lay there for a long time on the ice. The absolute cold of it was somehow comforting, the way it froze the thoughts, the way it turned bone and flesh to stone. This was not much different from how he had lived his life, after all, unable to touch or to make a connection. But now at least the anger was still, the rage frozen with all his other feelings, so that a kind of peace was still possible. It was only after he stood up and moved around that he discovered the giant face beneath the clear, cold surface.

The visage was somewhat transformed, as the eyes were closed, and the mouth made silent with all that language of hate locked inside. But there was the broken nose, the craggy lines beneath the ruined eyes, the rough ridges of the lips. It was his father's face, his angry expression, poised to keep Taylor company for all eternity.

August Freeze

As a child, Patrick had believed that you could see shapes in the clouds because they were people's dreams, risen high into the sky after sleeping heads had released them. In summer, he imagined they must travel fast and joyfully, the afternoon heat tickling their undersides. But in winter—as he was forced, inescapably, to realize—they had the disturbing tendency to stop in mid-flight. To freeze for an entire season, hanging oppressively over the dreamers. And there was nothing worse than an old, recurring dream, nothing more terrifying. Patrick knew.

Here, the canvas for these cloud patterns was immense, as wide as the horizon itself. The changing arrangements, the eye blink movements were much more chaotic than at any other place Patrick had lived. As if once the boundaries of city skyline or mountain range were removed the clouds returned to a more natural state, became wild, mad, uncivilized. You could not watch them for long. You couldn't just sit out in your backyard and study them for hours. The clouds drove you inside.

Once as a child, Patrick had looked up at the sky just after dark. God had looked down at him, and there was darkness in His eyes, thunder in His cheeks. God looked just like Father.

At least once a day after he and Michelle arrived at the farm, Patrick would wonder whatever possessed them to move. They had virtually nothing to do in eastern Colorado, except try to keep the wind out—out of their house, out of their heads. The wind maintained a river of dust some ten feet deep flowing willfully, incessantly, outside their adobe-style home. It was soon no wonder to him that pioneers left alone on the plains too long sometimes went mad. The wind here was an irritating, undirected passion—it dried your hair to hemp so that the frayed rope-ends constantly flailed at forehead and cheeks. There was always grit in your eyes and a whistling in your ears. At least this time of year it was a warm wind; snow was still months away.

This house had been his father's a long time ago, years after the divorce and years since the man had seen either Patrick or Patrick's mother. What Patrick could remember about his father was cloaked in shadow: the dark slumped shoulders after a day at the garage, the still form out on the porch with the cigarette glow marking the direction of his gaze, the restless shadow reclined on the bed—checking the watch, staring at the ceiling, arising before anyone else to begins its ritualistic pacing. Patrick couldn't remember ever playing with that shadow or talking for a time on matters important and inconsequential, their contact had been limited to the briefest of inquiries and pleasantries.

Their house was filled with thoughts when Father was home; you could feel them brushing your cheeks, pressing against your head in their futile attempts to force their way in. The temperature seemed to rise as they swarmed around his parents' bedroom, breaking suddenly when his mother began to yell, his father to shut down, turn off the light, pretend she wasn't there.

This house in eastern Colorado stayed empty for years after his father's death. The will had been contested—some of the local relatives on his father's side of the family just couldn't believe old man Martin would have left two hundred acres and a barn full of machinery and a perfectly fine house to a son he hadn't seen since the boy was a teenager, and a city boy at that.

Patrick had figured if he got the house and land, he'd just

resell it to one of those puzzled relatives. He had a good house in Denver, and architectural consultations kept him and Michelle well provided for. But when the will finally cleared Patrick balked.

He told Michelle it would make a great retreat, a vacation spot. Something they desperately needed at this point in their lives. She'd looked at him doubtfully—there was nothing to see out there but the raw effects of the wind, and endless flat fields. There was nothing to do. "You'll like it, just wait," he had said, knowing full well she never would. He couldn't imagine enjoying it himself. They liked being around people; they both needed a constant stream of planned activity.

He had a local agent sell the farm equipment at auction, and the same agent converted the income into canned goods, powdered milk, and other nonperishables. An expensive underground water storage tank exhausted the rest of the profits.

"Kind of far away for a fall-out shelter, ain't it?" The agent had chuckled over the phone. Patrick didn't laugh. The stored goods made the "retreat" more self-sufficient; you didn't have to go into town for supplies all the time. But the explanation wasn't fully satisfactory, even to him. "Storing nuts for winter." The man had laughed again, a thin, strained kind of laugh. Then he'd coughed and left as quickly as possible.

The house on the plains had been stocked and ready less than ten days before Patrick wanted to take Michelle there for a week's vacation. His vacation wasn't scheduled for another six months—they were supposed to go to Hawaii this year. It cost him two major clients whose jobs were at a crucial stage, and almost cost him his marriage. Not because of Hawaii, not because he wanted to go some place she had no interest in, but simply because Patrick couldn't give Michelle a straight answer when she asked him why he wanted to go there now, so soon.

"We need the time away from here, to think things out," he had said.

We can't leave now! she had said, a harsh whisper. Had repeated it again and again. We can't just leave him at a time like this! She had said, again and again and again. But Patrick had finally gotten her away from Denver, by wearing her down.

"A little chilly in here, don't you think?" Michelle was wearing her sweater, her arms folded tightly over her chest. She sat huddled in a flower print chair in the middle of the living room, her long brown hair almost covering her face, as if that too might warm her. She had been sitting almost constantly since their arrival here, sometimes huddled in the chair or on the couch, other times wedged child-like back into the enormous antique rocker, drifting back and forth into light and shadow as the curved runners moved silently over the rug.

The sweater irritated him. "It's August, Michelle. It doesn't get cold out here in August, for Christ's sake!"

"I don't care what it's supposed to do! I'm cold, dammit!"

Patrick opened the door to the basement.

"Where are you going?"

"There's some storm windows down here. Thought I'd put them up."

"I thought you said . . ." But he had already slammed the door and was pounding down the stairs. "It never gets cold this time of year!" she shouted after him. She stopped, as if the house had swallowed her words.

A chill entered his body, as if it had wriggled across the basement floor and climbed his leg. He thought he could hear her speaking above him, but the sound of her words shouldn't have carried that far, that clearly. "It'll be too dark to see out there, Patrick," he thought he heard her say. "You can't see in the dark, can you?"

Patrick was careful not to wake his wife when he climbed into bed at midnight that night. The storm windows had taken longer than he had planned. He had forgotten there were no streetlights out here, and his father's old spotlight, mounted on the south edge of the roof, had gone bad. The wiring was probably rotted out; he wondered if he could get an electrician out to fix it first thing tomorrow.

He lay in bed for hours without sleeping, staring into the dark, listening. It was a long time before it came to him what was bothering him so—it was so silent in the house. In Denver, their old house creaked and sighed and groaned in the dark. But here in this bedroom out on the plains, he couldn't even hear the wind outside. He slapped at his ear, afraid he'd gone deaf. Michelle stirred restlessly beside him. And then, suddenly, the wind was back.

It slapped and pummeled the outside of the house. It whipped at the shingles and rattled the windows. Patrick could hear a high-pitched squeal off in the distance, like a train gone mad. Something bounced off the roof above their bed, followed by something heavier. He pulled closer to Michelle, but she drew away with a protesting moan. She didn't trust him; he supposed he couldn't blame her.

He tried to imagine his father in this house, sleeping in this bed. He tried to think of him getting up early mornings to milk the cows or feed the pigs. Patrick had kept the pigs and was paying a local teenager to come over every day to feed them. He didn't know why.

He could hear the pigs squealing beneath the wind. He could hear tractor engines turning over, harvesters gunning their big diesels. He could hear the screech of metal, the muffled thunder as tons of earth were moved. "Michelle?" he whispered. "I need you." There was no answer. Why had his father left him? What had he found out here on the plains?

The next morning it was colder than before. A soupy fog hugged the ground in all directions. Patrick had a great deal of repair work to do around the house, but he just didn't feel up to it. Michelle didn't speak to him all the morning; she kept a coat on and curled up on the couch to read.

He came in from an afternoon of laying extra feed into the barn, fixing up the shelter over the pig pen, and caulking every crack and break in the outside walls of his father's house. Despite the early morning fog, it had been a hot day, at a hundred and four one of the hottest of the year. Michelle was standing in the kitchen, waiting for him, looking far more tired than he could remember.

"I want to go back and see Johnny."

The words came out slowly, with difficulty; he seemed to be having a hard time hearing her. As if each syllable turned to slush on contact with the air in the house.

"I don't think that's a good idea. A little more time."

"He's your son, Patrick."

He'd never heard her sound so cold. "He's making progress . . . they know what they're doing there. We'll see him as soon as we get back. We need a little break, a vacation, don't you think?" She said nothing. "The decision to put him in the hospital was a mutual one, Michelle. I don't like it any more than you do."

When she finally spoke, he could barely hear her. There was a roaring in his ears. He imagined his blood singing through his head. "You haven't mentioned him one time since we've been here, Patrick. Not once."

The gray cloud swept in the following day, a sky full of dust trapped in a choking stream of cold, damp air. Michelle had been the first to see it. Patrick was in the back yard, transferring the last massive load of foodstuffs delivered from town into their cellar. He hadn't told Michelle about this latest order, and when it arrived, she'd looked at him as if he were a madman. He'd given up hope she'd ever understand what he was doing here.

He'd seen her standing at the back door, staring off across the fields, toward Denver. She insisted on wearing the sweater, even though the temperature was still in the high nineties. When she cried out, it wasn't entirely unexpected—

after all, she'd been upset and acting strangely all week—so he ignored her at first, working a little harder to get all the supplies properly stowed. As he got the last box of cans into the cellar, he felt the first hint of cold lap at his ankles.

He turned to face a gray wall of cloud spilling over the fields to the north. With awful suddenness, the wind had picked up, and grit was riddling the windbreak of trees surrounding the house. Michelle was screaming something, but he couldn't hear her above the roar. He watched the trees bend, branches breaking and rocketing past him. The air seemed full of grayish smoke.

Patrick ran toward the back door. Michelle had disappeared; he hoped she had enough sense left to go back inside. The air turned to steel around him . . . he could feel it slipping coldly through his cupped hands. He grabbed the doorknob and at the same time slapped his palm against the wooden door. It seemed to have turned to metal and stuck to his skin, making it painful to pull away. As he opened the door, he could feel darkness falling rapidly behind him.

He found Michelle in the living room. All the lights were out; all he could see was the silver-frost outline of her face against the dark blue couch. "We'll never get out now," the face said. "We'll never see him again."

Johnny had stopped talking at the age of twelve. He'd always been an unusually quiet boy, reticent to talk of his feelings, but for two years he didn't say a word. He stole, he struck, he destroyed, slashed his wrists, got drunk and set fire to his room. He communicated in every way imaginable except for the spoken, or even written, word.

You couldn't predict what Johnny was going to do next; There was no way even to theorize what the boy might be thinking, what was going on behind the blank architecture of his face. Patrick had grown afraid of his son.

After he set fire to the room, and almost burned down the house when Patrick and Michelle hadn't awakened, they'd decided to put him into residential treatment. The hospital was a good one—they spared no expense, Patrick constantly reminded himself. But he had seen no improvement in his son's condition.

He wasn't sure he was sorry about that. God help him, he wasn't sure he wanted his son home ever again. Something as intangible, and cold, as a Colorado winter wind had slipped behind the boy's eyes and filled him quite completely.

Michelle's breath turned to puffs of steam in the darkened house. Patrick could hear the roof creaking under the weight of the spreading ice.

Michelle wouldn't sleep with him that night. Instead she pulled all her clothes out of the closet and slept under a great pile of them on the couch. He tried to tell her that wasn't necessary—he'd stocked the shelter with dozens of wool blankets and parkas and sleeping bags. "I'm not sure why I got all that winter stuff down there, it being the hottest time of the year. But I guess we're just lucky I did. It's just a freak storm, Michelle. I'm sure it'll be gone in a couple of days."

She stopped arranging her clothes on the couch, turned, and looked at him. And stood that way a few minutes without saying anything. It angered him . . . Just like Johnny, he realized . . . maybe she was going crazy just like him. Maybe it was genetic. The doctors, as good as they were supposed to be, hadn't yet figured out the cause.

As he was finally drifting off to sleep that night Patrick became afraid he wasn't going to be able to breathe the new air that had filled this house. His father's house. The cold mist was like misery filling his lungs, forcing the tears out. The subtle eddies of wind swarmed around his ears.

By the next morning a glassy skin glittered on the trees, the fence rails, the tools abandoned in his rush to get inside. Spikes of glass rattled as they fell from the barn roof and struck thicker glass sheeting the water tank. The old red pickup in the yard looked dazed under its icy varnish. Everywhere he looked, the world was locked up tight with cold. He was careful not to move too quickly through the still, cool air of the house, afraid the trapped atmosphere in these rooms, once owned by his father and now passed too eagerly to him, might break. The windows glared at him, their curtains hanging stiff-armed at their sides. The morning was silent, still, mute. Patrick wondered if anything would ever speak to him again.

Michelle was at the living room window, staring through a steamed circle she'd made in the pane. Patrick stepped closer and breathed on the back of her head, imagined he saw two or three hairs go dull and break. He gazed past her. A pheasant stood upright on the frosted grass, one leg slightly cocked, whitened neck twisted so it could face the window. It did not move. Its beak was pulled stiffly apart, tongue protruding as if to recall the voice that had been stolen from it. One eye was frozen to the glass.

Although he'd thought about Johnny almost constantly, he felt the urge to apologize to Michelle for not thinking about him enough. Maybe he'd been acting as if he'd never had a son. But the boy scared him; Patrick couldn't tell what was going on. It was as if they were playing this elaborate, powerful game, and Johnny hadn't bothered to tell Patrick the rules.

Patrick spoke those thoughts silently to himself, moving his lips against the frosted window, as if to retrieve those ideas from darkness.

He realized he'd tried much the same technique with Johnny that first year the boy had shut down and shut up. He'd voiced theories, postulations, wild guesses to the boy. Patrick told his son what he thought he might be thinking, but not saying. He told his son how he understood, how he understood that he needed secrets, that he needed to have some power, even if it were simply power over his own speech. How that was all okay, but you shouldn't let it go too far, shouldn't let it go too far or it could hurt you, and hurt those around you. Destroy the family.

Patrick had talked, talked, talked, his lips growing weary from the strain, his throat tense and sore, but still attempting to get something important said, to get his son to speak himself up out of the void, say the magic words that would lift himself out of the nameless emptiness we all, in our aloneness, ultimately contain.

But the boy remained obstinately silent, and powerful in his muteness.

The snow fell all that day. Patrick didn't notice it until sometime after noon, but it had obviously been going on for quite a while.

It wrapped the ice that covered everything with a fluffy white insulation, as if to preserve it for all time. Patrick had never seen flakes so large, or so light. They covered the ground far more quickly than he imagined a normal snowfall would. He wondered if snowfalls out here in the country were always more expansive than he had been used to in the city, as if only here—away from buildings and traffic—they could manifest their natural condition. He could hear the pigs in the distance. He could hear Michelle sliding the antique rocking chair in front of the living room window and beginning to rock, rock, and rock and stare out that window. Like a sentry. By dark the snow was up to their windowsills, the outside doors were blocked, and the pigs were screaming.

About ten o'clock Michelle left the rocker and returned to her sleeping place under her clothes on the couch. Patrick watched the rocker continue its back and forth motion in front of the window, from shadow to snow glare, for the next hour. And then for an hour more. Finally, he walked over and laid a hand on the arm to stop it. It settled into stillness with a low, creaky sigh. The wood must be warping with all this damp, he thought. He sat down in the rocker and it started rocking again. Out beyond the window snow was shifting, groaning, making a trail of sunken hollows that circled the house. He could see the small collapses of snow crust as he stared through the glass. He wondered how many times his father had sat in this very same rocker, watching the snow eddy, wondering what was out there seeking him.

Patrick wondered if he had haunted his own father.

Patrick was still awake in the rocker when Michelle got up the next morning. She looked puzzled. Patrick realized it was, in part, because the house was still quite dark. "The snow is up over the windows now, you see. It's morning . . . but I guess we'll have to turn on some lights." She continued to stare at him. "Good thing I was so well prepared, don't you think?"

She walked over to him, so close her hair stung his face as she swept it out of her eyes. "How did you know, Patrick? How did you know?"

The wind was picking up outside. They were in for more snow. The lights flickered once, twice, and then went out. He could hear Michelle returning to the couch. He could see the puffs of her wet sobs drifting in the near darkness. She struggled with speech but could not quite manage it.

Patrick woke up several times during the night, fighting for breath. Each time he searched for the rocking chair. Each time it was rocking, navigating through the cold dark night. He wondered how long his father had kept it up, when he had given in to the silence out on these cold plains and stopped talking.

He walked to the window behind the rocker and noticed how the snow against the pane seemed to glow, but he didn't know whether it was illuminated by sun or by moon. He started to speak . . . he suddenly wanted to incant and rave at the night . . . something, anything that might stay the darkness and fill the hollow opening inside him. But he was afraid. He was afraid he might discover he could no longer speak.

The next morning he found Michelle at the window,

touching it, stroking it, beating it, and crying to get out. The window was solid with white—the ice was pushing its way through the frame. There was ice on the curtains.

The rocking chair still drifted through its private dream.

Patrick stared at the front door, walked to it, and twisted the knob. Then turned his shoulder and rammed it as hard as he could. The door stopped eight inches out, jammed into a snowbank. Patrick slipped through into the brilliant cold glare.

It took almost two hours, but he finally made it to the pig pen. He looked back down at his father's house. Snow drifts gnawed halfway up the roof. He looked past his father's land, at the distant fields, and there were gleaming fields of wheat and corn, red and green harvesters under the brilliant August sun. The hottest time of the year down here. The snow stirred all around him, eddying, forming rivers of powder, sinkholes, caved-in impressions, as if it were alive. The breath froze in his throat.

As he had expected, but was compelled to find out for sure, half the pigs were dead. He had to dig out several feet of snow with his bare hands to find the bodies. But his hands had been so numb, for days, it didn't matter.

The others, the larger mothers, the enormous fathers, had been gnawing on the smaller dead ones. Trapped within the freeze, they had devoured their young.

The snow eddied. The icy crust groaned from unseen pressures, unheard presences. His father stalked him silently, invisibly.

He tried to scream, but the freeze broke up the words.

By the Sea

When a very young and precocious Sarah Kingsley first learned the word "solvent" she thought of that vast sea beyond her home, *limitless* as far as she could determine, *incomprehensible*, *unforgiving*. These were all vocabulary words Mother gave her to keep her occupied.

The family lived on a small Carolina vegetable and apple farm near the Atlantic coast, along with a few cows and chickens, a goat, and a goose or two. Despite the general smallness of her world there was a great deal of serious trouble a child could stumble into if insufficiently engaged. Farm animals weren't always the best-natured playmates, the fields nearby had snakes and foxes and the occasional sinkhole, and further out were the high cliffs and caves along the shore.

Her father worked continuously sun up to sun down, but always began and ended each day with a joke and a hug. Because of the hard work of the farm Mother didn't always have time for Sarah. A *taciturn* woman by nature, she doled out her affections sparingly. So when Mother was busy in the gardens and orchards she delegated Sarah's supervision to her three older siblings: two brothers who had never had much to do with her, and her sister Peggy, who at least spared a kind word now and then and seemed to enjoy brushing Sarah's hair.

The farm was not far from an isolated stretch of beach where the four would play nearly every afternoon after morning chores were done. Her siblings insisted on it, and since they had been properly delegated the authority, Sarah had no choice. Her brothers and sisters loved building sand castles and splashing around in the edges of the ocean. It's where they learned how to swim. It's where they escaped from the hard work of the farm.

Sarah, of course, had never learned how to swim. And when their father, trying to help, told her *Sweetheart, there's no reason to be afraid. Did you know that human beings are mostly water?*— she had been *appalled*.

For Sarah, the ocean was a very different experience. She hated the way the sand got in between her toes and stayed there. On the walk back to the farm the tiny bits of stubborn grit burned into her skin, and so the journey was almost always accompanied by tears. And her siblings, often sour about having to leave this favorite place, called her "crybaby," which at that point in her short life was the foulest insult.

There was always a certain repellent *persistence* about the sea, a quality which back then she had no words for—how it would invariably chase after her when she felt brave enough to approach it, the long distorted fingers of it relentless no matter how fast she ran. And how, when the others sculpted fine castles and farm houses, and even people, out of sand the perfect degree of damp, the sea always returned and destroyed them, intolerant of anything humans attempted to build along its shores. What was even worse was how her siblings laughed at the destruction of what had taken them hours to create. It was left to little Sarah to mourn, to be devastated as all that hard work was washed away.

At least these daily trips to the beach only went on for a few years, and when Sarah was old enough to stay at home while the others went off to tease the ocean, she did, content to pick apples or plant flowers with Mother in the gardens around the house, or remain in her room and read of far off lands, some with a coast and some without, but at least when there was a coast it wasn't *her* coast, not the one she could hear at night in the midst of some fitful dream.

When there was a storm in her childhood, it seemed that storm almost always came out of the sea, the mountains of cloud rising somewhere out over the middle of the ocean, then rolling in with much darkness and the drama of lightning and torrential rain. The storms always left things worse off than they had been before—plants flattened, branches snapped, and trees down, sometimes shingles and even entire roofs blown away. She often heard that the destruction was more terrible the closer you got to shore, and along the shoreline itself. Sarah took their word for it, unwilling to venture close enough to see.

Her oldest brother went out before one such storm, on a small boat with friends. He never came back. A few weeks later some fishermen pulled his body out of the water, or so she was told. Because she did not witness these things herself she could always believe they weren't quite true, that facts had been exaggerated or misinterpreted. The last she saw of him was that long box in the church. Mother had laid out his good Sunday suit for the occasion but the undertaker told her sadly that because of the body's *engorgement* it would no longer fit. The casket would be closed. Sarah had understood very little of what was going on. She'd seen a dead cat once, and a few birds, and one of their cows had died giving birth to a stillborn calf. And how could she grieve when all she had was a box to stand over? And what was grief anyway but a sadness over the unseeable, the untouchable, when the one you knew now seemed someone only imagined? And her brother had been so much older they could hardly be called friends. He'd paid very little attention to her, from what she could remember, and never offered any particularly memorable kindness.

What had struck her most about the funeral was how the box had been so short, when he had always seemed so tall. Hadn't the undertaker talked about swelling? Something was obviously awry. Sarah eventually decided the casket must have been empty, and simply there so the preacher could say some words. In truth the ocean had taken her brother, and selfishly hadn't thrown back even a shoe for the family to take home.

After a year had passed she had almost forgotten what he looked like, and had completely forgotten the sound of his voice, which made her feel badly about herself. Certainly, she thought, she was the most heartless sister who had ever lived. Of course she told no one she had become this awful human being. It was a dark secret known only to her and the sea. People might not have believed her and she would have felt compelled to provide them with all the terrible details, having to confess the worst thoughts that had ever passed through her *corrupted* brain.

A few years later, at the end of high school, and before she was to board a train for the different life to come, Sarah walked down to that private stretch of beach for what she intended to be the last time. What bothered her most was discovering how very close it had been, much nearer than she had remembered. When she was a child it had been such an arduous journey, but the fact that this dangerous place was actually so *proximate* was almost too much to bear. No wonder the ocean had invaded her dreams. What had ever possessed her parents to raise a family in such a place?

Still, this was something she needed to face before leaving home, possibly forever. Her train wasn't leaving until late in the evening, but she wanted to get to the beach hours earlier, in the fullness of daylight, when she could see more and avoid its most unpleasant associations. But she'd been delayed, mostly because of entreaties from her father that she not go. Mother said nothing during her father's speech, but left the room from time to time to hide, returning a little more red-eyed and *haggard* each time.

She did not enjoy disappointing either of them, but even more she hated the emotional fuss, the secret tears and the attempts to make her feel as if she were doing them some terrible wrong. They'd lost one child—how could they afford to lose another? By the time Sarah was finally able to *extricate* herself the sun had set, and she required a lantern for most of the way to the shore.

She took the dark path down to the water. Years of coastal erosion had steepened the trail. Lowering the lamp was necessary to make sure she placed her feet safely. At the bottom she discovered a much wider band of sand than the one she remembered. It wasn't until she raised the lantern again that she fully appreciated the vastness of the fluid body stretched out before her. Because it *was* a body. It was impossible, staring out at that distant horizon, its edge softly illuminated by a fallen moon, to think of this as a collection of individual waves, of cells or bits or droplets of water. This was all one *ravenous* creature, moving sluggishly as if asleep, pushing its appendages here and there experimentally in response to some half-considered thought or hungry dream. There was a soft murmuring noise as its edges pushed up and nibbled on the beach, the sounds of some *thing* ingesting the world at its own lackadaisical pace, unconscious of all the damage it was doing, uncaring of the human lives it might destroy.

This was where the world ended, she thought. This was where, if you went too far, it was impossible to come back. Her brother had journeyed too far out over the skin of it, and like a great annoyed beast it had swatted him down. All that kept this from devouring the rest of the globe, she supposed, was an ancient inbred laziness, a lack of ambition. Wake it up too much and one day it would take away everything we knew.

She walked closer to the water, intent on staring it down. Tonight it seemed intent on keeping its distance. The tide was out further than she expected, and some tiny creatures moved and flapped about where it used to be, waving claws and segmented limbs, struggling for purchase on the *insubstantial* ground. There were also the usual bits of both ragged and smoothed wood, polished stones, twisted sodden bits of seaweed or some other plant, some other being, creatively destroyed.

She almost gagged from the reek of it. Out in the distant black the silver edges of the waves looked razor-sharp and eager.

"Come," she said softly. "Take me or leave me. I can't stand the waiting."

She paused as long as she could, but still with no answer she turned away.

When Sarah Kingsley next returned fifty years had passed. Not a good fifty years, but half a century just the same. She had had several careers, various love affairs, lost a husband, lost an only child. She had also traveled widely, roaming through Europe and Asia numerous times—although she never liked flying over the ocean, and always found ways to distract herself until that necessary passage was done. She liked to imagine what lay below as some vast, painted backdrop (or more accurately, drop cloth), covering the great *abyss* between what is and what is not.

She thought often about the deaths of others, both the ones she had loved and the ones she'd only encountered briefly. No one she'd ever known was a person of note. None of them were people you'd ever read about in the paper or see on the news. Like her parents, her siblings, and herself, they were people who lived their entire lives without notice, subject to the whims of the planet, of the weather and climate change, of the politicians and the governments and the armies which—as far as these insignificant people were concerned— were every bit as elemental as the weather, as *obstinate* as the ocean.

But rarely did she consider her own death. What was there to think about? You were there, and then you were snatched away into the *unfathomable*. Or perhaps "snatched" was the wrong word, because some people appeared to be inevitably drawn there, pulled by forces beyond their control. Sarah had long suspected that something in the sea—some parasite, some nearly extinct creature, some consciousness—knew all about what lay waiting in the worlds beyond, but she was quite sure this being was not someone she wanted to meet.

Decades before, her parents had moved off the farm into a small town nearby. There they died—first her father and then Mother years later. She'd been there for her father's last illness. They talked and laughed and even now she still couldn't believe he wasn't somewhere in the world waiting for her to visit. She missed Mother's final years but hadn't been surprised when sister Peggy told her the dying woman had had very little to say.

The farm had remained in the family—Peggy owned the land and whatever was left. From her wheelchair she gave Sarah her blessing but declined to join her on this final journey back to that *insignificant* stretch of coast.

The last two Carolina hurricanes had transformed or *expunged* entirely most of the landmarks Sarah could recall. The orchards were gone except for the occasional twisted trunk, denuded branches bent in a desperate reach for the ground. The farmhouse itself had vanished except for scattered piles of stone tracing the pulverized foundation. The landscape beyond was runneled and carved into a network of gullies and washouts. She maneuvered through them as best she could, her old bones hardly up to the task. Overhead the screams of gulls followed her down to sea level, where the landscape ended in a series of low dunes and a broad expanse of beach. The water here was calm, the horizon line a blur of silver haze. She recognized nothing. With this final *dislocation* she sank to her knees in the sand.

She struggled to find the words, and then remembered. "Come," she whispered. And when nothing changed, she closed her eyes and said it louder, "come," seeing all that she had lost and what little she had left to lose. "I can no longer stand the waiting."

Then she felt that distant change in the world, that fundamental shift deep in the bowels underground, heard the telegraphed rumble, and opened her eyes to see that the ocean had finally stood up to speak.

The Way Station

Homage to Stefan Grabiński

The decision to attend his father's funeral was hastily made and he was surprised at his own willingness to go. They had been estranged for decades. Polk had burned all pictures and belongings reminding him of his father. One day he'd built a grand bonfire in the field behind his house and been gratified by the impressive volume and intensity of the flames. Their beauty and barely controlled passion, the too-real possibility of their escape, had almost brought him to tears.

But when he received the note from his sister a trip home felt required. He had no idea how he would get there. He didn't really know anyone in the area. He'd said hello to a few of his neighbors in the five years he'd lived in this distant and isolated community, and asked for directions a time or two, but had no friends here, or even anyone he might call, honestly, an acquaintance. Out of necessity he rang the one neighbor whose name he recalled.

"Can you drive me to the train station? I no longer own a car."

There was an awkward pause and then the old man haltingly replied. "I haven't been by there in years. Do we still have train service? I believe—well, didn't the station burn down some time ago?"

"I have no idea. You can take me there, and if the station is no longer operational you can bring me back. I will pay you either way, of course. I have . . . familial obligations."

"I see. Of course . . . family. I know all about families, the things you have to do, the things which must be tolerated, even beyond the bounds of good taste. I will drive you. And there's no need to pay me. I was looking for an excuse to get away from my own family for a few hours, to see some of the countryside, the freedom of the open road and all that."

His neighbor was obviously a fool, but Polk had no choice. The old man arrived in a dusty yellow car blaring music out the open windows. On the long drive the neighbor chattered on about a variety of subjects—family life, town gossip, politics—without turning the music down. Polk gazed out at low-lying scrub and malnourished patches of weed and wildflowers. Now and then he spied bits of rusted train track. It was impossible to determine if any of it was still in use—certainly it looked poorly maintained. But the paths away from a place were often subtle and underutilized. He closed his eyes and was almost asleep when the man's tone changed. "So, is it . . . peaceful, out where you live?"

"I suppose so. I never think about it in those terms."

"Well, it's just that no one ever sees you. We thought you might be dead."

"I have always lived . . ." Polk considered, then continued, "in a condition of privacy." The old man said no more, and Polk fell asleep.

Polk dreamed he boarded the train and subsequently traveled for weeks, following the streams in low-lying river valleys, climbing mountains and dropping down steep rocky inclines. At the end of the line he was met by his sister and his father, still alive.

Polk woke up as they pulled in front of the dilapidated train station. There were no other cars in the dirt and gravel lot. Portions of the outside of the building were scorched and a pile of burnt timbers lay near the entrance, but the exterior at least appeared to be intact. There was no one around to ask if the building was still in use.

"See? As I remembered! There's been a fire!" The neighbor shouted above the music.

Polk reached over and turned off the key. The neighbor stared at him. "You can leave me here. I thank you for the ride."

"But can't you see? There's been a fire."

"There is still a building. I appreciate your concern." Polk felt anxious to get away. He climbed out of the car and walked around to the entrance. He saw no lights on inside, but the door opened easily enough. The sour taste of smoke filled his mouth, but none was visible.

At first glance the interior appeared to be abandoned. Dirt and leaves filled the corners, and the overhead beams were populated with the nests of wasps and small birds. The chalkboard where departures and arrivals were once recorded was blank except for faint, ghostly smears. There was a single bench pushed up against a wall layered in advertisements and notices many years old. The bench was painted with dust. One side of the building was open, and only a few feet away was the platform and the tracks below. It seemed an unusual arrangement to Polk, that close proximity to where people would be waiting for their trains less than safe.

Polk felt vaguely annoyed, even though he had fully anticipated this. Not that he actually wanted to make the trip, but he believed in options, even though he never used them. Why was there no "Closed" notice posted either on the outside of the building or somewhere in its interior? There was no way to call anyone—the payphones had been removed and he did not own a cell.

Good enough. He had tried to do the right thing by his dead father, but unavoidable circumstances had prevented it. It was completely out of his control. He would rest for a few moments and then begin the long trek home. Perhaps someone would drive by and he would ask for a lift, but he had no idea what kind of traffic could be expected this late in the day. Nor did he have any sense whether he was the kind of person likely to get a ride in this community. He realized he was somewhat scruffy and unkempt. It had been a very long time since he'd cared about his appearance. Did this make him look dangerous? He had no idea.

He dusted off the bench as best he could with his hands, clapping them together afterwards. The dust rose up in puffs so copious someone might have thought his palms were on fire. He sat down and gazed ahead. The old ticket window was directly in front of him, the filthy glass like a gray filter. He noticed a darker gray area somewhere beyond the glass, a distant murky corner of that room. As his eyes adjusted that gloomier gray area appeared to enlarge. He couldn't take his eyes away—the strain made the vision wobble ever so slightly. And then out of that obscurity a face bearing a mustache resolved, fixed above a shabby uniform. Dusky eyes blinked. The pale lips moved. "May I help you?"

He stumbled off the bench and approached the man behind the window. "You're open for business?"

"Sporadically," the lips said, "when there is a need. Do you have such a need? Where do you wish to go?"

"Somewhere East. There's a funeral—my father has died." Polk thought the information might obtain more sympathetic service.

"The closest terminal is a two-hour journey. There you can acquire a ticket to a number of eastern destinations."

"Well then, that's what I'd like to do."

The man took his money and handed him a ticket. Polk thought the price remarkably cheap. "You will have a bit of a wait before your train arrives. A number of other trains will pass through. Some will stop and some will not. Your train will be the only one to open its doors. Do you have luggage?"

"Just my book," he said, and pulled a thin volume of poetry out of his coat pocket. "It was a spur of the moment decision. I brought nothing else."

But the ticket seller had already receded from the window. Polk put his face against the glass to see where the man had gone, but the glass was so grimy and the interior so dim he couldn't find him. He returned to the bench and sat.

After several minutes he became cognizant of a slight vibration in the bench, and a subtle change in the air as sometimes accompanies an approaching storm front. Then a distant sound that made him want to hurry somewhere, anywhere but where he was sitting.

Then the train was there, filling the gap in that side of the station, traveling too fast, obviously, to stop. Due to an optical effect Polk did not understand, the outside of the train was blurred, but the interior—and the passengers moving around in that interior—were perfectly clear. What was even more peculiar was the attitudes of those passengers. Many were gathered at the windows, their faces pressed against the glass, looking out, looking at him. He could see others running around inside the cars as if in a panic, gesturing toward the windows, recruiting more passengers to gather at the windows and gaze, at him. By the time the last car arrived the windows were full of staring faces.

Polk had no idea what to make of it. He waited a few minutes for another train to arrive, and with none forthcoming he got up and paced the waiting area. He hoped he wouldn't go to all this trouble and then be late to his father's funeral. His sister had not revealed the date or the time of the service, and because of this he assumed she would wait for his arrival. But how would she know he was even coming? He didn't have her phone number and she didn't have his. Both were unlisted, or at least his was—he knew—was he sure about hers? Too late in any case. He was on his way, or soon would be, and there hadn't been time to write her a letter.

Would they really wait for him before burying his father? It seemed unlikely, after all this time of non-communication. Still, Polk would follow through.

The next train came by so slowly Polk thought it was going to stop. He went out on the platform, ready to board. All the cars were full of smoke. He could see here and there the occasional ashen face among the gray clouds. Were all these people smoking? Was this a train of nothing but smokers in their smoking cars? The train never stopped, and left the station without his discovering the answer.

He wasn't actually sure his father wanted to be buried. He vaguely remembered some talk of cremation. His mother had been cremated—it had been her wish. Would his father follow suit?

Two more trains passed at such speed he thought he might have hallucinated their presence. A haunting, drawn-out memory of sound, and then they were gone, leaving behind not even a whiff of their exhaust. He sat back down on the bench and closed his eyes.

When he opened them again another train was passing. He was alarmed at the way it had sneaked up on him, making not even a breath or a sigh of sound. Cattle cars, one after another, sheathed in wooden slats, tiny windows at the top. Here and there the slats had warped, and fingers protruded from the resulting spaces. The fingers moved back and forth, as if in admonishment, or simply to maximize their contact with the air. There were sounds coming from the cars he couldn't quite identify. Soft—moans, perhaps? Perhaps weeping, or something from a despair far beyond the point of weeping.

No more trains appeared for a very long time. Polk was ready to abandon the attempt, even though it meant a long trek back to the isolated ramshackle structure which he had made his home. It occurred to him that the ticket seller might have cheated him and simply pocketed his money, that indeed trains did not stop here. Why would they, at such a desolate place?

But then there was a sudden roaring sound, and something thunderous rolling down the tracks. Polk felt the wall of intense heat before it came into view: car after car completely consumed by flames. There were dark charcoal shapes inside the flames, and these shapes appeared to be moving, but he could not tell whether these were actually people, or what had been people, or the collapse of internal furnishings instead.

Polk jumped up and ran to the ticket window and began beating on the glass, shouting and begging for that apparently sole employee to do something, anything, to somehow fix this terrible circumstance. Getting no response, he picked up a nearby trashcan and used it to beat on the glass, but no matter how hard he struck it the window would not shatter. He dropped the trashcan and ran around the waiting room, jerking open cabinet and closet doors, then out to the front of the building looking for a hose or some kind of fire extinguisher. He found nothing.

He walked back into the station only to discover that another train had arrived, now waiting at the platform, the doors open. He hesitated only briefly, then raced through the opening before he—or it—could reconsider. The doors closed behind him with a snapping sound.

This particular car was empty, which pleased him initially, and he sprawled across the wide bench, feeling luxurious, although the bench in fact was not that comfortable. Both the seat and back were rock hard, and soon enough he found himself fidgeting, moving around, seeking some sort of comfort which was not there. Finally he sat up straight and focused on the passing countryside.

This was the one part of the journey back into his father's influence that Polk had been looking forward to. When he left his father's house it was in the middle of the night in an automobile that barely ran. He had made his goodbyes with no one, and he'd been so concerned that his vehicle might break down he'd paid very little attention to the passing countryside. And what he did see he could not trust—anger and upset had often made him see the unexplainable.

He was anxious now to see normal beings in their native habitat, performing their daily rituals, doing the things which all good people felt they had to do.

But after an hour or so Polk realized he was to be disappointed. The train tracks veered far from most developed areas, and when the train did come near a town he searched the streets for the inhabitants to no avail. Perhaps it was a holiday—he had not kept up with the usual calendrical landmarks in some time. Not that he felt completely alone out there—he did see the signs of human activity—trucks and cars moving on distant highways, other trains, a large tractor or two plowing or whatever such machines do. But he wasn't close enough to see the drivers, or any other human beings around. Automation seemed a distant and unlikely possibility. It had only been a scattering of years since last he came this way. There had been a population then—there had to be one now.

Polk stood up and proceeded to explore the rest of the train. There was no one in the first few cars, but he had determined—based on a look out his window as the train wrapped around a wide curve—that his car was near the end, and perhaps the forward cars were considered more desirable. He did not know that this was so, but it certainly seemed plausible.

Polk traveled from car to car, and actually enjoyed those more unsteady sections between cars, where the floors bounced up and down. He proceeded up the train until he reached a locked door near the engine and could proceed no further.

Perhaps he had figured incorrectly, and in fact he was progressing away from the more desirable train cars. He retraced his steps until he had reached the car he had originally entered (and a good thing, since he discovered he had left his ticket behind on the seat). Retrieving his ticket, he passed through that car and worked his way toward the end of the train where he was stopped by another locked door after passing through a dozen or more empty cars.

All the cars were empty. Polk was the only passenger on board. He returned to his seat and tried to relax into the inevitability of it. This had been his decision, of course. All his decisions had led him here, to this particular empty train. He refused to have any regrets.

The train bent its way around another long curve, and gazing out the window he could see that it was approaching another station. He stood up, curious, and pressed his face against the glass.

As the train entered the station he had the peculiar sensation that everything was speeding up around him, and yet he, in his car at this window, remained still for a time. So as the train passed the platform he was able to remain motionless, and get a good, long look into that platform, and at whoever might be waiting on the benches inside.

An old man sat by himself on the bench, dressed in a familiar gray suit and hunched over a battered suitcase Polk would have recognized anywhere. The fool thought he could actually take a bag where he was going. It was his father, who now raised a bottle of whiskey to his lips. But the bottle proved empty, and the old man threw it at the train in disgust.

Polk laughed and waved his hands. He jumped up and down. And before his train finally whipped him away he saw the old man's oh so pale look of alarm.

The Walls Are Trembling

The key to her good days was finding as many things to do as possible, and then not going to bed until you could barely hold your head up. That way you still fell asleep even though the worst things were happening.

Phyllis was relieved when people finally stopped asking how she was doing. She did appreciate their concern; it would have been much worse if they'd completely ignored her. But it was a challenge coming up with an honest answer every time. She didn't know how she was doing. She was nervous, certainly, much of the time, but she'd always had her nervous spells, even before her husband's death. She had depression, too, but didn't she have reason? Most people have their sad days. Sometimes she took pills for it. Sometimes they worked.

Today she was exhausted even before her day began. This particular fatigue occurred several times a week. She was always reluctant to go to bed, and even when she got there sleep rarely came easily. Her eyes wept from fatigue, and sometimes a glimpse of even the most common household objects, seen in her vision's periphery, could be alarming.

The wall with the fireplace shook. Soot drifted down from the chimney. An ornate blue and orange plate on a hanger above the mantle rattled. She'd been told to expect this until the project was complete. A cracked foundation was one of many repairs her husband had left behind, but at least he had identified the need for them before he died. It was a long list. He had worried over this list for several years and made copious notes. Now, with all the insurance money, she was getting these repairs done one at a time. Phyllis didn't know how Oliver would have felt about that. But she liked to think it honored him in some way.

Each morning she went over Oliver's list at breakfast, making notes as to progress, expenses, and intermediate goals. After that she did some sort of exercise, running up and down the stairs perhaps, or finding something heavy to lift. There was too much clutter to run through the house, but she conscientiously kept the stairs clear. She never stopped until she was in pain.

A horn blared suddenly. Her body seized and she almost fell down the steps. It sounded as if it was right outside her windows. She thought she heard a cracking sound, but a quick search found no broken glass. Maybe the damage was somewhere she couldn't see, inside a wall or hidden in a crawl space. Traffic patterns had recently altered, so larger trucks were using the roads nearby. Another change she had no control over. She could have had a heart attack. She might have broken her back on the stairs. Living alone, anything might happen. She would be the next to go.

She tripped over a glass on the dining room floor. She couldn't remember how it had gotten there. She rolled it under the table with her foot. She should make a list of where everything was in the house. She would compile it room by room. No telling how long it would take, but it would take a very long time.

He had not been a perfect husband and theirs had not been a perfect marriage. There had been disappointments, at least for her. He'd always seemed content with what they had. She supposed their marriage had been better than some. He'd never raised his hand to her, never even shouted. She'd been the shouter in the family. Sometimes a shout would fill her body until she had to let it go.

At least he had admitted to many of his failings, and made

promises to change. Oliver said he had even made a list, although he never showed it to her. But he had never been very good at repairing himself, or anything else. There had been little improvement overall. Was that a terrible thing to think now that he was gone? No matter—it was true.

Of course she could have cleaned the house to kill some time. She supposed it was long overdue and would eat up a huge portion of the hours she wasted worrying. But still, she was reluctant to touch anything. A clean house would also be an emptier house, and she didn't know if she could bear it. Outside, a trench now went around the entire house, even under the concrete walks that led up to the front and back doors. This trench exposed the foundation, whose cracks were being mended, whose bulges and displacements were being corrected by new steel bracing. More concrete would be added to create a ledge that would eventually be buried when the trench was filled in. The contractor said the ledge would add more stability. And of course stability was something she longed for.

But for now everything lay exposed: the crumbling foundation blocks, tree roots, pipes whose function she had no sure knowledge of. As exposed as her nerves, she thought, all of it so fragile. When heavy trucks passed on the adjacent streets the whole house shook. To make matters worse it had been raining for days, filling the trench and delaying the completion of the job. The outside smelled of garbage and mud. She kept the windows tightly shut. She felt trapped here, unable to enjoy the world, assuming she was still capable of enjoyment. Her marriage had been joyless for so long, perhaps whatever organs were involved with happiness had atrophied.

After Oliver died she had been desperate to fill the time, and attempted to develop new interests, read more deeply into subjects she knew little about, signed up for an online computer course (despite her ineptness with all things electronic), began clipping pictures from newspapers and magazines for scrapbooks she hadn't gotten around to buying. Lately she had been reading about climate change. Apparently the seas were rising all around the world. There were unusual spells of drought in some regions, unseasonable damp in others. Apparently an increased chance of famine and disease was also involved, although she'd missed some of the pieces that made these connections.

She didn't know if these recent rains had anything to do with climate change, but she supposed it was possible. Of course it wasn't fair, but sometimes she felt as if her husband had abandoned her to face a new and terrible, evolving reality. She remembered, with some resentment, how he had always slept like the dead. The thought made her laugh until she stopped herself. She'd become a terrible person, or perhaps she'd always been a terrible person. Maybe that was why he wouldn't touch her.

Phyllis had not kissed a man, or seen a man's naked body, since her husband died—so pale there in the bed they'd shared for more than thirty-five years, as pale as the sheets, a dried froth of blood on his lips. This scene had been so unexpected, even though she had been expecting it for years.

Phyllis detected an odd stench in the air. She wondered if perhaps the vibrations had cracked one of the toilets, or broken the sewer line. She didn't exactly know where her sewer line ran—it was just buried somewhere beneath the house. She couldn't imagine what would be required to fix it—it didn't appear on any of Oliver's lists. Perhaps she could live with it, as she had learned to live with so many disappointments in her life, but no doubt it would get worse over time. Most things did.

She went into different rooms and sniffed. At least the odor wasn't everywhere. It was obviously stronger in the kitchen. She walked over to the counter and found a pile of dirty dishes, glasses, silverware. Some were encrusted with mold. She didn't remember leaving them out like this—could someone else be using her kitchen?

Oliver had never taken very good care of himself. He just ate what he wanted to eat, did whatever he was moved to, and didn't do anything that didn't suit him. "I'm sorry, but I just have to have that last piece." That could have been his motto. She should have had it engraved on his headstone. She wondered if it was too late. Perhaps she would spray paint it on. At least he apologized—he always knew he would be the first to die.

He'd almost never felt well. He'd often used that as an excuse not to touch her. But even before that he'd been a selfish lover, behaving as if his own pleasure was the only point. She'd wanted so much more out of the marriage, but apparently Oliver couldn't even imagine it.

Phyllis was stomping her way through the house now, shaking. She was still angry with him, how he had held her, held the both of them, back. There were things scattered across the floor—a lamp, some books, several grocery items, the contents of her purse—had the traffic vibrations caused all this? Some of it perhaps, initially. She vaguely remembered leaving some items on the floor where they'd fallen, because what was the point, really, if the house's shaking would just make them fall again? And once she had been searching for her car keys, and frustrated that she hadn't been able to find them, she'd dumped everything from her purse onto the floor. And then she'd liked the way the purse had looked empty, so spacious and full of possibility, so she hadn't put any of those things back.

She ought to take a nap. She might feel better with more rest. But if she lay down she would be forced to contend with those thoughts she always had when lying down, and that thing that happened to her when trying to let go and relax. She couldn't risk dealing with that experience more than once a day.

She really should take a long drive; she couldn't remember the last time she'd gone out for no other reason than to see a little bit of the world that wasn't part of the troubles of her own life. She hadn't driven in several weeks. The increased traffic made her nervous. And she wasn't sure she was even safe to drive. She probably wasn't. She would probably kill herself and who knew how many others. And she had no idea where her car keys were.

If she still had family she could visit them. But she hadn't had family in quite a while. Oliver had been the last to go, if you considered a spouse a member of the family. Sometimes they were and sometimes they weren't. Sometimes they were that final mistake which separated you from family.

Phyllis was Irish on her mother's side, and her grandmother had told her the old stories about leprechauns, the cluricaun, fear gorta, and the banshee, that horrible fairy woman who was supposed to warn you of an impending death. Supposedly the banshee only shrieked for certain old Irish families, but her grandmother always said "If you've 'eart enoof, oi expect yer wud 'ear 'er well enoof!"

But of course the fairy woman had let Phyllis down, and she'd received no such warning preceding Oliver's death. Perhaps Phyllis didn't have enough heart. Perhaps it had transmogrified from lack of affection. No doubt all she had left inside was an ugly piece of stone at the center of her body. People would not have guessed from just looking at her. It was bitter to speculate about. If for no other reason she was glad she hadn't died with her poor excuse for a husband. She needed to live a very long time, she supposed, just so that people wouldn't suspect she'd died from grief.

If she had only heard a scream that warned her not to marry him in the first place, that might have been some help. Maybe there had been such a scream and she'd just ignored it. There was a great deal of crime in the city—perhaps she had heard such a scream and misunderstood its significance.

People were always getting warnings. Rarely were they screams—more often they were isolated episodes of high anxiety, premonitions of disaster, dreams of apocalypse. People learned to ignore such misgivings and chalked them up to some neurosis or other. Perhaps they shouldn't.

She walked into the living room and stared at the ceiling. Now and again over the years she'd seen a drip coming from one corner. Oliver always said it was a flaw in the roof design and no solution would last for long. "We can't exactly take off the entire roof and rebuild everything!" He always had a reason why some idea or solution wouldn't work or wasn't worth the expense. Almost always he shot down her ideas and complaints. Still, he could have called someone, asked for another opinion. "I know I'm stubborn. I'm lucky you put up with me." Again, at least he more or less apologized. But it didn't change anything.

She replaced the almost full bucket with an empty one. The stain in the ceiling was twice as large as it had been only a few weeks before. She carried the bucket to the back door and poured it into the flooded trench. The trench looked wider than it had before. She didn't think she could step across it if she needed to. If the concrete walks at both the back and front doors failed she would be trapped inside her house. She watched as some more of the rim of the trench slid off into the water. A large truck rumbled by in the street, causing even more erosion. The whole house began to vibrate. She clutched the doorframe, took a deep breath, then shut the door.

She'd always seemed to know that something bad was going to happen. Her whole life, but especially since she'd married Oliver. And eventually, of course, something always did. But she was always afraid. She was always uneasy. If she'd been the fairy woman she'd be shrieking all the time.

She went back through the house looking for damage. With all that quaking and shuddering there was always damage: pictures fallen off the walls, little knickknacks on the floor with corners and delicate details chipped, although nothing had yet shattered beyond repair. Everything about her life was just a bit shabbier. It was her nerves that had taken the worst beating. But none of it had broken her, not the trembling walls, and certainly not Oliver's death.

She felt some guilt about that. She'd always believed people should be shattered by the death of a spouse. She'd had this romantic notion that she'd feel compelled to spend years picking up the pieces, pulling her life together, before she could be reasonably expected to move on. But her marriage had been fracturing for years. The worst damage had already been done.

The storm continued unabated all afternoon. Phyllis went down and checked the basement. There was a lot of leaking around the edges of the floor, but actually not as bad as she'd expected. She'd moved much of Oliver's stuff down here: boxes of clothing, all of his books, bits of his various collections—minerals, stamps, some antique toys, a few coins, and old mechanical gear whose purposes she couldn't begin to imagine. She also had several boxes full of his notes and plans, reminders and lists, and whatever private correspondence she could find in his little office off the side porch. She imagined that if she read through all this material she'd acquire a better understanding of this man she'd lived with all these years. Perhaps she might even discover why he had lost interest in sex, or at least in sex with her. But at the moment she couldn't face that. She wasn't even sure it was worth all the trouble. If the water damaged some of his things then so be it. It would mean less for her to deal with.

Back upstairs she sat down in his living room chair—he'd been very particular about that—and watched the rain streaming down the windows. She looked around the room. Papers were scattered everywhere. Books were off the shelves and grouped into little piles. Not stacked, but piled. Piles made them look more relaxed, more receptive to being read. The dining room table was covered with dirty dishes, tissues, pill bottles. Again she wondered if someone was sneaking into various rooms and creating these astonishing messes. She really had no idea how things had gotten so bad. She had no memory of it. Small handwritten notes were everywhere— on the table, on the other furniture, on the carpet, even taped here and there to the wall. But they weren't Oliver's—they were all in her handwriting. She had made all these notes about what she needed to do with her life now that she was alone. Now she was the note maker in the house—she felt some pleasure in that.

She'd stopped picking up after herself sometime after Oliver died. She couldn't remember exactly when. But she needed to figure out her new place in the world, and she quickly discovered that she couldn't figure all that out and pick up after herself at the same time.

Abruptly the ceiling began to wiggle. There was a roaring noise outside. She imagined a whole fleet of enormous trucks rolling by. The chandelier swung back and forth. It made her dizzy to watch, so she looked away. The house resembled distant earthquake footage she had seen on the evening news. As soon as she figured out who and where she was in life she would clean everything up. She would move furniture around. By the time the workers were done, by the time she was done, it would be as if she were living in a completely different home. Perhaps even a residential paradise suitable for a major magazine spread.

Theoretically, Oliver's death should have freed her. She should have had new opportunities; she should have met many new people. She wasn't a young woman anymore. But she wasn't dead yet. Oliver never fully appreciated her. It should have been time to find someone who did.

If the fairy woman really wanted to help her, she could have warned her about that. She could have screamed "Pay attention!" Perhaps that was all Phyllis had needed. One good scream like that might have woken her up. But the warnings had all been low and off in the distance, too soft to comprehend completely, and too easily misunderstood as being meant for someone else.

She still wasn't quite ready to fall asleep, if she could fall asleep. She needed just a little more aimless activity, a little more useless movement before attempting to go to bed. She tried watching some television, but she didn't think she really understood television anymore. Why were these people acting so foolishly? Was this what the human race had come to? She turned it off after less than thirty minutes. She grabbed an ink pen and some paper and started to draw, something she hadn't done in years. She didn't think she was very good at it, but there was something soothing in looking at her house and attempting to abstract what she saw into a series of lines and shading. Inevitably things began working their way into her drawings that she didn't intend: cats and rabbits and giant millipedes which stretched from one drawing into the next. She wadded up the drawings and threw them over her shoulder, hoping she would never find them again.

So now she was dead on her feet. She could barely keep her eyes open. As usual, fatigue was quickly filling her, squeezing out everything else. She stumbled through piles of her possessions on her way to the staircase. She stepped on a variety of objects—she could hear them break or squeak, she could feel them fracture, but she didn't have it in her to determine what damage had been done. She desperately wanted to lie down, but didn't want to do it here, with everything encroaching. Besides, there was no empty floor space. Every square inch was filled with the daily debris of the shaking, the bits worn off as she trembled in her struggles to get through the day.

Finally she made it into her bedroom. She managed to kick off her shoes but removed nothing else. She used sweeping movements of her arms to knock a miscellanea of objects off the covers. She didn't know where they'd come from. She didn't think they were even hers. She crawled up on the bed and pulled the sheet and blanket over her as best she could. And she waited. It never took long.

As it happened every night, Phyllis first heard the distant sounds of weeping, and then somewhat closer the ripping of either cloth or flesh. And then the rapid sound of bare feet ascending the stairs.

Once again the woman came out of nowhere, rushing off the stairs with hair flying and nightgown torn to ribbons, and through the open door to plant herself at the foot of Phyllis's bed. Leaning over, the woman opened her mouth and screamed directly into Phyllis's face. It did no good for Phyllis to cover herself—the scream always blew away the covers and forced Phyllis's hands away when she tried to shield herself.

Sometimes she just lay there and cowered. Other times she would sit up and attempt to stare at the woman eye to eye.

Phyllis wanted to tell her *you're too late! You're too late! What could you possibly be warning me of now?*

But up that close, the woman's familiar scream made her tremble. Up that close, all she could see was that mouth stretched to its extremes, and that throat with its dark center surrounded by vibrating walls of skin.

And the woman screamed, and she screamed, and although Phyllis had grown accustomed to it, she could not avoid noticing the woman's intense resemblance to the face she saw in the mirror every day, or her unaccountable admiration of the shrillness which had no top, or the emptiness which had no bottom.

The Grandmother & The Rest

The grandmother hunches over the bag containing everything she still owns. "Mr. Bell has died. Cancer. I felt him go." She takes out some jewelry and swallows it.

Her friend Alice cries, "Wait! Save something for your grandchildren!"

"They never visit," the grandmother replies. "If one did I might eat her instead. By the way, Mrs. James has passed away." The rest turn toward the wheelchair holding the dead woman. "I heard her heart stop." She places her old car keys on her tongue.

"At least she escaped the nurses. Last week I saw one try to smother her." Mr. Willow was once a pilot and has excellent eyes. No one in the nursing home believes him but these friends.

"I'd rather be strangled by their lovely hands," Mr. Campbell says winking.

"At least those wicked girls believe you when you talk about your lovers," Mrs. Dean replies. She spits on the sidewalk and her teeth tumble out. Mr. Campbell laughs so hard he turns blue and falls.

"I feel him coming," the grandmother says, chewing up the last of the comb her mother gave her as a child. While the grandmother devours her beaded scarf the giant gray bird lands in Mrs. Dean's lap and plucks out her eyes.

"At last. But you'll have to wait," the grandmother admonishes the bird. "I haven't finished my meal. Please attend these others first. I don't want to leave anything behind!"

The bird stares at her sullenly, but drifts from resident to resident, a blunt puff of smoke taking lives.

"Disgusting isn't it, how none of them object? Here, you eat this one," she says, trying to hand Alice a shiny coin. "Wait! Don't tell me you've already dined!"

But Alice says nothing, having swallowed her tongue.

Forwarded

Tom received the first letter postmarked from his hometown in May, and continued to get them at irregular intervals throughout the summer. All had been forwarded a half-dozen times or more, addresses crossed out and heavily edited, having passed through various film studios and the offices of former agents. One had been forwarded by the editor of an obscure reference book on horror films. Tom met the man once at a party years ago. So odds were he shouldn't have gotten any of these letters. But he did. They took an improbably circuitous route to get to him, all originally postmarked a year or more ago. Now they were here he'd spent hours trying to decipher them.

They weren't conventional letters, but childlike, chaotic drawings, scratched out and multilayered, covered with multiple loops and rough cross-hatching in both blue and black ballpoint, ferociously applied, as if with a pen in each angry fist. A few alphanumeric characters did rise out of this tangle, crude misspelled words (if word-making was the intention): *owt* and *dammem* and *fulohell* and others.

It was only after multiple examinations that he detected an evolving imagery from drawing to drawing, like the individual shots of an animation: something desperate and ugly and angry emerging.

He was born Thomas Tobin, later changing it to Thomas Tobin Greene as a stage name for his mostly unsuccessful acting career. He was known for a few small parts on television, cop shows, a well-reviewed play in New York for a nine-month run, and toward the end of his career, a handful of horror movies in which he was featured. He wasn't half bad at playing dangerous characters, manic villains, the evil or the insane. Not much else. But those roles always came naturally to him.

At age sixty his small talent appeared exhausted and he spent his few years before retirement editing technical manuals. He didn't mind so much; he'd lost his taste for acting. The small paychecks never felt adequate for the deep sense of exposure he felt, and the anxiety and vulnerability he experienced preparing for his last few roles became intolerable. He had to keep reminding himself he was still a good person.

He liked and kept his stage name, Greene sounding so positive—Tobin was his father's name, and hating his father, he wanted to bury it.

The name on the return address of those letters was "Toby Tobin." That was the real problem. Toby was someone he used to talk to, long ago, when he was a kid who found comfort in talking to himself. Not an imaginary friend exactly, because they'd never been friends. And he wasn't Toby; he just couldn't be. "You be good now, Toby Tobin," he'd say, or sometimes, futilely, "Behave yourself Toby." No one knew that name besides Tom.

Tom had not been home in years, but his brother Will was retiring from the police force, and would be honored in a special ceremony. Despite their differences Will said he wanted Tom present. His brother was a brave man, a good and decent man, no doubt about it. The last thing Tom wanted was to go home, but he felt obligated to make an appearance. Besides, there were those letters.

Hanover was four hours from the airport. His brother offered to pick him up, but Tom didn't want to be stuck without a car. Besides, neither liked the way the other drove. "I'd pull you over for driving too slow. It's a hazard." Will never said that in a light-hearted way, but then he rarely said anything in a light-hearted way. Will's driving was typically angry and aggressive; Tom was terrified to ride with him.

Hanover was smaller than he remembered. Smaller and duller and shabbier: fewer people on the streets, many stores shuttered. In front of the drug store an older man waved vigorously. Tom didn't recognize him, but waved back.

A man stood in his brother's yard with his back to the street, hands on hips, apparently studying the garden which spread from the side of the house up the hill to the wild overgrowth above, where the bushes shuddered and branches swayed. He had late stage male pattern baldness, a classic horseshoe or cul-de-sac hairline. He wore a civilian shirt with uniform pants.

Tom caught his breath—this was a vivid recreation of his father, dead fifteen years. But when his father turned around it was Will's face on the other side. Will grinned and walked across the yard, growing taller with each stride. He was a good eight inches taller than either Tom or their dad.

His brother opened the car door, reached in and pulled Tom out for a hug. Tom barely had time to get his seat belt unbuckled. He let himself be swallowed inside his brother's embrace, his tears flowing uncontrollably.

"Hey there you old so-and-so," his brother whispered huskily into his ear. An expression their dad used to use. He smelled of liquor and aftershave. Tom pulled away.

"You're drinking again?" He'd decided not to talk about his brother's drinking in order to keep the peace, but here it was, first thing out of his mouth.

Will scowled. "I retire tomorrow, big brother. I think I'm entitled to a few drinks at the end of a long career putting my ass on the line. Doesn't mean I have a problem. I see you haven't stopped eating. How much do you weigh now, anyway?"

Tom felt a flash of shame. "I've let myself go, I know. There are reasons, but I intend to do better. I'm sorry, I just worry about you."

"Yeah, well, feeling's mutual. I'm doing okay. Amy's got dinner on, let's go eat."

The dining room was furnished with his mother's dining room set. Tom hadn't known, but he didn't care. He didn't want anything from the old house. He had too much of his own stuff he was trying to get rid of. He didn't want to leave a lot for people to dispose of after he was gone. Nothing in their house in particular reminded him of their father, and yet everything did. His brother looked and talked just like his father, sitting in his father's place at the table, holding forth with his grievances.

"So I'm retiring not because I'm old or because I want to *enjoy* myself, whatever that is, but because I can't take the bullshit anymore. People who can't do their jobs. People who won't let you do *your* job. They may be giving me this big sendoff, but half the town is just as glad to see me go. Those folks never understood what I did for them anyway, how I kept them safe. Now that bunch of hypocrites want to *hono*r me. Well, fuck them. I'll take their watch or their gift card or whatever, but fuck them." Most of the dinner had been that kind of conversation, or monologue of complaint. Their father had done the same thing every night. Tom could hardly get his food down. Just like old times.

"Will." Amy kept patting the table nervously, as if signaling her husband to tone it down.

Tom tried to find some way to defuse his brother. It wasn't one of his talents. "You can't read their minds. Most people don't say anything, good *or* bad, do they, when people are doing their job? It takes something like tomorrow's ceremony to get them to tell you how much they appreciate you."

"You don't live here, big brother. You escaped to Hollywood. This isn't Hollywood."

"I never lived in Hollywood, Will. Still don't."

"You know what I mean. You had Hollywood money."

"Actually, I never—"

"Okay, I know you're not rich. But you have a name people might know. They see you in those movies, and they can look up your name in books and on the internet. Me, people will forget me the day after I retire. By the time I die it will be as if I never existed." The way he scowled, with his head down, uncanny how much he looked like their dad. Tom averted his eyes.

Amy hurried into the kitchen to get their dessert. Tom started to get up to help, but saw an opportunity to talk to his brother alone. "How's the old house? Do you know the current owners?"

Will shook his head. "It's been empty for years. Not worth saving. You'd know if you visited more often. I told the town council they should tear the place down—I sure won't shed a tear. But as always they're not going to do anything until some kid hurts himself in there, or a vagrant burns it down."

"Lots of bad memories, I know. I know I was just terrible to you growing up, the way I bullied you. I think a lot about those days, and I want you to know how regretful, how sorry—"

Will raised his hand. "We don't need to reminisce about the *good old days*."

"I'm just so sorry, I need to apologize. I'm not like that anymore. I'm a good man. There was just a brief period—"

"You know in my job I work with troubled kids all the time, and not one of them did the kinds of things you tried to do to me." Will had never said that to him before.

Tom felt sickened, but pressed on. "I've tried to remember what I was thinking at the time, and I can't, but I don't think I intended to hurt you. Maybe I was resentful, I don't really know. Maybe I was just trying to scare you. I never imagined—"

"I said no reminiscing!" Will pushed back from the table and left.

The guest room was a converted porch at the back of the house. It was a humid evening, with a hot breeze making it even more uncomfortable. Tom sat on the steps and watched the sunset over the untamed trees and wild scrub at the top of the garden. He remembered they didn't trim things back here, so there were plenty of opportunities for hideouts, for places kids could get lost in. The town lay in a wide valley between two mountain ranges covered with forest. The sky was a blue velvet blanket stretched out between them. Despite its drawbacks (and those were immense) he'd always thought it one of the most beautiful places on earth. But he could hardly bear to be here.

He kept looking at a particular tangle—vines and stems and narrow branches making a swirly, loopy pattern just inside the thickest part of the scrub. It appeared as if the air had been scratched, worn thin at the one spot. He kept watching it for movement, and although he couldn't find any, he kept expecting it to be there.

"Got a minute, Tom?" It was Amy, walking around the side of the house in her housecoat, her head in a scarf. He noticed how thin she'd gotten since the last time he'd seen her. He wanted to blame Will, but that wasn't fair. He didn't know.

"I'm sorry I upset Will. I was trying to apologize, but I guess I shouldn't have brought those things up."

She lit a cigarette, stuck it in her mouth with a frown. He'd never seen her smoke before. He remembered her beautiful sand-colored hair. Now gray, it didn't look that different. But he'd noticed she didn't smile as much as she used to. He thought she was beautiful and kind and Tom had never had anyone remotely like her his whole life. "I never had siblings." She threw the cigarette down and nudged it into the damp grass. "I don't really get this brother stuff. Did you know he got closer to your dad toward the end? They weren't buddies, but they talked a lot. But I know they didn't talk about what happened when you were kids. He doesn't talk about that ever. So it's hard for him. And now you're famous."

"I'm *not* famous."

"Well, the most famous person *we* know. He's actually very proud of you. We both are." She smiled then. "He doesn't know how to make things right between you. He hates it when bad things happen to kids. Has he told you what's been going on?"

"What? No. Not a word."

"Two kids dead, scratched up and clawed, their bodies dragged around through the fields, into the woods. It might have been post-mortem, but still. Two others—older, teen-agers—missing. All this last year. He's been up all hours patrolling, every single day, and he must have interviewed everyone in town and most of the county. Just nothing. And he's retiring tomorrow. I've told him someone else can handle it, a younger officer, but he believes it's all on him. He thinks he's a failure."

The next morning Tom drove his rental over to the old house. He didn't want to tell Will; he wasn't sure where the conversation might go. So he said he just wanted to drive around and refresh his memory, maybe drop in on a few friends.

"You think you still have friends here? No offense, but you've been gone forever, and I don't imagine you were stay-ing in touch with anyone. Were you?"

"No. But maybe somebody will be glad to see me."

"Remember my big do is tonight and I expect you to be there. Do I need to remind you to leave yourself enough time to clean up?"

"I won't be late. I won't embarrass you."

Little in the area felt familiar until Tom was within a few blocks of the old neighborhood. People were generally poor here. Derelict houses were sometimes pulled down but new homes were rarely put up to replace them. A lot of empty lots. Many of the landmarks he recalled appeared to be missing. The Adams' house on the corner remained well-kept, still the yellow color it had been during his childhood. The next previously small home had added a second story and a large garage. He'd never known the quiet couple who'd lived there. The next two houses were missing, or he thought they were missing. He remembered two Victorians with wraparound porches, an antique birdbath in front of one, an ornate gazebo before the other, but had he just imagined them? Instead a large field deep in weeds and ragged bushes nibbled at the road. Nearby were the ruins of a structure which had burned to the ground. A chimney and a few blackened uprights remained. He couldn't remember if it had been a house or something else.

Following the overgrown, vaguely paved remnants of an alley, where Tom remembered trimmed lawns and brightly painted houses, there was another wild field, mounds of earth and ash, a red-rusted vehicle carcass, the collapsed remains of a couch, a small dilapidated structure enveloped in vines. He was disoriented and couldn't quite place what part of the neighborhood he was in, or where their house might be.

Then past another tall mound of refuse he saw a familiar tree, the swing still attached, but a pendant of shattered gray boards now, then the moss-covered concrete runner that had been the front walk, the crushed corner of a blonde brick garage, its unpainted door sprung open and bent sideways, and the attached house with its missing doors and windows, stark naked openings swimming with shadow.

He watched his feet as he stepped around splintered planks and piles of brick and drywall rubble, nervous when his shoes appeared to sink too far into the twisted weeds. Inside, several walls leaned, with detached sheetrock and ceiling panels pan-caked over sections of the floor. This disassembly confused him, and he had difficulty matching up the rooms with the ones in his memory. Spindly little trees, binding weed, and other bits of snarled vegetation had taken hold, outlining the broken rectangles in vivid green and skeletal gray and black, spreading through the interior and invading the structure in trails which felt oddly familiar.

He heard the occasional scurry, a scrape and a light squeak, which suggested an infestation of rodents. Now and then some larger bump sounded with a shifting of materials, which made him suspect a creature of more gravity. He picked up a broken stick and swung it a few times, wondering what he could do if attacked. He perceived some soft complaints, as if from something wounded, and thought he heard a distant whine and maybe crying, but all that might be in some other place or even imagined from memory.

Scavengers had raided the place, dragging the copper wire and pipe out of the walls, there were signs of a campfire, and fast food wrappers and beer cans and other trash had been pushed into corners by the constant drafts. There was also a great deal of unexplainable wire, coat hanger or electrical or fencing, some of which he would have thought the scavengers would have taken but for some reason had not. Most of it was bent into circles and loops, and he thought of those drawings he'd received, with all their complicated swirls. These created visible passages throughout the ruin, wire tunnels which had snagged bits of clothing, clumps of fur, and threads of flesh. A portion of the wire was reddish, both dull and glistening, as if something had repeatedly wounded itself in passing.

And everywhere on walls, floors, and ceilings, the graffiti: pencil and crayon and ink, paint and lipstick, crayon and smeared mud and something thick that stank horribly, whirls and coils and furious crossings of lines, obliterated words and words needing obliteration, massed and laid over and over

until the eye couldn't help but find shapes moving and grov-
eling for escape.

He heard something in a space far back behind the thickest
wreckage. Like a sigh forced out from pain. Tom couldn't
bring himself to move closer, but whispered "Toby?" before
stepping back.

When a familiar voice answered, although he couldn't
have sworn with which words, Tom made a stumbling retreat
until he was outside the house, and upon further consideration went back to the car and locked himself in. He watched
the house and yard for some time, thinking since he'd come
all this way he should really pin down what was actually
there, but knew he could never go back inside. Still he felt
unable to drive away, and sat there as the afternoon wore on,
sun baking the interior until it was unbearable, and him too
anxious to roll down a window for air.

No one would have ever said Tom was a bad kid. He was
quiet and obedient in school, and too shy to enter into any
conflicts with the other kids. He had a few pals he hung out
with, but none on a regular basis, no "besties," none he ever
invited over to spend time in his room, around his house, or
in their yard. Will had lots of friends and sometimes brought
a few by, but they never stayed long. Will didn't want them
to.

It was embarrassing to have friends over when your dad
was drunk and passed out on the couch. Embarrassing but
bearable. They figured it was no secret to the rest of the town
that one of the town cops was a drunk. But sober, and often
raging, their father was impossible to be around. People
kept their distance. No one wanted to be arrested by Officer
Tobin. People said yessir and nosir and kept their heads down
and prayed for the best. He'd been written up dozens of times
for what happened to prisoners in his custody. Their mother,
barely remembered, ran away when the boys were little. Tom

couldn't really blame her, but why had she left them behind? Tom had tried to imagine what he might have done to drive his mother away, but those years were simply too far away.

Will claimed not to recall much from those years. Tom's memory was vivid, but there were gaps, and some events came back unfocused. He recalled nasty arguments with his father, denials he'd done anything (whether he had or not). Other days it was all about screaming and running through the house, dodging and falling and escaping outside, covering up, protecting his face.

There was a time—he was eight, maybe nine or so—when Tom fancied himself a sort of mad scientist. Will, up until then always anxious to play, readily agreed to be his assistant, or lab rat, until it became clear what that entailed. This was a couple of years after he stopped talking to himself, after he stopped talking to Toby. His dad caught him a few times mid-conversation, and he'd been slapped for it. "Stop acting crazy!" his dad told him. Tom wasn't sure he could tell whether he was acting crazy or not, but he sure would try.

Once, claiming to be studying "air-o-magnets," Tom attempted to throw a dart past his brother's head into a target. It would have impressed everybody if he'd been able to pull it off, but the dart lodged in Will's ear.

A few early electrical experiments had been relatively harmless, given Tom knew so little about electricity. He ran an extension cord with exposed wire through a brass tube and had Will hold the tube while he plugged it in. Will panicked, dropped the tube, and there was a shower of sparks, but the brass hadn't been connected to the wire.

A few months later Tom acquired magnesium powder, potassium salts, and some chemicals from a chemistry set, mixed them together in a coffee can in their living room and gave the can to his brother to hold. "Hold it real still," he told him. Tom took a step back and shouted "Presto chango!" as he tossed a lit match into the can.

Thankfully Will dropped the can before it erupted into white light and purple flames. He stumbled back onto the couch in shock, waving his hands as if they were on fire. Flames burst through the bottom of the can as it hit the floor and spun, setting fire to a corner of the shag rug. Tom stomped on the flames, yelling for Will to help, but Will just pushed himself farther back onto the couch.

Tom didn't think he ever meant to hurt his brother. He screwed things up a lot but he was sure he was a good kid—how could he not be a good kid?—and he never imagined these experiments would actually injure Will. But this time Tom terrified himself.

He spent an hour trying to clean everything up. He went into the kitchen looking for heavy-duty scissors, thinking he'd cut the burnt corner off the rug and hide it at the bottom of the trash. When he came back his father was standing there, his hands on Will's shoulders. The worst thing was the way Will looked at him, his head down and forehead all wrinkled up, eyes mad and frightened at the same time. Tom tried to find something to say that would make everything right again. Finding nothing, he ran. As he broke through the back screen door he could hear his father bellowing behind him.

He was never able to remember how he got from the house to whatever place he would spend the next few days. He was so scared, wondering what craziness his father might do to him. His dad continued to yell, a sound more bull than human, loud enough his voice was cracking, turning into a hoarse scream. The scream continued with little drop in volume as Tom crossed street after street, doubling back, running through people's yards, stumbling over ditches and straight through bushes. Even part way into the woods he heard his father hurtling through the brush behind him, enraged and shouting. Tom didn't look back, but he imagined his father's face warping into something swollen and split open. He never knew his dad could run so fast. He must have been *so* angry to be able to run so fast.

For one strange moment he wasn't quite sure why he was being chased. Was it because of the fire and the mess in the living room? Or because of what he'd done to his little brother? Had he really hurt Will? He didn't think so but with all the panic and confusion he might have missed it. If he had, he deserved to be punished of course. He deserved to be hurt.

Tom had no idea where he was. He'd been down and across numerous streets, through the back yards of families he didn't know, in and out of dark sections of forest, sometimes crawling on his hands and knees through the scrub, so scared, the most afraid he'd ever been in his life, terrified because he couldn't imagine what he was in for.

When he finally stopped to rest he was in some overgrown place, a patch of woods between neighborhoods maybe, or in a backlot behind the factories and warehouses on this end of town. He could just barely see the glistening reflection of a metal roof between the trees, but it was some distance away, maybe miles. There were places like this in town—he'd seen them from the back seat of his dad's patrol car, but he'd never visited any of those places, didn't even know how to get to those places.

He didn't hear any traffic though, so at least he wasn't out near the highway, or maybe he had crossed the highway somehow and now it was behind him. He just didn't know.

It was cold and the weeds were wet. Everything was damp and dripping even though he didn't think it had rained in days. It was incredibly dark. Wherever he was, there weren't any streetlights or house lights. The only reason he could see at all was because of the moon hanging up there in the trees like a white balloon snagged in the branches.

He might have run so far he was out in the country, maybe out on somebody's farm, somebody's property. Maybe he was a trespasser, and he'd always heard farmers didn't like people trespassing on their land, not even kids.

It was mostly quiet except for occasional scratching, and now and then something sliding, and sometimes a thump or two, or several in a row like a runaway heartbeat, a scrape and a thud, and he thought he might scream if it didn't stop. Maybe he was making all those sounds. He could hear his own ragged breathing with a little bit of crying in it, and sometimes he made a little hurt sound as if someone had punched him and now there was something broken inside. Not as if he didn't deserve it, scaring his brother and almost hurting him or hurting him and pretending he didn't know. He was so sorry now and didn't want to be broken anymore.

It was all so stupid. He was stupid for being out here where he didn't belong, but maybe he belonged nowhere and maybe nowhere was where he was.

The night seemed to get darker and darker but to his surprise he could see better and better. Bodies lay under the trees and bodies hung from the trees with their eyes beginning to open, one at a time like individual fire flies, then two at a time, blink and blink all the dark animals from nowhere staring back at him but he couldn't see their bodies just their stares.

Blink and blink and blink and blink they all closed their eyes and went back to sleep or went back where they belonged but he stayed because he didn't belong anywhere. Blink and blink until there was just the one pair of eyes staring back at him. "Go away," Tom whispered, but instead of going away the eyes burned into him like two bright suns.

"Toby?" he said, and although Toby didn't answer he knew that was who it was. This angry Toby now lived out here in the dark and didn't even try to be good. This angry Toby hated the world and what it had done to him, crawling around all night and eating out of people's trashcans and stealing food wherever he could find it, so weak and hungry when they finally found him Tom was almost dead.

He didn't hate the world. Tom was a good kid. He could be so good. People wouldn't believe it he'd be so good.

Amy was outside the courthouse waiting when Tom pulled up. She looked extremely upset, racing toward his car with a bundle of clothing in her arms. He stared at her as she slapped at the driver's side window. *Of course*, he thought. *I'm really late.* He rolled the window down.

"Where the hell have you been? Will's beside himself! Today of *all* days! What's *wrong* with you?" That's what their dad said when he threw the dart into Will's ear. *Stop acting crazy!*

"I'm sorry. I don't. I just lost time."

She looked at him strangely. "What's happened? My god, you're soaked and your shirt's torn. Are you sick?"

Tom struggled to get out of the car. He stood up and—dizzy—leaned heavily against the door. He noticed blood streaked across the back of his hands. Several of his nails were torn. Grime had turned to mud between his fingers. Scratches ran round and round his wrists and scored loops across his palms. "Maybe. I fell asleep in the car. It was so hot, and I couldn't, I couldn't get the window down." She looked skeptical. "You don't believe me."

"No." She stared at him. "No, why would you lie? I just don't understand how you could get yourself in this condition. Tom, this isn't right."

"Did I miss everything?"

"There's still time. When I left the house I brought some of your good clothes in case you showed up late. We just have to find a bathroom." She put her arm around his waist and made him lean onto her shoulder. She might have looked slight, but she was very strong.

There was nothing shy about Amy. She found a bathroom on the bottom floor of the courthouse near the town's police offices, told the woman inside who was freshening her makeup she had to get out, and dragged Tom inside. Now and again someone came in, looked confused about what was going on, and left.

"After I clean you up a little I'll leave and you can change your clothes. You might as well trash what you're wearing. They're ruined. But we have to hurry."

Tom sat on the floor as Amy took soap and wet paper towels and wiped down his face. "Some of these scratches are still bleeding. I'll leave some wet paper on them and see if they clot. Not much else I can do. God, did you tangle with a cat?"

He didn't answer. She washed his hair as best she could and combed it back, clipped the hanging nails and scrubbed his hands between hers. He had vague memories of his mother doing something like this for him when he was small, but no one else had ministered to him like this, and so gently, since then. He wanted to cry.

"I'm sorry I screwed up so badly. Sometimes I do crazy things."

"Hush. Don't say things like that. Just do better, okay? You two are grown men. Good men, both of you. You're not boys anymore."

He came out after he'd changed clothes, feeling bruised and rumpled, but more human. "Where is it going to be?"

"The main courtroom, but you need to let Will know you're here. I don't want him to go out in front of his fellow officers and all those other people worried about what's happened to you. He went up the old back staircase. He's sitting on the second landing working on his speech. No one uses those stairs except for emergencies, so he goes there if he needs some place quiet to figure things out. I warned him not to put off writing his speech, but you know how he is."

The antique and ill-proportioned stairs were difficult for Tom. He was already out of shape, and of course he was extremely sore. He wondered if Amy had thought about any of that. Maybe she had and maybe this was his punishment, to climb these treacherous stairs and then to supplicate himself at his brother's feet. If so it was fair punishment.

"Well, look who's here." Will sat perched on the edge of the landing, a pad and pen on his knee. He was wearing a dark blue dress uniform. Tom thought he looked the most impressive he'd ever seen him. No wonder he'd been able to attract a woman like Amy. "I could have used your help with this speech, but there's not enough time now."

"Looks as if I'm doing nothing but apologizing to you this weekend."

Will shook his head. "Don't. You went to the old house, didn't you? Or what's left of it? I knew you would. I'm not stupid, you know."

"I know. Sorry—nevermind. I'm late."

"You're not late. You're just in time." Will started down the stairs toward him. "I hope you found whatever you needed to find."

"It was a full afternoon I guess."

Will stopped on the same step and gazed at Tom. "Just don't tell me about it, okay? And don't tell me how you got those scratches." He went down two more steps. "Are you coming, bro? Watch your step."

Tom turned around and followed his brother down the stairs. Will might be getting old, but he still had broad shoulders, a thick muscular neck. Still looked good in his uniform. Tom admired all that. He admired almost everything about his little brother.

When Tom reached out his torn hands, and even as his fingers first touched the back of Will's shirt, he didn't know yet if he was going to push, or pull him backwards into safety.

The Parts Man

The car was right out of the mid-thirties: jet black with a chrome grill, skirted fenders, multibar bumpers, and the dashboard rich in shiny silver knobs and trim. Cranks on either side of the dash allowed him to tilt the two halves of the split windshield. Christian loved that classic look, but this vehicle, with its endless lines and confusing interior shadows, not so much.

The car stretched as it roared through intersections and bent around corners. The side windows were so short it appeared to be squinting. The inside, so full of dark, had enough room to fit pretty much every person Christian had ever wronged.

"Drive faster. You have limited time, and so many passengers to pick up," said the parts man from one of the back seats. The parts man moved around in the car by means of unfathomable physics. He seemed everywhere at once. Sometimes he appeared large enough to fill the interior, other times so thin and two-dimensional he disappeared when turning his head.

Christian kept a nervous eye on the rear-view mirror. "I'm still getting used to the shifter."

"Push the gas pedal down, Christian." The voice was close behind him, breath stinking of spoiled meat and cigar. Christian gazed into the rear-view and the parts man stared back, only his sleepy brown eyes and a twisted stretch of pale nose showing. Thankfully not the mouth of no lips, the saw-like teeth, the long white tongue. "Or are you having second thoughts?"

Christian glanced into the mirror again, this time seeing his own face, sixty-eight years of deep lines and broken blood vessels. Or was it sixty-nine? When he first slipped into the driver's seat his arthritis made his joints scream as he bent his legs. "No. A deal's a deal."

He counted off the intersections, scanning the sides of the street for landmarks, looking for that certain spot he remembered from decades ago. He couldn't remember precisely where, until the parts man said, "Stop!"

Christian hit the brakes and saw the church through the split windshield, and that tan apartment building still standing on the corner. He remembered. This was more or less where it occurred.

"First, the payment," the parts man said, and reached around the back seat and between the buttons of Christian's shirt.

Christian gasped as he saw the fingers go in—so terribly long and pointed, spider-leg narrow, slim enough to go through a keyhole. They entered somewhere below his heart, pinched, and withdrew. The sensation of a cold wind leaking into his insides consumed him. "What was it?"

"I took nothing you cannot live without. A surgeon's exam would find nothing missing. Still, you have paid a dear price."

Christian reached under his shirt but felt neither blood or wound. But that notion of a cold leakage continued. He stared out the driver's side window. A glossy spot shimmered in the pavement a few feet away, an oil stain perhaps. But as he watched it spread into a pool, shimmered, and then long tendrils of smoke and liquid rose into the air, entwined, filling in with patches of pale mesh, dripping, bleeding into veins and arteries and the brilliant white of bone, red of muscle, wrapped rapidly by umber flesh, flowering into a brain, eyes, tongue and head, the coiled corkscrews of her Afro, and then that face that still haunted his dreams: it was Cheryl, still wearing the yellow sundress she'd died in.

The rear driver side door opened and Cheryl staggered toward the car with a dazed expression. The door closed around her as if she'd been swallowed. Christian watched her in the mirror. When he caught her eye she leaned forward and grabbed his arm. "Christian? What happened?"

The parts man was now seated in the front passenger seat. His head was long and triangular-shaped, snailskin pale, topping a long too-pliable neck whose many creases suggested segments. He was enveloped in a soft gray coat which flapped and shuddered with a life of its own. The parts man murmured with his lipless mouth, "Tell her she had a bad moment, but that she's fine now. She will be, until tonight's ride is over."

Christian shook his head, more at the parts man's proximity than the lie he had to tell his long-dead girlfriend. "It's okay, honey," Christian said. "You're okay. You just had a bad moment. Everything's fine—just enjoy the ride."

She laughed hazily. "I'm just so tired. Don't take it personally if I can't hold up my end of the conversation, 'kay?"

Christian watched her reflection as her eyes closed, then caught a glimpse of himself: the smooth brow and the clear eyes, maybe eighteen years old. He'd been driving a '71 Mercury Comet back then, blue as the sky. He and Cheryl had been arguing all afternoon about something—he couldn't even remember what—something unimportant, with him not understanding what she was even talking about, and her furious with him for not caring enough to understand. She'd shouted at him to stop the car—she was getting out. He'd been so mad he'd foolishly slammed on the brakes, right there in traffic. He knew he'd made a terrible mistake when she grabbed the door handle. Before he could object she'd opened the door and was standing out there on the pavement, not even a second before something large and silver slapped her away.

So forty-five plus years later when the parts man dragged

Christian out of bed and made his offer, how could he refuse? A few hours more life for Cheryl, and for all the others he'd let down over the years, the ones he'd left behind dead or dying while he survived. And at such a reasonable cost for an old man, although the pricing details had not yet been specified when he'd accepted the deal.

He heard the sounds behind him, and twisted around as the parts man touched her with his spider-leg fingers, pulling her close for an intimate whisper. Christian wanted to object, but had no idea what he was objecting to.

A half-hour later they were parked in front of a block-long brick box of a building. It looked grayish, wrapped in dirty fog. The upper story was ragged and transparent. It was the old YMCA building, torn down ten years ago.

"We're here for Tommy, aren't we?"

"Thomas O'Toole. Less accomplished than your other friends. 'Slow,' you thought."

Actually they'd called Tommy much worse. It wasn't that they disliked him. Tommy had been quiet, didn't defend himself, and they had no one else to pick on.

"I don't think he was even slow. He was probably as smart as the rest of us. Maybe if we'd left him alone he would have been okay."

They walked up the steps and a slight tug opened the double doors. The parts man apparently knew the way, guiding them through a series of halls until they entered the dusty gym. Christian avoided looking at the far end of the court. The bleachers on both sides were partially collapsed, the wall banners in tatters. Moonlight made a series of narrow vertical shadows on the far wall. One of the vertical shadows suddenly began to swing.

He followed the parts man until they were almost under the hoop. A small boy hung from a clothesline tied to the rim. Christian hadn't looked at the body when it happened; he felt he had to now. The noose made such a deep crease in the neck the folds of skin obscured it. "There's a ladder leading up to the beams," Christian said. "He must have climbed up with the clothesline, walked the beam to where the backboard supports are attached, and then shimmied down those supports to the hoop. That took a lot of guts.

"We didn't know why, if it was something we did. There was no obvious . . . *precipitating* incident."

The parts man ignored him. He was staring at the little boy. "Thomas? Are you ready to come down and join us?"

Tommy's head rose from its hinged position. Small hands dug into the groove in dull pewter flesh and pulled the noose out. He dropped gently to his feet and looked around. He stared at Christian but said nothing.

The parts man came up to Christian and one hand went deep into his upper belly, fumbling around. Christian heard a loud snap and felt intense pain. He doubled over as the parts man brought out a bloody piece of rib.

"Not *so* bad," the parts man said. "I understand that some starlets *choose* to have the lower ones removed. It makes them look thinner."

Tommy and the parts man strode for the doors. Christian, still in pain, struggled to keep up. When they got to the car Cheryl looked curious as Tommy climbed in. Later, when Christian checked his rear-view, the parts man was whispering to Tommy, who appeared to be laughing hysterically, but no sound came out.

Several more stops followed, picking up people Christian hardly knew. The choices surprised him: former neighbors and distant relatives, casual college friends, a remote co-worker. The locations weren't always familiar; some he didn't remember at all, but they stirred feelings strong enough to make him weep.

The fares for these passengers were modest. Whatever the parts man took from Christian caused barely a twitch or strain. Yet damage adds up, as someone of Christian's age knew all too well. Soon enough he suffered from a constant barrage of aches.

The bald man with the sad eyes waited at the curb in front of his decaying cottage as if this was a ride he'd expected. He stepped gingerly onto the running board and then appeared confused as to what to do next. After a rush of offered hands and a tangle of advice he stumbled in and navigated to the back, so far into the rear of the vehicle the car appeared to stretch to accommodate his desire for isolation.

Christian said to the parts man, "I think this is a mistake. I don't recognize him."

"You were a child. Perhaps you recognize his home."

The cottage had a partially collapsed roof and sagging windows, large water spots patterning the warped lap siding. "I've dreamed about this house."

The parts man was now in his ear, whispering. "When you first read that John Donne poem in college, you thought of him. 'Any man's death . . .'"

". . . Diminishes me," Christian finished. The man's name had been Wilson, and he'd lived at the end of their street. The neighborhood kids teased the poor man, ringing the doorbell and running away, throwing trash in his yard, calling him names as they hid in the bushes. Christian didn't know why they'd singled the guy out. Maybe because he was one of the few adults they knew who seemed totally powerless, and who was so frustrated by their actions.

Then one day the man was gone, and Christian's parents said he died. It was the first time he could attach a face to death. Some of the other kids laughed about it—a forced, embarrassed laughter—and he remembered he'd tried to join in, but couldn't.

"What's the fare for . . . for Mister Wilson?"

"Hmmm, first tell me, when you first heard about his *demise*, did you cry?"

"I didn't really *know* him. I didn't know *how* to feel. I was just a child."

"Very well then." The parts man reached for Christian's face, fingers hovering over Christian's right eye. Thinking the parts man aimed to take it he closed his eyes tightly. Then he felt a tug on a single eyelash, and the swift pluck that forced a single tear. "That will do," the parts man cooed, and Christian felt ashamed.

As he drove the car full of passengers through the long dark night and into the day and again into dusk he tried fruitlessly to keep track of where they were, in what part of his current city or in what part of his past, down narrow lantern-lit lanes where lovers strolled, past saloon-lined blocks playing the best jazz he'd heard in decades, out into the dusty roadways between fields where the headlights were the only illumination.

Behind him in the seats the revived chattered on as if speech were a gift soon to be taken away (which, of course, it was). He wondered how their mouths felt to be active again. He didn't listen, too busy wondering about the next stop, the next passenger. Once you've lived more than six decades you become accustomed to friends disappearing from the world a few every year, and then a few every month, and then every week seems to be this march of everyone familiar into everything unknown.

Was he expected to mourn them all? Was he supposed to think he was the one deserving to go and not them? Christian could barely remember their names. There were moments when he would wonder what so and so was up to these days before remembering that so and so had died ages ago.

They picked up his grandfather coming out of a dilapidated church. Christian thought it might have been the church where they'd held the old man's funeral, but he couldn't be sure; he hadn't attended. He'd been so busy with his own life he hardly remembered getting the news. This man had been the only grandparent Christian ever knew, the others dead before he was born.

His grandfather was dressed in a snug-fitting sand-colored suit, blue shirt, and bright red tie. The outfit made his tawny complexion resemble gold. He sat down next to Cheryl and immediately struck up a conversation. She looked enthralled. Christian was so glad to see him he almost didn't mind losing a kidney for it, although the taking of it proved to be a long and lingering extraction.

Soon thereafter, the car found the factory where Christian's father died. The angry-looking man in the blood-stained coveralls at first refused to get in when he saw that Christian was driving. Christian saw the side of his father's face and his left hand, both chewed to pieces when he'd fallen into the machinery, and looked away. The casket at the funeral had been closed. He wondered what age he was in his father's eyes. In his mid-twenties was when their relationship fell apart.

He watched as the parts man tried to talk his father into getting into the car. He looked at his grandfather, who appeared to have lost his good humor. His grandfather had never approved of his son-in-law.

Eventually the parts man re-entered the vehicle, holding onto his father's good hand, leading him like a child. His father settled somewhere near the back, pressing himself so tightly against the window Christian could only see parts of his bloody coveralls.

Christian clutched the wheel and jerked recklessly into traffic. It appeared as if the hood passed through a Ford station wagon without a ripple. He heard random complaints from the back but paid no attention as he hit the gas and floated into the passing lane. He was furious, but not sure why, except that his father was present. He'd been the same way at the funeral, staring at the back of the pew in front and clenching his teeth as a succession of speakers attempted to find something nice to say.

"For this passenger you have a choice of payments," the parts man abruptly said from nearby.

"For *him*? I'm not paying. I didn't request his resurrection, and I'm aware of no guilt over his death. *His* was the funeral I should have skipped."

The parts man said nothing more, but Christian felt the long fingers inside his back, and the twist and jerk as additional bone was taken away. He bit into his tongue, choked on the thick metallic liquid that filled his mouth, but uttered not a sound. After a few more miles the fire of the pain had dampened, but he felt as if the parts man's fingers were still in his back, prodding.

The car had become so hot and humid Christian was having trouble thinking. Assuming a little air on his face would clear his head he looked for the AC controls before realizing a car of this age had none. He began to turn the crank to tilt the split windshield on the driver's side. But after only half a turn the handle broke off. Frustrated, he tossed it to the floor.

"No worries," the parts man said, reaching past him with one hand and playing with the dashboard. When he took his hand away Christian could see that the broken handle had been replaced by the bloody rib the parts man had taken earlier. He couldn't bring himself to touch it and cranked up the other half of the windshield instead.

It dawned on him where they were. Large, aging maples obscured most of the houses from the street, but regularly spaced narrow driveways cutting between dark lawns led up to each one. "You must turn soon," the parts man said, so close behind him he might have been inside Christian's head. "Remember? The alley behind the back yard."

The parts man didn't have to guide him. This was where his mother moved after Christian married and moved out west, about twenty years after his father died. He turned into the alley and drove until he was behind the fourth house on the right. He could see the brilliant orange glow coming over the top of her fence.

His mother had started to fail the next to last year of her

life. It wasn't anything obvious at first: the occasional lost name, a little more observable awkwardness, the random fall. She claimed to be okay, just a bit "distracted."

Christian had noticed these things, but they hadn't worried him. She wasn't that old, and she'd been living by herself for over fifteen years and doing fine. She had her friends and her volunteer work. She didn't need him looking after her. She'd told him so herself, "I have lots to do, too much. You have your own life now, a family to start."

But something *had* changed. He'd noticed the accumulating differences. But he *did* have his own life to worry about, and a marriage to nurture, a new wife who demanded most of his attention. When he came back to visit at Christmas they would have more time together; he would be able to observe his mother and evaluate whether there was any real cause for alarm.

There were no witnesses but the fire department was able to piece together an approximation of what must have happened. She'd been cleaning house, getting rid of outdated files, tax returns and bank statements. She'd talked about doing that for years. The problem was how to dispose of so much paper. "I don't want some criminal stealing my information." That had become a constant worry. Apparently she decided to carry it all into the back yard and burn it. It must have exhausted her. The fire was going strong when she decided to add one more box to the flames. She either became unsteady and fell, or tripped.

The parts man joined Christian at the gate. The glow was so bright it showed through the narrow spaces between the boards, casting tiger-stripe shadows over both them and the car.

"What are you charging me for her?" Christian asked.

The parts man didn't answer right away. Then, so softly Christian could barely hear him, "The price will need to be a grave one."

"Then take it now. The pain will help me focus."

The parts man circled in front of him. The invasion of Christian's chest was immediate and devastating. Afterwards, the parts man held up a shapeless bag of pinkish gray organ meat. "You can live with only one lung. You don't need this one." He stuffed it into his coat pocket.

A corrosive ache filled the cavity where his lung had been. Christian dwelled on that as he pushed open the gate.

What he witnessed was not fire, although it did project a kind of heat. A large volume of what was not fire but perhaps the idea of fire occupied the middle of the yard. It had much of the brilliance and the color, but was a little too transparent. It warped and mutated like some kind of amorphous organism made of light, filling the air with the smell of frying beef. Down at the bottom of it a darkened figure lay writhing, featureless head drawn back and white teeth gleaming across the gaping mouth. One cindered arm stretched in his direction.

"We have to drag her out of there!" His father was standing beside him, fresh blood like a shimmering veil obscuring the ruined part of his head. His one remaining eye locked onto Christian's gaze. "Help me boy!" His father entered the flaming apparition and grabbed his mother's arm, suffering no apparent harm. Christian's remaining lung raged with pain as he involuntarily sucked in air. He stepped into the center of the flames and grabbed her around the shoulders and the two of them carried her out of the flaming illusion. It withered into nothing with a whistling sound.

They helped her into the front passenger seat and his father retreated wordlessly into the back of the vehicle. Ridiculously, Christian buckled his mother's seatbelt with care.

She attempted to speak. "You've ... gotten ... old." Her voice was like crackling leaves at the height of autumn.

He glanced at her head. Two narrow slits had opened in the scales of black crust to expose the whites of her eyes, but her iris and pupils had partially adhered to the underside of her lids so she couldn't look directly at him. He focused on the road ahead. "I thought you would see me as younger, the way I was when you were alive."

"I'm your mother. I see you as you are."

"M—mama. Was it bad, my bringing you b-back?"

He heard her teeth clack together and didn't know if it was involuntary or some version of mirth. "I'm glad I . . . can see you again."

As they drove on the sky was no longer completely dark and the last faint stars disappeared. Christian felt fatigue unlike anything he'd ever experienced, and wondered if he might be dying. His passengers had little to say, although his mother and Cheryl did exchange pleasantries about the brief time they'd once known each other.

Christian had given everything possible to give, and if the guilt had not been thoroughly exorcised it never would be. Like so many days in his life which he had anticipated with either excitement or trepidation, this one had devolved into yet another day he just had to get through.

Someone stepped in front of the car. She was tall and gangly, with little flesh on her frame. Her nursing uniform swallowed her. She carried a small bundle. He stopped. Beside him his mother clacked her teeth.

The skeletal nurse stood wobbly, one hand reached for the hood for stability as she fixed him with an angry glare.

"Ba-by," his mother croaked. "She has a ba-by."

Then Christian recognized who she used to be. "No, this is *not* something I need to do. He wasn't a child yet, more like our *hopes* for a child."

The parts man was then so close Christian could feel the tongue's moist touch on his earlobe, and the soft scrape of those well-sharpened teeth. "Can you say you felt *no* guilt when they took him away? Which did you regret more, looking at him, or not looking at him *long* enough?"

He and Grace had been trying to have a child for a long

time, had almost given up when Grace became pregnant. She was wearing one of those oversized T-shirts that said "Baby On Board"—she joked about how odd it looked on someone her age—when her water broke months too early. Her voice was broken when she called for him from the bathroom. He remembered looking at her as she stood awkwardly with her feet apart on the wet floor, her eyes tightly closed. He didn't know what to say, and that became his mode for the rest of the evening.

In the car on the way to the hospital she kept saying it was far too early and they were going to lose the baby. He kept repeating that she wasn't a doctor and she didn't *know* that. But at the hospital the doctor said the baby was dead or dying and for her sake recommended that they remove it rather than wait. *Dead or dying?* He would always wonder if he'd heard that correctly, and if there was significance in the difference they should have paid more attention to. Grace would later say she could remember nothing about that conversation.

From that point on—even as they took her into the delivery room and allowed him to sit beside her—he held her hand and kept whispering "we'll get through this day." He could hear the sounds of babies being born in nearby rooms, the mothers' cries of both joy and pain.

The tall nurse with the piercing eyes stood at the end of the bed and stared at him with what he thought was disapproval, but it was a very bad time—probably her stares meant nothing. She narrated the procedure in an oddly matter-of-fact way. As they removed the small body there was a moment of silence, then she said "a boy, perfectly formed, approximately . . ." and Grace cried out "please, I don't want to hear this," and the nurse replied, "it's just for the record" and Christian wanted to call her a liar, and realized they were in a Catholic hospital and wondered if that made any difference.

Before they took him away, Christian stood up clumsily and stretched so that he could see his son. It was only a momentary glimpse, but he thought the skin was a dark red, almost purple, and the closed eyes looked molded on, doll-like and unreal. He sat down feeling like an awkward teenager. He thought he'd done something wrong—either he shouldn't have gotten up, or he should have taken a longer look.

As they wheeled Grace into another room he'd kissed her, and the lethargic way she looked at him, the stillness of her body, convinced him he would one day lose her, but at least not that night.

Now the skeletal nurse was handing him the bundle through the window, and unwilling to hold him Christian passed the child into his mother's charbroiled arms, who carried him into the back to share with the others, and although they all exclaimed at the delicacy of his fingers as he held on to theirs, at the beauty of his eyes and of his smile, the baby made not a sound. Christian got out and walked around struggling for breath. The nurse had disappeared.

"It is time for my payment, Christian."

Christian stared at the parts man, who huddled in his great coat as if cold, only his sad eyes and part of his twisted nose showing above the tall collar. "I didn't *need* to see him again! Haven't I paid you *enough*?"

"I do not make the rules."

Christian sat down in the road, his arms hugging his knees. "Then *who* does?" Getting no answer, he stretched out on the pavement and looked up. Color had flowed back into the sky. He was seeing the dim edges of different clouds, and he struggled to find resemblances.

"This will be the last time I charge you." The parts man loomed over him. "After this we will return you to your home." Then the parts man hunkered down, and serious exchanges were made, essential and irretrievable items were taken, and secret locations within Christian's body made empty. He knew he would never be the same. The pain was . . . *clarifying*, and although Christian cried he did not scream.

The worst of it was glancing over and seeing that all his passengers were watching from the car.

They pulled up to his house in the drowsy light of morning. It was difficult climbing out of the car. Whatever adrenalin had driven him through this journey had dissipated, and all he had left was this constant mental haze of deterioration enlivened occasionally by an ambush of pain. He wondered how much of his future had been amputated, but of course there was no sensible math for such things.

He didn't say goodbye to any of them. He wondered if they recognized the kind of bargain he had made.

They'd bought this small house almost ten years ago. They'd gotten rid of much of their belongings, keeping only a few pieces in remembrance of their best of times. This place required little maintenance. Grace had fallen in love with the tree-shaded porch, and they'd spent many evenings there during her final few years. He'd liked the well-lit corner where he could read his much reduced collection of books.

He'd left the house tidy when he went away with the parts man; he always liked to leave rooms picked up and put away. Now the surfaces were cluttered with tissues and pill bottles and a variety of medical debris. The air smelled of strong disinfectant, but not so strong as to hide the basic sourness underneath. A wheelchair sat in one corner of the living room, a walker and a potty chair in another—everything he'd thrown away the week after Grace died.

The woman sitting in the green wing-backed chair was not the Grace of her last few days—thin and suddenly older and breathing explosively—but the Grace from a few weeks before, smiling and teary-eyed and still able to speak her mind.

With some effort he got down on his knees in front of her and cupped her trembling hands inside his own. They stilled immediately and she smiled at him. "Christian, where were you? I've been waiting."

"I had . . . errands." He struggled not to cry and it made him almost laugh. "But I'm here now. We never said . . . our proper goodbyes. I wanted to tell you how grateful I was, for all those years. And how, now I ache for you every day." And then he rose awkwardly and embraced her, kissed her desperately on her eyelids, her lips, and when she failed to respond he sagged onto the floor.

"I'm sorry," she whispered.

"You didn't speak your last few days," he said, "and you could hardly tolerate my voice. I assumed it was because, in a way, you had gone on to another . . . life, and were done with this one. Is that the case? This . . . place, it means nothing to you now?"

She was silent for a very long time. Then the words came slowly, but at least they came. "I remember . . . going away, to college. I saw no one from home for three years. Not my parents, not the boyfriend I left behind. Then I came back for a week. I still . . . loved my parents. They were the same. But I was different. I cared not a bit for my hometown, my old friends, even my old boyfriend. They meant nothing because I was now in another place. It wasn't as if I'd fallen out of love, out of anything. They'd just become . . . irrelevant."

She'd angered him. "You're saying I'm like some high school flame? Our marriage was, what? Trivial?"

"You're upset. No, it is *not* the same. But I'm just trying . . . to find some words you might understand. Take my memory of going away to college. Multiply it a thousand. Times ten thousand. Imagine that. It's not that I don't want to care. It's that I cannot. Want, or care. Now."

He took this in, and found he wasn't surprised. He didn't know what else to say to her. But then he thought about what he really wanted to know. "So tell me this. You're the only one I can ask. We weren't believers, either of us. So is it like heaven? Is it like hell? Something else? What is it? What is it like?"

She stared at him blankly, and then there was a slight tremor in her mouth. She looked as if she were in pain. "Don't ask me that. That is something you cannot ask. What good . . ." She stopped, glancing around as if she'd forgotten where she was. "What good would it do you? There's nothing I can do to save you from it. Just . . . live your life, Christian. Live your life as long as you can."

He sat there without speaking. Occasionally he would glance at her, expecting her to be gone, but she still sat there with no expression, occupying the chair. He struggled to his feet and went to the front window. To his surprise the car was still out there, the parts man standing beside it, watching the house. Christian opened the door and limped down to the street. "You're still here," he said.

"I wanted to see how your visit went," the parts man said.

"Is that humor? Is that the way you see us?"

The parts man grinned a toothy grin. "That is life—make of it what you will. Enjoy the rest of your journey. Now that our arrangement has completed it is time that I ended *theirs*."

The parts man spread his great coat, making it appear as if he'd increased his size. He re-entered the car, but instead of getting into the driver's seat he climbed in through one of the back doors and joined the full complement of passengers. Christian couldn't tell what was happening inside the car— the interior was too dark and the windows were too small— but there was a great deal of movement and a great number of teeth and when the car glided away it appeared to be empty.

Sleepwalking with Angels

This is the way you leave the world.

"Dad, I've filled your refrigerator. I got that soft cheese you like. They were all out of fresh peaches, but the produce guy said he'll have more next week. I've sorted out your pills. Are you sure you don't want me to stay and read to you? Is there anything else I can do? We all love you very much—don't we kids? Say goodbye to Grandpa. Say goodbye."

A memory stands somewhere in the room waiting for your acknowledgement. For the longest time you've resisted looking, but this effort costs you more than you can say. Closing your eyes doesn't help. That's when the recollection burns the brightest.

You value your solitude. It's impossible to be yourself around other people; you always find some role to play. You crave those moments when you're missing, when no one is watching, where nothing you do is a mistake.

But you clench your teeth every time you go to bed alone. Falling asleep is like a dive into the abyss. Your adult children say they are worried about you. You could take care of things yourself if they would only give you time. For now, you sleep with your back to that side of the bed.

"We can buy you a whole new bedroom suite, paint the walls a different color. Whatever you want. At least let the cleaners in here, open the windows and air things out, dust and polish and pick up all these clothes and towels and sheets, run the vacuum over these rugs. How long has it been, Dad? How long?"

But you won't let anyone else inside. This difficult life is still yours to handle. You wonder if you should change the sheets. You suspect things may be getting out of hand. You're so tired of everyone's advice you have to stop yourself from screaming.

You haven't told them how the bed creaks at night, how the mattress shifts, and the covers pull away. How every mysterious draft comes with a whisper attached. How someone on that other side has grown cold and needs your warmth.

Once a day a man in a white suit delivers a hot meal to your door. You have no idea how much this costs them. You're a grown man, and you're ashamed to say you've never learned how to cook. You keep busy with nothing. Your hair is usually disappointing. You try to ignore these inexplicable swings in light and shadow, these unfamiliar odors, these unexpected swells of emotion. You don't need to see everything, nor do you want to.

"I know you don't believe, but wouldn't it be wonderful to see her again? We miss her too, and that's what we hope for, that some day we'll all be together again."

Both the walls and your skin resemble old newspaper. But in every lustrous surface: a piece of silhouette, a hint of eye, the suggestion of a moving form. Some of these reflections are not yours. Walking through this house has become an exercise in disintegration. You grow weary of the flies and stink.

"For a long time, I wanted nothing to do with you. I regret all the time we missed. Why do we go through that with our parents when there is so little time left?"

A long-lost cat glides in as if it might finally stay. You caress it, knowing its life to be short and brutal. You try to look out the window for the time of day, but those panes are full of confusion.

Thick tassels of dust hang from doorways and the corners of ceilings. You never learned how to manage such visible neglect. You swing at them with a broom but have no idea if it does any good. You intend to take more showers. Cleanliness will keep you healthy and hopeful. You believe these perceptions may not be your own.

"Dad? Please pick up. Are you okay? I'll try to drive down next weekend. We'll go to the movies. You loved taking me to movies. Remember how you said they were almost as good as dreams? I'll always remember that. I hope you're doing okay."

The phone rings many times a day, but it is always someone pretending to be someone they are not. Sometimes you can barely hear them. They act as if they know you when they don't know you at all. Sometimes when you answer no one is there but everyone is listening.

You are now old enough to understand there is a line which can be crossed, a balance which can be upended. You should not be here, and yet there seems to be no good solution for it. Everything you have done up until now has been improvised.

"Are you sure you want to give all this stuff away? How are you going to remember the life you two had together?"

"Dad? Please pick up the phone. I've been trying to reach you for two days. I'm going to have to drive down and check on you. We had a deal, remember? I may have to call the police for a welfare check, and I know that may embarrass you, but I don't have a choice. I'm hanging up now. Someone will be there soon."

You haven't been outside in ages and you have no desire to go, but something compels you to open the door. You search your closets for some magical suit you can wear but traveling unprotected seems your only choice.

You are surprised how dark the world has become. You had no idea the hour was so late. But at least all the tiny cracks are obscured. You start to go back inside, afraid to walk the city at night. Still you are driven to take another step, and then more.

The neighborhood has changed but you can't quite pin down the details. Your sense of balance is compromised and you're not sure how to land your feet. Someone calls to you with a name which although familiar isn't quite your own. You pick up the pace even though you have no specific destination in mind. Each time someone speaks to you it comes from a further distance away.

"When you first taught me how to drive, I thought I'd want to drive all the time, remember? I asked you to send me on errands. I took my friends anywhere they wanted to go. Now I dread it. People drive like they're at war."

Cars are densely parked on both sides of the narrow street, people jammed into their shadowed interiors. You wonder what they are waiting for. You stopped driving years ago. You could no longer trust yourself not to kill someone.

Something moves among the trees along the parkway. A dark figure stands in the shadows between two buildings, whispering advice you can't quite hear. You would step closer and challenge them if you were sufficiently brave. Everyone here has a great deal to answer for.

"You forgot to eat dinner again? Dad, how can you just forget to eat?"

On the next corner a once-favorite restaurant is shuttered. You press your face against the window. The space appears to be completely empty, occupied by successive layers of dark. The black silhouette reflected isn't yours, but you may have seen him somewhere before. You cannot remember the last time you looked at a photograph of yourself. The family pictures were stored in cardboard boxes at the back of a closet. You don't know what happened to them all. They might have been burned or donated to thrift stores. You worry that someone else might be passing them off as their own. In any case these images no longer resemble you. Your history isn't yours any more.

"Have you made any friends? We worry that you're so isolated. All these old men sitting around the rec center—maybe some of them can be your friends."

You are aware of other people walking these streets, conversing and conducting business, but they're always so far away. No matter how far you walk you never appear any closer. You can't account for the many discrepancies in time or distance. You can't explain the general scarcity of pedestrians. You stopped paying attention to news reports a long time ago. Perhaps this is the consequence of choosing to be the last one to know.

"Did you see it, Dad? They showed the whole thing on TV. All those poor people dead. The media could use better judgment—it only encourages the terrorists when they see their names everywhere. Do you think it really happened? We all saw it on TV, but today they can fake anything, did you know that? You never know what to believe. You can't trust your own eyes anymore."

More than once you perceive a witness staring from some distant window. You are pretty sure they know something you do not. As you get closer you search for an opportunity to say hello, just so they know you're aware, but every window is empty, and every door closed. Even if you wanted to start a conversation you could not. You may already know some of these people. But you're not sure you can still tell strangers from friends.

The city is consumed by the anticipation of its own decay. You want to let everyone know the first thing you lose is the meaning. Don't make any rash assumptions. Withhold interpretation until you've seen enough. Most of what you believe about other people will prove to be incorrect. Everyone has the right to suffer in silence.

While walking you have a dream in which you meet several people constructed entirely out of garbage. They follow you home and try to get in. They leave their nasty handprints all over your front door. You hide in the dark pretending you're not there. You're ashamed of your own reluctance to care.

"Why can't we invite them in for dinner, Dad? You always say we should do whatever we can to help. There's so many of them now and they have nowhere else to go."

When you awaken, you're still walking and there is no one left anywhere. Row upon row of architecture recedes into clouds of dust. All around your feet bits of life scurry by. You don't know what they are, if they are even edible, but you snatch and swallow them while you still have the opportunity. This doesn't satisfy you, but then you know nothing will. This is what it's like, you think, to outlive your home.

You burn. You burn.

Tiny insects crawl out of your eyes and down your face like tears. Their overabundant legs mark permanent trails in your cheeks.

You try to remember the last time you spoke to her. You don't know if the failure is in your recollection or with your calendar. This is the life you've always had. Anything important either happens unexpectedly or is ill-prepared for.

You remember other times when walking through the city was like reading a novel or watching a movie, finding yourself in another person's head as you both negotiated an unfamiliar landscape. But not like this. Not for hours, not for days.

Eventually you reach the suburbs of this place. Here all the doors have been left open. All the houses have been emptied; everyone's things gathered into piles by the street. All of humanity is moving. The dead leave their houses for the living and the living are restless because they can be. Still, you see no one. Perhaps they've all gone out to dinner, you think, dinner and a show and the life to come with someone they used to love. You sift through their piles of everything, and yet nothing interests you.

When you reach the bridge, you are terrified of its shuddering construction, so high there is nothing you can see below you but the obscuring fog. This may be the same bridge which brought you here so many years ago, but you really can't remember. You gaze down through the layers of mist, where you imagine the drowning continents lie.

"Have you met your new neighbors? Go out there and introduce yourself. At this point in life you need your friends."

Acknowledgements

"Thanatrauma," originally published in *New Fears 2*, edited by Mark Morris, Titan Books, 2018.

"Field of Shoes," originally published in *Daily Science Fiction*, May 28, 2018.

"The Dead Outside My Door," originally published in *Black Static #77*, November 2020.

"Saudade," originally published in *The Devil and the Deep*, edited by Ellen Datlow, Night Shade Books, 2018.

"Sleepless," originally published in *Crimewave* 13.

"A Stay at the Shores," originally published in *Necronomicon 2019 Memento Book*, edited by Justin Steele and Victoria Dalpe.

"Reflections in Black," originally published in *The Mammoth Book of Halloween Stories*, edited by Stephen Jones, Skyhorse Publishing, 2018.

"Whatever You Want," originally published in *Exploring Dark Short Fiction 1: A Primer to Steve Rasnic Tem*, edited by Eric Guignard, Dark Moon Books, 2017.

"Ladybird, Ladybird" is original to this collection.

"For All His Eyes Can See," originally published in *The Dark*, August 2018.

"Heterocera" is original to this collection.

"Sleepover" is original to this collection.

"Torn," originally published in *I Am the Abyss*, edited by Chris Morey, Dark Regions Press, 2019.

"August Freeze," originally published in *Weird Tales* 2, Winter 1985.

"By the Sea," originally published in *Nightscript* IV, 2018.

"The Way Station," originally published in *In Stefan's House*, edited by Jordan Krall, Dunhams Manor Press, 2019.

"The Walls Are Trembling," *Apostles of the Weird*, edited by S. T. Joshi, PS Publishing, 2020.

"The Grandmother & The Rest" is original to this collection.

"Forwarded," originally published in *The Dark*, January 2020.

"The Parts Man," originally published in *The Valancourt Book of Horror Stories, Volume Three*, edited by James D. Jenkins and Ryan Cagle, Valancourt Books, 2018.

"Sleepwalking with Angels," originally published in *Shadows & Tall Trees 8*, edited by Michael Kelly, Undertow Publications, 2020.